the Off-Season

a Washington Rampage novel

megan green

xoxo,
Megan Green

Copyright © 2017 by Megan Green
All rights reserved.

Visit my website at: www.authormegangreen.com
Cover Designer: Megan Gunter at Mischievous Designs
Editor: Jovana Shirley, Unforeseen Editing, www.unforeseenediting.com
Formatting: Alexandria Bishop at AB Formatting

No part of this book may be reproduced or transmitted in any form or by any means, electronic or mechanical, including photocopying, recording, or by any information storage and retrieval system without the written permission of the author, except for the use of brief quotations in a book review.

This book is a work of fiction. Names, characters, places, and incidents either are products of the author's imagination or are used fictitiously. Any resemblance to actual persons, living or dead, events, or locales is entirely coincidental.

ISBN-13: 978-1983983658

chapter one
tag

I'll never forget where I was the day my world came crashing down around me.

I wish I had a better story. Something like, *I was volunteering at a hospital, visiting sick children, when the news first hit*. Or, *I had just finished saving an old woman and her forty-two cats from a burning building when my agent called*.

But no. I was sitting in the fucking drive-through at McDonald's, waiting for my daily fix of salty goodness, when the radio newscaster interrupted coverage of the Seahawks game to drop what would turn out to be the most defining moment of my life thus far.

"Charges have been filed against MLB star Ian Taggart, better known as Tag Taggart, of the Washington Rampage. Our sources say a young woman has come forward with allegations that Taggart sexually assaulted her after their

division win last season."

I didn't hear what he said after that, my Bluetooth kicking on in my truck as I answered the call from Ray, my agent.

What had started as a simple stop through a pick-up window ended up being the catalyst to the worst period of my entire life. And, now, six months and hours and hours of turmoil, frustration, and a hell of a lot of anger later, it all comes down to this moment.

My career.

My life.

My future.

Coach Peters is sitting across from me with Nathan Shelton, the Rampage's GM, to his left.

Lucky for me, Mr. Lane couldn't be here today. As the owner of the team, he generally tries to stay abreast of anything involving his players. He's a little *too* involved, if you ask me. I've had far more meetings with the man in the past few months than I ever cared to have in my life. Add in the fact that he's a class-A douche canoe, and…well, let's just say, there are times when I've had to wonder if this is my punishment for the crime I didn't even commit. Having to deal with Tyler Lane on the regular has to be worse than any prison cell could ever be.

And that's right; you heard me correctly. I know that's the standard answer all assholes give when they're hit with a rape charge. And I know, ninety percent of the time, they're lying through their teeth. Being a professional athlete seems to make some guys think they're untouchable—a fact I can attest to from the hundreds, if not thousands, of times I've witnessed unwanted advances, unpaid tabs, drugs, and dozens of other less than savory activities. But I digress.

The fact is, *I* am not that guy. I love women. I respect women. Fuck, if I could build a shrine to women and worship at the altar of femininity, I would. Because, if there's one thing in this world I love more than baseball, it's the female body. But I would *never* touch a woman in any way that was unwanted or untoward.

The night I met Angela Hancock was the best night of my life.

We'd just won our division championship—a first in my seven years with the Rampage—and I was riding high. And I could think of no better way to celebrate than a night out with my teammates, a few bottles of Jack split between us, and a couple of willing females to keep us company.

I set my sights on Angela the moment I spotted her on the dance floor, her short black skirt and low-cut red top too mouthwatering to resist. When she took a break from her friends and headed to the bar to refresh her drink, I made my move.

Now, I'm not going to lie and say I had to work to get her attention. To be totally honest, I've never had any trouble finding a woman to warm my bed. With my muscular build, tan skin, and fucking adorable smile—you try to tell me dimples aren't cute—I know I fit the mold of what women consider hot. And, before you start to think I'm a cocky asshole, let me stop you right there. There's a difference between conceit and confidence. My teammate, Simon Weaver, is an arrogant fuckwit. Me, on the other hand? I radiate a smooth assurance women can't help but be attracted to.

To say getting Angela back to my room was easy would be an understatement. After one quick dance—if you could even call it that—we basically just dry-humped the shit out of each other for three minutes and another shot of Jack for the road, we were on our way.

I might have had a few drinks, but I wasn't drunk. And I can say with absolute certainty that everything that happened that night was completely consensual.

Angela slammed the door behind us and had my shirt off and her hand down my pants faster than you could say, *Do you have a condom?* I've always been a sucker for a girl who knows what she wants and isn't afraid to take control.

But, even in my lust-fueled state, I wasn't too far gone to stop for protection and to make sure she understood what this was.

"This is only for tonight. You got that, right?"

Not exactly the most romantic thing in the world to hear two seconds before some dude shoves his cock inside you, but as I said, I like to make sure a woman knows exactly what she's getting with me.

She made no bones about my declaration, and the next few hours were pretty fucking amazing, if I do say so myself.

We parted the next morning with a quick hug and a, *"Thanks for the fun night."* No awkward lingering or pretending like one of us was going to call when we both knew it would never happen.

Angela seemed like a really cool chick, and I had a brief pang of regret that it was the last time I'd ever see her.

Or so I thought. Just over six months after the night I walked out of that hotel room, Angela came back with a vengeance.

My life has been hell since that fucktastic day. Because, regardless of how many times I say I didn't do it and despite the fact that Angela has zero evidence against me, just the implication has been enough to almost ruin my career. I lost several of my sponsors the same day the news broke, a few others following suit shortly thereafter. Reporters have been watching my every move, thrusting cameras and microphones in my face the second I step outside the stadium or my home.

The only people who have stood by me through the whole ordeal are my teammates. No matter how hard my name has gotten raked through the mud, they know it's all a load of bullshit. Without those men, Coach Peters, and Ray, I'm not sure I could have survived the whole ordeal. I sure as hell wouldn't be sane; I can tell you that much.

As if he can sense I'm thinking about him, Ray reaches over and gives me a pat on the back. He's been by my side every step of the way—both literally and figuratively. So, it only makes sense to have him next to me as we wait for the call that will either make or break my future.

My lawyer met with Angela's today in one last-ditch effort to keep this out of the courtroom. If it goes to trial, even if I'm found not guilty, it will be the final nail in the coffin for me. I'd be finished in the MLB, and I probably wouldn't even be able to get a job coaching little league to underprivileged kids in the projects.

I've worked too damn hard to let that happen.

Leaning forward, I prop my elbows on my knees and start gnawing on my thumbnail, my eyes never leaving the phone on Coach's desk, as if I can somehow will it into ringing. Coach, Ray, Shelton, and I are silent, none of us wanting to be the one to break the tension filling the room. I have a feeling that, once broken, it might be impossible to repair.

At that thought, a harsh ring shrills through the air, the sound causing a deep tremble to rattle my bones. Coach looks at me, and I give him a stiff nod. The four of us decided earlier he would be the one to take the call.

"Peters," he answers, his voice gruff and his tone clipped.

His eyes dart to mine after only a few seconds, but I'm unable to read them. There's concern there, but also something else. Relief maybe? Or is that just wishful thinking on my part?

He grunts out a few responses, never giving any indication as to which way the call is going. By the time he ends the call, I'm ready to rip the damn phone out of his hand and chuck it at the fucking wall.

After setting the handset back on the base, he leans back in his chair and lets out a long, slow breath. "She's dropped the charges."

The relief that rushes through me is palpable. It's as if, to use the most cliché expression on earth, the weight of the world has been lifted off my shoulders. But that's exactly how I felt over the last six months. A soul-crushing heaviness had settled over me since the day I was first hit with the charges. And, for the first time in what feels like forever, I can finally breathe.

Ray gets up and gives me a hug, Coach and Shelton both throwing in their relieved congratulations. It's then that the door to Coach's office flies open, and Brandon Jeffers—my best friend and teammate—bolts into the room.

"For fuck's sake, can someone please let a guy know what's going on? I've been dying out there."

I had no problem with Brandon being in the room when the call came, but Coach and Shelton insisted that, since the matter didn't directly involve him, he didn't need to be here. B wasn't even supposed to be in the building at all, but he's never let a little thing like rules stand in his way.

Coach shakes his head. "Should've known you wouldn't stay away, Jeffers. Don't know why I even bothered trying."

Brandon plops his ass down on the corner of Coach's desk, picking up a stapler and tossing it in the air. Had it been anybody else, Coach would've reamed their ass for touching his shit. But, like I said, Brandon's never been one for following orders. I think Coach has pretty much written him off as a lost cause at this point. Good thing he's a damn good player; otherwise, the dumb fuck might be

the Off-Season

out on his ass.

The good mood continues though, Coach letting B join in on the celebration of my newfound freedom and even goes so far as to pop open a bottle of champagne he had stowed in the bottom drawer of his desk. This is a locker room though, so we have to make do with paper cups instead of crystal stemware.

Ray is the first to break up the party. "Not to be a downer—I'm truly happy she dropped the charges, Tag; I am—but we're far from out of the woods here. She took the cash, which, to a lot of people, will make her look like a money-hungry fame-seeker. Three mil isn't exactly chump change. But, to others, well, they're going to wonder why you felt the need to pay her off in the first place. If you had nothing to hide, why not let the case run its course, you know?"

My mouth drops open. "But you're the one who suggested we pay her off in the first place!"

"I know, I know," he replies, his tone even, almost placating. "And I still think it was the best possible solution. Now, she's gone, and we can work on getting you back to where you were before all this broke loose—the golden boy of the MLB."

I scoff. "You know I don't give a shit about that. I just want my good name back."

"And that's precisely what I'm talking about, Tag. We need to work on tamping down these rumors that are sure to start flying as soon as the story hits the press. And, as crazy as this might sound, I think it might be best if you weren't there in the spotlight for it all."

My brows furrow in confusion. "What the hell does that mean?"

"It means, I think you should lay low for a while. Take a vacation. God knows you've earned it after the last six months. Take a break. Relax. Let us do the talking. We'll tell everyone you're on sabbatical in order to find yourself after this whole ordeal."

"I'm not a fucking professor. I'm pretty sure baseball players don't go on sabbaticals. Besides, I need to be here, getting ready for next season. Tell him, Coach. Tell him what a stupid idea this is."

I turn my gaze over to Coach Peters, waiting for him to back me up. When his eyes don't meet mine, instead falling to a stack of papers on his desk, I know I'm not going to get the support I'm looking for.

"Sorry, Tag, but I think Ray is right. You need a break. You need to get your head on straight again. It's no secret that your mind wasn't exactly in the game this last season. Not saying I blame you," he quickly interjects when he sees I'm about to protest. "I don't think any of us gave it one hundred percent this year. Our boys care about you, Tag. None of them liked seeing you go through what you did. You're one of the best players and all-around people I've ever had the privilege of coaching. This might have affected you the worst, but believe me when I say, we all felt your pain."

And he's right. I played like complete dog shit this entire last season. As shortstop, I have one of the most pivotal roles on the field. My quick hands and ability to catch and tag a runner are what earned me my nickname. No, it's not just a play on my last name. Though that might have helped inspire it.

But, this last season, I had more errors than outs. My batting average was virtually nonexistent. And I didn't score a single run. All. Season.

Maybe they're right. Maybe I do need a break. A few months to myself to clear my mind and get my head right. But where in the hell would I go? Seattle is my home now. My hometown is out of the question. The thought of going back after the events of the last six months and facing all those people who were so proud when I was drafted is unbearable. My dad has called once a week, like clockwork, since this nightmare began. But I always manage to keep the conversations short and sweet. Hearing any sort of disappointment in his voice would crush me.

So, where? I can't hide in my house for a few months. Not only would I go stir-crazy, but there's also no way the paps wouldn't get wind of it eventually. I need to go somewhere nobody has ever heard of me.

An idea pops into my head.

"Hey, B, you still got that cabin in Bumfuck, Colorado?"

A slow smile spreads across his face. "Sure do, buddy. Perfect place to get away for a while. Nobody will find you there."

Looks like I'm going to be spending some time at the lake.

I'd better learn how to fish.

chapter two

lexi

"You're sure you don't need my help, Lex? I'm more than happy to hang around a bit longer."

I let out a deep breath, blowing away the strand of hair that fell across my face, as I scrub the kitchen floor. "I told you, Ella, I'm fine. Get your ass out of here, and get back to those babies of yours. Drew is probably going out of his mind by now."

My sister pulls her bottom lip in between her teeth, her eyes darting from where I'm kneeling on the floor to the stacks of boxes arranged haphazardly around the room. "I feel bad, leaving you like this. I was the one who convinced you to move all the way out here. The least I can do is help you unpack."

Dropping the scrub brush back into the bucket of soapy water, I push myself up off my knees and take in my sister. For a woman who had twins only six months ago, she looks amazing. In blue leggings and a white T-shirt, you'd never guess that, only half a year ago, the woman looked like she'd swallowed an entire watermelon. Maybe two. I've always envied her for that. Throughout our childhood and teen years, she was able to eat anything she wanted without a second thought to what it might do to her thighs while, if I even looked at a cheeseburger, I would gain ten pounds. I've spent my entire life counting calories and watching everything I put into my mouth, and I still never look as good as she does without any effort.

Until now anyway. I haven't exactly had much of an appetite this past year. That's one perk of everything that's happened. I'm the thinnest I've ever been in my life. Probably too thin, if there is such a thing.

I walk across the room, circling my arms around Ella's shoulders when I reach her, giving her a brief, firm hug. "I appreciate everything you've done for me, Ells. You believed in me when nobody else did. You stood by my side when everyone else turned the other cheek. And you helped me find my dream house without even knowing it was what I was looking for."

Ella's brows rise in a skeptical look as she takes in the run-down condition of my new home. "Dream house, huh? I think you should set your sights a little higher next time, Lex."

I laugh as I spin her around and shuffle her toward the door. "You just wait. Fixing this place up is exactly what I need. It's going to be freaking spectacular."

My hand closes around the doorknob, pulling hard to open the front door that I already know sticks slightly. It's one of the many things on my list of to-dos for this place. When the door still doesn't budge, I brace my foot up on the frame for leverage, giving it another strong tug.

My sister's laugh registers before the fact that I'm now planted squarely on my ass, doorknob in hand. I look between it and the new hole in the door where the knob used to be, and before I can help myself, I join in.

"God, this place is a dump," I say between breaths, wiping the tears developing in my eyes. It's the first time in a long time that the tears are from laughter and not pain and anguish. It feels so good to laugh.

And then the guilt hits.

Do I deserve to feel good after what I did? Do I deserve to laugh with my sister after almost taking that privilege from someone else? I ruined someone's life. What in the hell am I thinking, sitting here in a fit of giggles while that person is still going through hours of pain and therapy?

Ella sees the change in my face almost instantly. And, like all the best big sisters, she knows me better than anyone. She knows exactly where my thoughts went without me even having to say a word.

"Lexi, don't. You need to stop punishing yourself. You made a mistake, and you paid the price. But you can't keep wallowing. You need to live. You need to laugh. You need to be happy." She reaches her hand down to me, pulling me to my feet with ease. "And you need to fucking eat something. You're too damn skinny. I can practically count your ribs, even through that damn shirt," she admonishes, pointing to the top I put on this morning.

It's a size small, and even still, it's slightly baggy around my midsection.

I wrap my arms around my waist, trying to hide the evidence. "I'm fine, Ells. Besides, you of all people aren't one to talk about being too thin. You just had twins, for Christ's sake. Look at you."

the Off-Season

She shakes her head. "Not going to happen, Lex. You're not changing the subject that easy. You need to get some help. I'm worried about you."

This isn't the first time she's lectured me, and it certainly won't be the last. I know she's concerned. And I know the way I'm living my life isn't healthy. But knowing something and doing something about it are two entirely different things.

"Can we not do this right now, Ella? I've had a long day, and I've got a long-ass night ahead of me. I understand your concern, and I swear I'm going to do something about it. But, for now, I need to focus on this place. Once I'm settled, I promise we'll talk."

She eyes me with another skeptical look, her gaze giving me an assessing once-over. She must believe me because, a moment later, she exhales a loud sigh. "Fine. But don't think I won't remember this conversation. I'll give you some space and let you get settled. But, Lexi," she adds, eyes narrowed and lips set in a hard line, "I'm always just a phone call away. If you need *anything*, you call me. I don't give a shit if it's two in the morning. You need me, you call me."

I give her another quick hug, so grateful she's my sister. I don't know what I did to deserve her, but every day, I'm thankful that she's mine. Even when we lived in different states, she never failed to make sure I knew she loved me and would do anything for me. Every damn day.

"Thanks, Ells. I love you. And I'll be over to squeeze my nieces as soon as this place somewhat resembles livable space."

She gives the room another glance. "So, we'll see you at their graduation?"

I playfully smack her on the arm. "Oh, stop. It's not *that* bad. I'm telling you—in a few weeks, you won't even recognize this place.

Now, get the hell out of here, and let me get to work."

She laughs, slipping her fingers into the notch where the doorknob was five minutes ago, pulling the door open. "You'd better get this fixed ASAP. This might be a safe town, but that doesn't mean you should have a hole in your front door."

"Got it, chief. I've seen *Friday the 13th*. I know what lives in these weird lakes. First up, fix the hole in the door to keep psycho serial killers out."

Ella rolls her eyes at me. "Oh, great, one more thing to worry about. Try to stay away from men in hockey masks, m'kay, sis?"

"I make no promises. You know I've always had a thing for jocks."

"I'll stop by tomorrow. Try to still be alive."

"You don't have to—" I start, but she shoots me a dirty look, telling me exactly what she thinks about my protest. "Fine. See you tomorrow. But don't bring those kiddos here until the place is a little more habitable."

"Don't worry. My babies aren't coming within a mile of this place until I know they won't die of toxic mold poisoning."

"You're so dramatic. There's no mold here. I had it checked. It just needs some sprucing up."

She lifts an eyebrow at me. But, before she can open her mouth, I spin her around again and smack her on the butt.

"Stop insulting my house, and get the hell out of here. See you tomorrow."

"Bye, Lex!" she shouts over her shoulder as she descends the front porch steps.

I cross every appendage I have that one of those dilapidated steps doesn't give out under her feet, giving her further fuel to the fire against this place.

the Off-Season

Once she's safely in her car, I close the door, leaning back against it as I assess the situation.

Long-ass night might have been an understatement.

Four hours later, the door is fixed, the kitchen floor is gunk-free—I don't even want to know what was causing my feet to stick to it like glue—and my bed is set up. That's about as good as it's going to get for tonight.

It's past midnight, and I want nothing more than to crawl into my bed and sleep for about twelve hours straight. I hustle down the stairs, grabbing a bottle of water from the old fridge that luckily still works, and guzzle half of it while standing in front of the sink.

The glare of the moon on the lake catches my eye, and an idea pops into my head. *What better way to unwind after a long day of cleaning and unpacking than to relax by the water for a few minutes?*

I grab another water and a bushel of grapes I picked up from the supermarket when I first got to town. Then, I head down to the dock.

When I flew down to look at houses with Ella last month, I fell for this place the moment the realtor pulled into the driveway. I didn't even need to go inside. The second I stepped out of the car and saw this dock, I knew I wouldn't be living anywhere else.

It's true; the house needs work—a hell of a lot of it. But it has good bones. It's old, but it was built at a time when quality was more important that quantity. There is no doubt in my mind that the structure itself is fine—a fact I had confirmed by the home inspector before I closed.

It's small and cozy—only a living room, kitchen, and guest bath downstairs and a small bed and bath upstairs—but it's perfect for me. Add in the fact that it's only about fifteen minutes from Ella's house in Grover—the next town over—and it was a no brainer.

And the dock that shoots off the back of the house and right out onto the lake?

Pure heaven.

I step out onto said dock, the bite of the October air washing over my overheated skin. I walk out to the very end, sitting down on the edge and dangling my feet out over the water. I momentarily think about diving in. Nothing would feel better than a cool dip after hours of sweating over boxes and running around the house. But even I'm not dumb enough to jump in black water in fifty-degree temps. I'll just have to make do with the cool breeze and gentle spray.

I munch on my snack, finishing off my first bottle of water and cracking open the second. A spark of desire for something a little stronger settles over me, but I quickly force it down. Alcohol is the last thing I need right now.

Setting aside the grapes, I lie back on the wood and stare up at the stars, letting the sounds of the woods take over. The lapping of the tiny ripples through the water, the whistle of the wind through the drying fall leaves, the snap of branches and twigs from the nearby wildlife—it's a symphony of nature. A soundtrack of meditation and relaxation.

I could get used to this.

Closing my eyes, I take it all in, reveling in every moment of peace. It's not something I'm familiar with, having moved here from the hustle and bustle of Chicago. I'm pretty sure the only wildlife I ever heard there was the scratching and clawing of rats. Not exactly the same thing.

the Off-Season

My eyes start to drift shut, and I know I need to get up and go inside, so I don't freeze to death. It might feel good at the moment, but sleeping out here would be an entirely different story.

I'll give myself five more minutes, and then it's back to the house.

I lace my fingers behind my head, inhaling deeply and holding the fresh air in my lungs. I'm halfway to the count of thirty when it happens.

Music breaks through my sanctuary, violently ripping me from my tranquil thoughts.

Okay, that might be a bit of an exaggeration. The sound is muffled, as if coming from inside one of the neighboring houses. And it's really not *that* loud. But, still, going from absolute silence to the sound of DJ Khaled singing about winning, no matter what, is jarring.

I jackknife up from the dock, glaring at the house that was dark as night when I first came out here. Now, every light in the place is blazing, the entire back wall a panel of windows, showcasing the extravagant decor on the inside. It makes my tiny lake house look like a dump in comparison.

Well, I guess that isn't hard.

The sound of the music increases for a moment, and I see the back door open as someone steps out. Strings of small, round lights illuminate the backyard, and I see the shape of a man as he walks along the grass.

It's pitch black outside, so I'm not able to make out his features, but judging from his frame and gait, I'd guess he's fairly young—under forty at least.

The annoyance I felt at the sound of the music evaporates as I watch him stroll down to the dock jutting off his property. His moves are tentative, almost tired. When he reaches the lake, he tucks his hands into his pockets, letting his head roll back on his shoulders as he lifts his face toward the sky. Even from fifty yards away, I can practically feel the tension and exhaustion radiating off him.

I don't say a word. I don't call out a greeting even though this man must be one of my new neighbors. I do nothing but watch as he stands there, soaking in the evening, just like I was doing moments ago.

And I can't help but wonder if he's running from something, too.

chapter three
tag

Seven hours into my *vacation*, and I'm already going out of my mind.

I thought getting away from the lights and sounds of the city would be soothing. I thought the peace and quiet would be good for me, giving me some time to refocus and be alone with my thoughts.

Turns out, that's the *last* place I want to be.

Being alone inside my head means thinking about everyone I've let down. It means dwelling on the past six months and what it means for my career. It means having to actually fucking think about what I'm going to do if baseball is no longer an option.

Being inside my head right now is really fucking depressing.

I need to get out.

Sliding out of the enormous bed—*seriously, did Brandon have this thing custom-made? You could fit ten people in it, easy*—I pull on a pair of gym shorts and a T-shirt. After lacing up my running shoes, I head downstairs and start a pot of coffee, so it'll be ready by the time I get back. I briefly check my phone, pulling up a few of the sites I know Ray was going to try to contact after I left. I see the usual headlines—people calling me an entitled playboy who got away with hurting an innocent girl. But then I realize that, despite my boredom, Ray was right. Because, among the negativity, there are a few new stories from people on my side. Ray has already started working his magic.

The early morning sun glinting off the lake catches my attention. I run every day, rain or shine. But what's the point of living at a lake house if you're not going to take advantage of the water, right? Kicking off my shoes, I strip off my shirt and step out onto the back patio.

I only ever saw this place in pictures before last night, and I have to say, they sure as shit didn't do it justice. The backyard is the stuff dreams are made of. A large fire pit with built-in benches sits right in the center of it, a volleyball net complete with sand off to the side. And the dock leading out onto the water is gorgeous—dark-stained wood with posts every few feet or so and strings of circular lights running along both sides. At the end, a sitting area is artfully arranged with yet another gas fire pit in the center.

It's an entertainer's wet dream. Too bad I don't know a fucking soul within a thousand miles.

The bite in the air gives me a moment's pause. It's mid-October, and while the days here still get up to the sixties and the occasional seventies, nights and mornings can get downright cold. I quickly shrug off my second thoughts though, knowing that, once I get in and going, I'll warm up in no time. Swimming works muscles that running doesn't even know about. It'll be a welcome change.

Looking around and finding nobody watching, I do something I haven't done since I was about twelve years old. I run full speed down the dock, leaping into the air and tucking into the perfect cannonball. Preteen me would've been in awe of the splash spraying up around me.

Adult me, however, immediately regrets this decision the second my skin comes into contact with the water. The water isn't just cold. It's fucking *frigid*. All the air rushes out of my lungs as the cold shock momentarily paralyzes me. And I'm pretty sure my balls are nestled somewhere up around my kidneys.

I shake off my temporary stupor, kicking my feet hard toward the surface. As soon as my head breaks free from the water, the cold air feeling about fifty degrees cooler than ten seconds ago, I wonder if I wouldn't be better off staying underneath. The thought of getting out of the freezing water and into the even more frosty air is about as desirable as voluntarily walking into a bear den after a long winter.

I sharply spin around, deciding the best course of action is to get my dumb ass back on the dock, make a mad dash toward the house, and cannonball into the hot tub waiting for me on the back patio.

But, to add insult to this already fantastic fuckup, I've somehow managed to drift away from the dock, and I am much farther away from it than I originally thought. I frantically search the area surrounding me, my eyes landing on another dock only a few yards away.

I have no clue who, if anybody, lives in that house. I can only hope they're not the inbred, redneck type you always hear about in these small backwoods towns. Getting shot for trespassing doesn't sound so fun. Then again, I'm so goddamn numb right now I probably wouldn't even feel it.

Deciding it's my best option because there's no way my frozen limbs will make it back the other forty yards, I force my arms to work and swim over to the battered dock. Climbing out, I shudder at the intense cold that settles into my bones and start running down the dock, toward the house.

It's not until I'm almost there that I notice the dock leads directly onto the back porch of the house. And sitting on that porch is a woman. A woman who, from the looks of it, is confused as hell as to what a half-naked wet dude is doing, running up to her house.

When I see a brief look of alarm flash across her features, her cup of coffee clattering against the old metal table beneath her as she starts to get to her feet, I call out, "Wait, I'm not going to hurt you."

She stills for a moment, her eyes narrowed as they scan my face. Sensing she's still half a second away from darting indoors and calling the police, I hold my hands up at my sides and take a step backward.

"See? Nothing on me. I made the mistake of thinking a nice cold swim was just what the doctor ordered. Learned real quick how stupid that was. Your dock saved my life. I didn't mean to scare you."

The woman looks down at my soaked gym shorts and shoeless feet, as if the fact that I'm dripping wet didn't even register until now. My teeth begin to chatter as I wait for her to finish her perusal of my person.

"You honestly thought it was a good idea to jump in that lake?" she asks, her lips turning up in the corners as she tries to stifle a laugh.

the Off-Season

I try to shrug but fail miserably, my muscles aching from the cold as I tremble. "What can I say? Not my finest moment. Now, if you'll excuse me, I need to get inside before I actually do turn into an icicle."

The woman's smile falls as she jumps into motion. "Oh, let me get you a towel. You can't walk through town like that."

Before I can object and tell her my house is next door, she's gone, the rusted screen door clanging shut behind her. I briefly debate on leaving without another word. I wasn't being overdramatic when I said I was about to turn into an icicle. A few more minutes out here, and I might be able to give Frosty a run for his money.

But the woman is back before I can take a step, a big, fluffy towel in her arms. I snatch it out of her hands as soon as she offers it to me, wrapping the soft warmth around my shoulders and exhaling in relief. I'm still cold as fuck. But the towel is a welcome comfort.

"Thanks," I sputter out through clenched teeth.

She gives me a sweet smile, her kind eyes sending a wave of heat through me as she looks me up and down. "Anytime. Though you might want to wait a while before you try swimming again. Like July maybe?"

I laugh at her bluntness. "Thanks. I'll be sure to keep that in mind. And I'll get this towel back to you as soon as possible…" I trail off, fishing for her name.

She waves me off. "No rush. I've got plenty of others. Housewarming gift from my sister. Apparently, she thinks there's going to be more than me living here. She gave me enough for the damn Brady Bunch."

My ears perk up at that. Hearing she's staying here by herself definitely piques my interest. Having a beautiful woman next door might make these next few months go by a little quicker.

No, Tag. No. That's not why you came out here. The last thing you need to do is start something with a sweet small-town girl after that shitstorm you just endured. Back the fuck off.

"Well, it was nice to meet you…" I realize she never supplied me with her name. I hold out my hand because, even though I'm cold as hell, I won't let it stand in the way of my manners.

"Lexi," she says after a moment, placing her hand in mine. "Lexi Barnes. And likewise. Maybe I'll see you around."

My fingers curl around hers, lingering a little longer than necessary. Something briefly flashes across her eyes, but it's gone before I can even get a good look at it. Pulling her hand from mine, Lexi spins around, grabbing the coffee mug from the table, and disappears through the door, not even bothering to say good-bye.

Well, that was weird.

She was nothing but nice—after she was convinced I wasn't there to kill her, that is—but then, as soon as her hand touched mine, it was as if she couldn't get away from me fast enough. And, despite her final words, I got the distinct impression that the last thing she wanted was to see me around.

Leave it alone, Tag. You're asking for trouble.

I know I should listen to reason. I should listen to that small part of my brain that evidently isn't frozen solid just yet. Lexi isn't like the girls I'm used to back in Seattle. She isn't going to roll over for me just because I'm Tag Taggart.

But the problem is…

I've always loved the chase.

chapter four
lexi

For the past three days, I've done nothing but clean, clean, clean, repair, repair, repair. The first day, it was fun. The second, a slight pain in the ass but still enjoyable. But, by day three, I'm about ready to burn the damn thing to the ground and claim the insurance money.

Why on earth did I think this was a good idea?

I woke up this morning, trudged my way to the kitchen to start a pot of coffee, took one look at the table I'd set up in the little breakfast nook—covered in various debris from my attempt to caulk the windows last night—and decided I was taking the morning off.

That is how I've found myself here, in downtown Maple Lake—if you can call a grocery/convenience/hardware store and a series of tiny storefronts downtown. There's not even a damn streetlight here.

As I walked the quarter mile from my house, I saw exactly three vehicles on the run-down road. And, when two of them came up to an intersection at the same time, I watched as each sat and tried to wave the other one through first. You'd never see something like that in Chicago. There, the only things waving out car windows are middle fingers.

I walk along the quiet street, smiling sweetly at each person who nods and waves to me. I'm not used to such politeness from strangers. It's a little overwhelming, to be honest—having to smile all the time. It's not something I've done much of during the past year and a half. But being surrounded by kindness is definitely a feeling I could get used to.

A hand-painted sign a few yards ahead of me catches my attention. It's nothing fancy, but the care that's gone into its upkeep, the paint looking almost brand-new despite the weathered wood, is evident, even from down the street. And, when the words on the sign register, I hustle the last remaining feet and duck inside.

Turn the Page bookstore is my childhood dream come to life. It might be a tiny space, but every single available surface area is covered in books. Shelves line every inch of the walls, thousands and thousands of pages begging to be read. There's an old cushioned chair in one corner and a small round table next to it with a dimly lit lamp and a stack of books resting beautifully on the top. I could spend hours in that chair, the musty, marvelous scent of books overtaking my senses and the wonderful adventures printed on those pages taking me to places I'd never been.

Just as I'm about to make my way over to my newfound,

the Off-Season

permanent perch, a man steps out of the back room, his arms laden with books and his shoulders covered in dust. He gives a little yelp when he turns and finds me standing here, obviously not expecting to see someone in his shop. I turn my face back toward the door, wondering if I maybe missed an hours sign.

Maybe they're not open yet?

"I'm sorry," I start, stepping forward to take some of the burden from his hold. "The door was unlocked, so I assumed you were open. I apologize for startling you."

The man lets me take some of the books slipping from his grip, giving me a grateful nod as I catch them just before they clatter to the floor.

Once we have them all set safely on the counter beside the register, he speaks, "No reason to be sorry, dear. We're open. We don't get many customers this time of year. I wasn't expecting to see you there."

I take in the man's appearance, a fleeting sense of glee filling my chest as I look him over. He's everything you'd expect a small-town bookstore employee to be. He looks to be around sixty years old, his gray hair unruly on his head. A pair of wire spectacles is perched on the end of his nose, and the worn cardigan adorning his shoulders has definitely seen better days. His short stature only enhances the little potbelly he's developed throughout the years. He reminds me of Belle's father, Maurice, in *Beauty and the Beast*. He's absolutely charming.

I hold my hand out to him. "I'm Lexi. I just moved to town."

The funny little man takes my hand in his, bringing it to his lips for a quick kiss. "Lexi. What a beautiful name for a beautiful girl. I'm Charlie."

I'm slightly disappointed his name isn't actually Maurice. But Charlie suits him, too. Not Charles, not Chuck, but Charlie. Unassuming and unpretentious. He seems like the kind of guy you could sit down with, holding a cup of tea and spilling all your troubles and strife.

If I were looking to do that sort of thing.

I shrug off the bleak thought and smile back at Charlie. "Thank you. This is a lovely place you've got here. Are you the owner?"

He beams at me before turning his gaze to the store around us. His face is prideful as his eyes fall back on mine. Not prideful in a boastful way, more like proud of the things he's accomplished, as if he's worked hard for every single thing around him.

"That, I am. She wasn't always something to look at; I'll tell you that much. But I couldn't be more satisfied with her now."

"She? You mean, the bookstore?"

He nods. "Yes. Much like a woman, this bookstore sure gave me a run for my money. There were times I wasn't sure I'd ever be able to turn it around. But she's never let me down. And every single drop of blood, sweat, and tears that went into this place made me a better man. Just like a great woman. Not always easy, but always, always worth it."

I smile at his response. I've only just met him, but he's already told me enough about himself for me to know that I like him. *He's a bit of a romantic, just like I used to be.*

My face falls at the realization, and I know Charlie sees it. But, before he can comment, luckily, the two of us are interrupted by a spritely woman.

My gaze shifts to the newcomer, and *spritely* really is the perfect word to describe her. Everything about her is petite—from her size to her features. Her long, gorgeous hair only adds to her ethereal appearance. And, when she opens her mouth to speak, the tone I hear is almost melodic.

Until the words she's saying register.

"Charlie, what are you—who the hell is this?"

Her words slice through the peaceful calm I've been feeling since stepping foot inside the bookstore. When I turn to Charlie, I find him shaking his head as his eyes fall on the girl.

"Olivia, what have I said about using such language? Especially in front of customers. It's not very becoming of a lady."

The evil fairy—Olivia apparently—rolls her eyes. "Lady, my left nut. Ask me how much I care if this *lady*," she drawls out the word, her negative tone letting me know how much of a lady she thinks I am, "approves of my 'language.'" She puts air quotes around the last word, shooting me a pointed glare.

And, even though she's been nothing but rude since the moment she stepped out of the back and I'm pretty sure she insulted me in her little tirade, I decide instantly that I like her, too. She's the hormonal imbalance to Charlie's kindness. The yin to his yang, so to speak.

And I can tell by the exasperated love in his eyes as he looks at her that I'm right. They might be as different as two people can be, but something tells me that either one would willingly take a bullet for the other. I wonder if they're related.

The sound of someone clearing their throat jars me from my thoughts, and I see Olivia still staring at me, waiting for me to say something.

"I'm Lexi," I say stupidly, holding my hand out to her.

She glances down at it briefly before bringing her eyes back to mine. When she doesn't reach to take my hand after a few moments, I drop it back to my side, embarrassment filling my face.

"Lexi just moved here, Livvy. Try to be nice."

"Moved here, huh? So, you're not a tourist who's going to try to con a free guidebook out of old Charlie here?"

I quickly shake my head. "Oh, no. I would never."

"Mmhmm. That's what they all say when I walk out and catch them in the act. Charlie is too damn nice for his own good. If it wasn't for me, this place would've closed up shop years ago. He wants to give everyone everything for free."

Charlie smiles at me. "Books are my passion. My life. Who am I to charge others for discovering their own love of words?"

"A man trying to run a business; that's who," Olivia says with a pinched expression, biting the inside of her cheek before finally turning and giving me a slight smile. "So, you're going to be sticking around a while?"

I nod. "Yep. I bought that old lake house up the road."

Olivia quirks an eyebrow at me. "The old Miller place? I heard someone had bought it. Didn't believe it at first. It's about one good windstorm away from falling into that lake."

I smirk. "Well, let's hope I can get it fixed up before that happens."

"You must be a glutton for punishment, girl."

"Probably," I say with a shrug.

She throws her head back and laughs. "Good. That gives us something in common. It's the only reason I still stick around here after almost ten years. No matter how much this old fart drives me insane, I can't seem to leave."

"Now, now," Charlie interrupts. "There's no need for name

calling. What do you say we give Lexi here a tour, Livvy? Want to do the honors?"

An hour later, I walk away with four new books to read, a belly full of coffee, and a job.

Despite the rough start between Liv and me, once she realized I wasn't trying to scam her surrogate father, the two of us hit it off pretty damn quick. I found out Liv—only Charlie is allowed to call her Livvy, a fact I learned the hard way after mistakenly using the nickname and receiving the look of death—had moved here with her mother when she was fourteen. Her mother had been more concerned with finding a husband than raising a child, so Liv had always had sort of a wild streak. One failed shoplifting attempt at the bookstore later, and she and Charlie had become inseparable. She liked to refer to him as the father she never had. And he called her the daughter he always wanted. They were beyond sweet.

When they offered me the job, I protested at first. Charlie had just told me that they didn't get a lot of customers this time of year, so why would they need to take on another employee? Despite how much I liked them both, I wasn't looking to be anybody's charity case. I'd managed to scrape together enough before moving out here that I didn't need to worry about money. Not for a few more months at least.

But they were insistent, telling me they were actually going to put a sign out front later today. They needed someone to help with inventory and reorganizing during the off-season. And, when

Charlie pulled me toward the back of the store, pressing his hand on a large book on one of the bookshelves there, my mind was made up for me. The shelf swung inward, revealing a small room hidden behind it. There was another soft chair—the twin to the one out in the main area—and a half-dozen tiny beanbag chairs arranged around the room.

"We have weekly story time here for the local children. They get a kick out of the hidden room. It seems to get them excited about reading. But an old man in a tattered sweater sure doesn't. I've tried to get Livvy to take over story time for me, but she refuses. I think you'd be perfect. Those kids would much rather listen to a bubbly blonde than this old codger any day."

I told him I wasn't so sure about that. He was like everyone's favorite grandpa. But, still, I couldn't turn down the opportunity. The thought of spending an hour or two every week in the hidden room was too good to pass up.

So, now, as I make my way back up the road to my house, I'm pretty pleased with myself. I might have taken the morning off, but it turned out not to be a waste. I made a few new friends, got a job, and found a few good books to unwind with in the evenings. And, after a few hours of intelligent conversation, I am ready to throw myself back into the repairs with renewed vigor.

All in all, I'd call today a success.

Ella would be so proud.

I look around at the changing leaves as I walk. This area really is gorgeous, and I can see why Ella and Drew love it here so much. I thought I'd have trouble adjusting after growing so accustomed to a large city like Chicago. But I have to say, I'm loving it.

I'm so lost in my thoughts and appreciation for the beautiful scenery around me that I don't even see him. Not until my body collides with his, his large hands closing around my upper arms to keep me from falling on my ass.

"Whoa there. You okay?" a familiar voice says as he lowers his face into my line of sight.

The man from the dock.

I avert my eyes, not wanting to face him.

First, I rushed off the other day like a crazy person the second he tried to be friendly. And, now, I just ran straight into him. In the bright light of day. I don't even have the excuse of darkness. He must think I'm a complete idiot.

"I'm fine," I murmur, keeping my eyes on the ground. "Sorry about that."

He laughs lightly. "No worries. Just be glad I wasn't a truck. I don't think you'd have fared so well."

"I'll pay better attention," I say dumbly, cringing as soon as the words leave my mouth. That makes it sound like this isn't the first time this has happened. Forget idiot; he must think I'm completely incompetent.

"You do that. Where are you headed?"

"Home."

He hasn't dropped his hold on my arms, which makes me slightly uncomfortable. It's been a long time since I've been touched by a man. The simple brush of his hand the other day on my back patio was enough to remind me how much I'd missed it. Now, with the feel of his strong fingers gripping me and the heat of his body radiating onto mine, I realize how much I *want* to be touched. How much I long to be held. But it's not something I can have.

I shrug out of his grasp, taking a step back. He easily lets go of me, not putting up any sort of fight. But, when my eyes still don't meet his, he reaches a hand out, his fingers coming into contact with my chin, tilting my face up to his.

"Can I walk you?"

I'm taken aback by the request. He's obviously headed toward town, and I'm going in the opposite direction. *Why would he turn around to walk me home?*

Oh, right, because he thinks I'm incompetent. Probably doesn't want the poor foolish girl who lives next door to get hit by a car and die on the way home.

"No, thank you. I'll be okay. Besides, you were obviously on your way somewhere," I say, gesturing at his slightly dressed up attire.

Dressed up might be a bit of an exaggeration. Back in Chicago, it wouldn't be unusual to see a man in dark jeans and a zippered charcoal-gray pullover. But, around here, where nobody seems to own anything but tattered Levi's and flannel shirts, he definitely looks out of place. That leads me to think he must be on the way to meet someone. *A date perhaps?*

"Nope. Just on my way into town to grab a loaf of bread and some PB and J. But that can wait if you'd like me to walk you home."

"You got all dressed up to run down to the corner store?"

He looks down at his clothes. "Believe it or not, this is probably the most casual thing I own. Guess I'd better rectify that if I don't want to be seen as an out-of-place tourist the whole time I'm here, huh?"

I smile. "We can be misfits together. I'm new here myself."

What. The. Fuck. Lexi? Did you just try to flirt *with him?*

"Well, it's nice to know I'm not alone. I like having a partner in crime," he says, his mouth widening into a devastating smile.

Oh God. I have to get out of here. Now, before I do something even more embarrassing than literally *running into him.*

"It was nice to see you again. Enjoy your peanut butter." I push past him before he can respond, my feet moving double time as I attempt to get away. I don't look behind me because I don't want to give him any indication that I might want him to follow me.

The man is gorgeous; that much is obvious. With his athletic build and broad shoulders, there's no doubting his strength. Add in those stunning eyes, chiseled cheekbones, and strong jawline, and he's everything I've always found attractive in a man. Old me would've been falling all over herself, trying to get a chance with a man like that.

But that's just it. That was the old me. The woman who hadn't made the mistake of a lifetime. The woman who deserved love. The woman who had a bright future ahead of herself but threw it all away with one terrible decision.

The woman I am today is a shell of that woman. On the outside, we might be the same. But on the inside? On the inside, we couldn't be more different. I don't deserve happiness. I don't deserve love. On the inside, I'm as ugly as the car crash I caused that night. On the inside, I don't deserve…

Anything at all.

chapter five
tag

"Can I give you a hand with that?"

Lexi screams as she drops the hammer, her feet jumping back before it has the chance to crush her toe.

Smooth, Tag. Real smooth. Way to give the poor girl a heart attack.

When I saw her outside from my kitchen window—well, B's kitchen window—trying like hell to reach up and hold a board in place with one hand while she maneuvered the hammer with the other, I couldn't help but smile. I'd only seen her on a few occasions, but this tiny blonde sure was different than anyone I'd met before.

Most women I knew wouldn't even know how to hold a hammer, let alone try to fix a broken shutter on her own. Yet here was Lexi, thin sweater rising up to expose her tiny waist as she reached, her round ass on full display for anyone to gawk at, trying her damnedest to do it all on her own.

the Off-Season

Okay, maybe that gawking part was just me since I seem to be the only perv within gawking distance.

After watching her for a few moments, I decided to stop being a creeper and go over to offer my assistance. And, instead of charming the pants right off her—which, let's be honest, was totally my intention—I almost caused spontaneous amputation.

Strike two when it comes to this girl. First, I showed up like an idiot on her back porch. And, now, on her front one, I almost cost her a toe.

Moral of the story—me, this girl, and porches do not mix.

She retrieves the hammer, allowing me a close-up view of that perfect ass as she bends over to pick it up, and then she blows her hair out of her face and gives me a pointed look. "Can I help you?"

Her irritation with me radiates off her in waves. Not exactly the usual response I elicit from the ladies, but then again, I normally don't come across as such a freaking idiot.

What is it about this girl that turns me into a fool the second she's near?

I shrug off the thought. It doesn't matter. I remind myself yet again that I'm not here for random hook-ups. I'm not here for anything other than reconnecting with myself and regrouping. And getting my game face back because, Lord knows, it was missing this last season. Screwing the neighbor is certainly not on the to-do list, no matter how hot she might be.

But that doesn't mean I need to be a dick and leave her here to fix this shit on her own.

I take a step forward. Her eyes narrow further as my hand extends toward hers, but rather than closing my fingers around her skin, I pull the hammer from her grip.

"I came over to see if you needed a hand. From over there, it looked like you might be having a hard time."

Lexi reaches for the hammer, but I lift my arm, holding it out of her grasp.

"I'm fine. Now, if you'll return my tool…"

I step past her, sure to keep the hammer elevated so that she's unable to snatch it out of my hand. I take a look at the shutter hanging precariously from a single nail. "Haven't you ever heard the expression, *Two heads are better than one*? Well, four *hands* are better than two. Let me help. You'll be done in half the time."

I don't wait for her to answer or protest. Instead, I twist the shutter around until it's upright, holding it in place as I look at her over my shoulder. "Hand me a nail, would ya?"

Lexi gives me another irritated look, her jaw setting a hard edge as she turns to the porch railing. Grabbing a handful of nails, she whirls around and stomps over to my side.

She really is cute when she's mad.

When she joins me, I flick my chin over to the lower corner of the shutter. "Hold on to that edge for me. Keep it steady while I secure this side."

I take a nail from her outstretched palm as she places her other hand where I instructed. Once she's in place, I drop my hold on the wood, lining up the nail in the perfect position before driving it home with a few well-placed hits.

I forgot how satisfying it could be to use your hands for something as mundane as fixing a shutter. My hands are my livelihood. Without them, I wouldn't be able to catch, field, or hit a ball. But there's a vast difference between using them to play a game versus using them to make something. I grew up helping my uncle with his construction business. I enjoyed it, but it was never the life I wanted. Looking back though, there was always a certain sense of pride that came from it. Not the same kind of pride that comes from a random stranger recognizing me on the street and asking for my autograph. But a pride that comes from knowing your hands helped create something that could change a person's life.

Fuck. It's a shutter, dude. Cool it with the philosophical bullshit.

I make quick work of the other two corners, testing the strength of the shutter with a firm tug. "All right, I think that'll do it. Unless we get hit by a freak lake hurricane, you should be good to go. Anything else I can help you out with?"

Lexi gives me an odd look. It's not exactly irritation, like it was before. But I wouldn't call it friendly either.

"What's in it for you?"

Her question catches me so off guard, I swear, I almost swallow my tongue. "Ex-excuse me?"

"You heard me," she says, her hip cocking to the side as her hand comes to rest on it.

I'd laugh at the ridiculousness of the motion if I wasn't sure she'd probably skin me alive for it. This girl is a paradox of sassy and adorable. I mean, I don't think I've ever witnessed a girl actually put her hand on her hip like she was Michelle Tanner or some shit. I half-expect her to stomp her foot at me. It's cute as hell.

But, on the other hand, she sort of scares the shit out of me. Every part of me is convinced that, if I made the wrong move, my testicles would be jammed so far up my body, my tonsils would be able to say hello. In the few times I've seen her, she's never once given me the impression that she'd fall for my shit.

She isn't a damsel in distress, waiting for the handsome prince to come and save the day.

She's a dragon. And she isn't afraid to burn anyone who gets in her way.

And fuck me if that isn't sexy as hell.

I hold my hands up, the thumb and forefinger circling the hammer to keep it from clattering to the ground again. "Nothing in it for me. Just trying to be neighborly."

Lexi's eyes roam me from head to toe, pausing every so often to pay special attention to some aspect of my appearance. When she finishes her perusal, her face is impassive. She turns on her heel without so much as a word, walking over to the window on the other side of the front door. She fidgets with the shutter on the right side of the window for a moment before looking back over her shoulder.

"Well, are you going to help me, or are you going to stand there and look pretty?"

Oh, God. I'm in so much trouble.

We work in near silence for the next few hours, the only words passing between us related to the task at hand. After fixing all the shutters, we move to the steps leading up to the front door. They're usable but in definite need of repair. If the creak under my feet is any indication, I'd say it's only a matter of time before someone's foot goes right through one of them.

I sit down on the cooling ground, starting with the bottom step and having no intention of stopping until we reach the top. Grabbing a hammer, I set about prying the old, rotted wood off the risers.

A pile of new wood and a miter saw are set up on the side of the house. When Lexi brought me over and showed me the area, I have to admit I was impressed. Impressed because she had some damn good materials picked out. And doubly impressed that she had intended to use that saw on her own.

I almost said as much but stopped myself before the words could escape. Something told me Lexi wouldn't take kindly to my male chauvinistic view of women and power tools. I didn't need to give her a reason to practice using that saw on, say…my balls.

Lexi disappears as I'm finishing the demolition of the first step, and I'm halfway through the second when she reappears a few minutes later, a plate of sandwiches in one hand and a glass of water in the other. When she takes a seat on the top step, setting the plate down next to her and picking up half a sandwich, I take that as my cue to join her.

I grab a sandwich, not even bothering to see what's on it, and inhale half of it before my butt even meets the stair. I hadn't realized how hungry I was until food was presented to me. All this hard work is…well, hard. I forgot how much it takes out of you.

I chew silently, not wanting to break the unsaid understanding we seem to have going on here. Lexi has made it clear she's not exactly a Chatty Cathy. Besides, this girl is already hard enough to be around, everything about her practically calling to me even though I know she's off-limits. If she actually acted like she might like me, who knows if I'd be able to resist? Better we keep up this all-business thing we've got going. Less temptation.

So, imagine my surprise when she finally speaks, "You said you were on your way to town for PB and J the other day, so I figured that was a safe bet. But, if you'd prefer something else, let me know. I've got some lunchmeat in the fridge."

The smile that spreads across my face is instantaneous. Not only did she speak to me, but she also remembered my favorite food. Okay, so maybe she didn't know it was my favorite. But it still makes me ridiculously happy that she remembered what I'd said.

I really am in so much fucking trouble.

I hold up my sandwich, turning my smile toward her. "This is great. Thank you."

A small laugh bubbles out of her, and it's the most contagious sound I've ever heard. I can't help but laugh with her.

"What's so funny?"

"You have peanut butter in your teeth."

Fuck. Me.

My lips snap shut, my tongue running across them to try to clear any remaining debris. The damage is done though. That's strike three.

I take a sip of the water, trying to buy some time to come up with something to say to explain to this girl that I'm not normally such a moron, when she surprises me again.

"So, forgive me for asking, but I think it's only fair, considering you know mine. What's your name?"

My eyes dart to hers, looking for any hint of sarcasm or impertinence. But her question appears genuine. I think back to our earlier conversations and realize she's right. I asked for her name but never offered mine. To be honest, the thought never occurred to me. I haven't had to introduce myself since my rookie year with the Rampage. Everywhere I go, people seem to know who I am. I never even thought about the fact that Lexi might not.

It's oddly refreshing.

To Lexi, I'm the guy next door. Not Tag Taggart, all-star shortstop for the Washington Rampage. I'm not a conquest, a chance for her fifteen minutes of fame. And I sure as hell am not a meal ticket, a man she can accuse of rape in exchange for three million dollars.

the Off-Season

"My name is Ian," I hear myself say.

It's not a lie. It's the name on my birth certificate. But it's a name I haven't gone by in years. My friends call me Tag. My teammates call me Tag. Hell, with the exception of my mom, my entire family calls me Tag.

But, while Lexi might not recognize me, she might recognize my name. And, now that I know she has no idea who I am, I want to keep it that way. At least for a little while longer.

"And what brings you to Maple Lake, Ian?"

"I, uh...I needed to get away for a bit. You?"

She raises a brow at me, as if she wasn't anticipating me to ask the same question. She thinks for a moment before saying, "I just needed to get away for a bit."

Right. I'd be willing to bet she's trying to get away from *something*, just like I am. But I'm not about to press the issue, not when I'm not in any rush to explain my reasoning either.

After finishing up lunch—she made me three sandwiches, and I ate every single bite—we get back to work on the stairs. Our semi-friendly chatter quickly dies off, the rest of the afternoon passing much like the morning did.

The sun is beginning to set behind the mountains as I hammer home the final nail. Setting the hammer down on the finished step, I take a step back, dusting my hands off and finding myself by Lexi's side. "Not too shabby, if I do say so myself."

She gives me a playful shove, almost knocking me to my ass out of shock. After spending all day with her, that's the last thing I expected her to do. She grabs my forearm and helps steady me. Her laughter and her smile, which lights her eyes in a way I haven't seen before, cause all the air to rush out of my lungs.

"Would you like to stay for dinner?"

It takes a second for her words to register. And, when they do, I'm convinced I imagined them.

"What?" I mutter like an idiot.

She smiles shyly at me.

Who in the hell is this girl, and what has she done with Lexi?

"Well, I figure I've stolen your entire Saturday. The least I can do is cook you dinner."

I'm not sure what has changed in the past few hours. When I arrived, I was convinced she was going to skin me alive. And, now, here she is, her cheeks blushing as she looks down at the ground beneath her feet, waiting for my answer.

I know I should leave. I should say, *Thanks, but no, thanks*, before turning and running my ass back to my place. Fuck, if I were smart, I'd get on the phone with Ray and tell him to find me someplace else to hide out for a few months before I could do something really stupid.

But, instead, I hear myself saying the words, "Dinner sounds great."

chapter six
lexi

What in the hell was I thinking? I ask myself for the millionth time since Ian left to go wash up. Standing under the spray of the shower, I can't help but wonder if I've lost my damn mind. Or maybe he has?

He agreed to dinner fairly quickly even though I'd been nothing but bitchy to him all day. Lucky for me, he asked if it would be okay if he went home and cleaned up first, and I didn't waste a second saying yes. I needed some time to wash up as well. And berate myself for being a goddamn idiot.

Why did I ask him to stay for dinner? Why had I let him stick around all day?

Well, I knew the answer to that one actually. Despite my resolve to do this all myself, it really was great to have some help. I'd expected those stairs to take me the rest of the weekend. And we were able to knock them out in a few hours.

But look at where it got me. I might have finished stairs, but now, I am going to have dinner with the gorgeous man who lives next door.

This is not good.

I tried scaring him away when he first showed up this morning. After my reaction to being close to him on the street the other day, I knew I needed to stay as far away from him as possible. So, I acted like a complete asshole. I was short, rude, and unfriendly as hell. And, still, he stayed to help. I thought giving him the silent treatment would get him to leave. But he seemed to accept it, working alongside me in an unspoken pact of silence. It was…odd. But nice. There was a certain comfort that came from being with someone who didn't feel the need to fill the silence with idle chatter all the time.

When lunchtime rolled around, I wasn't able to help myself from asking him a few questions. I didn't like not knowing my next-door neighbor's name, especially when he was doing so much to help me out. And then, by the end of the day, I'd gotten so comfortable with being around him, the invitation to dinner slipped out before I could stop it.

And therein lies the problem. In a few short hours, I've grown *comfortable* with Ian.

And that can't happen.

I can't exactly uninvite him now though. I'll just have to whip together something fast, feed him, and then feign exhaustion. Hopefully, he'll get the hint and get his ass out of my house before I have to resort to being rude again.

I finish rinsing off and step out of the shower, a twinge in my back indicating I might not have to pretend to be exhausted too much. A long, hard day of work certainly takes more of a toll on you at twenty-seven than it does at twenty-three.

My mind flashes briefly to the long days and nights I spent fixing up Simply Chic. The hours I devoted to painting and redecorating, making sure everything was perfect before opening. It was the first thing I could call all my own. And I couldn't have been prouder of the way it turned out.

Before I let it all go to hell.

Refusing to let myself go down that path right now, I hurry and get dressed, squashing down the memories in the back of my mind.

Where they belong.

I head downstairs, dumping some water into a pot, and set about making pasta. Simple, easy, and not exactly the type of meal you sit and savor. Ian can eat and run. Emphasis on the *run*.

Twenty minutes later, the noodles are done, and the sauce is simmering. And I'm stewing in a chair. It's been almost an hour since he said he'd be back *soon*. Evidently, his idea of soon is different than mine.

Or maybe I'm getting lucky, and he's decided not to show.

I try to tell myself that would be a good thing. It would save me a whole lot of trouble of trying to get him to leave and stay away. But I can't deny the soft pang of remorse that courses through me at the thought of him standing me up.

Don't be ridiculous, Lexi. It's better this way.

But what about the pasta? I can't eat it all myself. It'd be a shame to let it go to waste.

Pasta-schmasta. Pull your head out of your ass, and get your shit together.

Yep. I've officially lost my mind.

Before the fight in my head can come to blows—'cause, if anybody could go *that* crazy, it would be me—a knock sounds at the door. My internal bickering instantly quiets, the pounding of my heart overtaking my every breath.

I stare at the door, as if I can somehow both will him away and invite him inside with the power of my mind.

After a moment, he knocks again, his voice coming from the other side of the door. "Lexi? You in there?"

Hearing the confusion in his voice snaps me out of my trance, and I spring into action. Switching the burner on the stove off before the sauce scorches to the pan, I make my way over to the door. I plaster on a smile before I swing it open.

Big mistake.

My phony smile falls the moment I lay eyes on him. If I thought he was gorgeous in dark jeans and a sweater the other day, he's downright *mouthwatering* tonight.

His dark hair is still damp, the wet strands combed back, emphasizing his stylish undercut. He's wearing a pair of black jeans, a white T-shirt, and a fitted black blazer. A *very* fitted black blazer. The stretch of the fabric over his biceps is just plain obscene.

Whoever coined the term *arm porn* did so after seeing this man in a blazer.

Guaranteed.

Ian's soft chuckle forces my gaze away from his arms and back to his face where I find a soul-crushing smile waiting for me.

"Um, hi," I mutter, blushing like an idiot for being caught checking him out.

Ian has the decency to let it slide though, his dimples deepening as he looks at me. "You look great."

Heat flushes my cheeks, and if the glint in his eye is any indication, he sees it, too.

"Um, thank you."

He flicks his chin over my shoulder, looking at the living room behind me. "Can I come in?"

I look back, my brows furrowing as I take in the dingy space. I haven't been inside his place, but judging from the outside and the small part I can see through the windows from my dock, my tiny living room is not at all what he's used to.

"Um, yes. It's, um, still a work in progress though, so please excuse the dust."

Oh my God. How many times can one person say the word um? Pull yourself together, Lexi!

I step back, allowing Ian to step over the threshold. He's careful in his perusal, taking in every detail of the room around him. I twist my hands behind my back, suddenly even more self-conscious than before. If that's possible.

I wait by the door as he assesses the space. When he turns and smiles at me, I can't help but smile back.

"I like it. It's got a lot of charm. I'm sure, by the time you're finished with it, it'll be the nicest place in town."

I scoff. "Well, it's nothing compared to your house, of course. But I have high hopes."

Ian sits down on the couch, making himself comfortable. I didn't invite him to do so, but I guess the dinner invitation sort of implies a casual chat. I take a seat in the armchair across the room.

"That's actually my buddy Brandon's place. He's letting me stay there for a bit."

I'm not sure why, but hearing that the huge, ostentatious house isn't his fills me with a sense of relief. When he continues, that feeling only intensifies.

"I could never live in a place like that. Not long-term anyway. I mean, it's a beautiful house. But it's so...I don't know. Over the top? I'm not much for showing off. I prefer something much more cozy. Something like this," he adds, almost as an afterthought, his hand waving at the space around us.

I smile softly. "Thank you. My sister thinks I'm crazy for buying this place. But I know it's going to be great."

"You're not crazy. If I had more time, this is exactly the kind of thing I'd want to do. Fix up an old house. Restore former glory to a place that's fallen on hard times."

Something flashes behind his eyes as he says those words, making me think he's touched on a subject that delves deeper than simply renovating a home.

Before I can even consider asking him what he means, he stands, grabbing something from the floor by his feet. I was so dumbstruck by watching him as he looked around my living room, I didn't even notice he'd brought something with him.

When he holds up the six-pack of beer, he gives me another panty-melting smile. "I wasn't sure what your drink was, but I took a chance. I mean, who doesn't like an ice-cold beer after a long day of hard labor?"

My mouth goes dry at the sight of alcohol, my tongue feeling roughly twice its usual size. My fingers tremble as I curl them into fists and tuck them under my seated legs. "I'm fine, thank you."

He pouts his lower lip a tad. On any other man, it would look ridiculous. But, on Ian, it just looks…enticing.

"Come on, Lex. Don't make me drink alone."

My heart skips a beat at the use of the pet name. My sister calls me Lex. All my old friends back in Chicago called me Lex. But, coming from Ian's lips, it sounds more intimate. It sounds warm, like I could curl up around him and listen to him say my name over and over until I fell asleep.

the Off-Season

Holy fuck. What is wrong with me?

You need a few good rounds with Mr. Reliable; that's what's wrong with you.

Thinking of the nickname I gave my vibrator, the blush on my cheeks deepens even further. I shake myself out of it, getting to my feet and walking past Ian to the kitchen.

"I'm fine. I actually don't drink. But, please, don't let that stop you."

He grabs hold of my arm as I reach to open the cupboard for a few plates. "I'm sorry. I didn't mean to upset you."

"You didn't," I say shortly, turning back to the task at hand.

"I did. I thought I was being funny. It wasn't my intention to make you uncomfortable."

It kills me that he was able to read my reaction so easily. It only further solidifies the fact that I need to watch myself around this guy. He's already tearing down walls I thought were indestructible. And that's without even trying.

I turn and hand him a plate, trying my hardest to give him a genuine smile. "It's okay. You didn't know. But, really, don't let my teetotalism affect you. It won't bother me if you have a few beers with your dinner."

He turns and walks back over to the front door, and I briefly wonder if he might leave.

But, when he simply opens the door, depositing the six-pack on the porch before turning back and saying, "Water is great. I need to lose a few pounds anyway," I can't help but laugh.

"You didn't have to do that. And, believe me, the last thing you need is to lose a few pounds."

"Why, Lexi, have you been checking me out?" he asks, an amused smile spreading across his lips.

My cheeks must be the color of a boiled lobster at this point, but I can't seem to bring myself to care. I grin at him, rolling my eyes instead of looking away. "Oh, yes. You're such a stud; I couldn't help myself."

My words are laced with sarcasm, and Ian snickers right along with me. He doesn't have to know how much truth was also mixed into that statement.

"Come on, your dinner is getting cold," I say, leading him over to the colander and scooping out a generous portion of spaghetti noodles.

Dinner passes quickly, Ian making me laugh more often than he probably should—most times while I have a mouthful of food. At one point, I snort so hard, I'm almost positive a noodle passes through my nose. When I cover my face with my hands, Ian refuses to leave me alone until I tell him what's wrong, the two of us doubling over in a desperate attempt to catch our breaths as he tries to pry my hands from my face.

Luckily, no offending spaghetti is hanging from my nose. But, when I tell Ian what I was afraid of him finding, his hysterics only deepen.

Before I know it, the old clock on the wall behind me—one of the only possessions I'd had back in Chicago that made the journey to Maple Lake—chimes, indicating it's now nine o'clock. Ian seems to realize how late it's gotten at the same time I do, and he stands.

"I should get going. We've both had a long day. And I definitely need my beauty sleep."

I smile at his ridiculous statement. "Thank you for your help today, Ian. It was greatly appreciated."

He hits me with another dimpled smile, his eyes sparkling in the dim light of the living room. "It was my pleasure, Lexi. And thank you for dinner. I haven't laughed that hard in ages."

He takes my hand in his, lifting it to his lips and pressing a gentle kiss to my knuckles. "I'll see you soon."

After he leaves, I sink down onto the couch, thinking back over what he said.

"I haven't laughed that hard in ages."

Neither have I. I laughed with Ian—sometimes so hard, tears seeped out the corners of my eyes. I can't remember the last time I allowed myself to laugh like that.

For the first time in over a year, I let myself be...me.

The guilt that has been my ever-present companion for the past eighteen months is nowhere to be found.

Until now.

A guilt so deep that I feel it in my bones settles over me.

That's more like it.

chapter seven
tag

"What up, asshole? You miss me yet?"

Brandon's voice comes over the line before I even have a chance to utter the word *hello*. I'd say I'm shocked at his lack of proper phone etiquette, but who am I kidding? B is nothing if not inappropriate. I'd be more concerned for his well-being if I'd answered the phone and he'd asked me about the weather and how I was *feeling*.

Sign number one that your best friend has been replaced by a pod person: politeness.

I laugh as B doesn't wait for my answer, immediately launching into a story about his night out with Carter, the rookie we drafted this last summer.

"You should've seen it, dude. When that stripper came up to him, I thought he was going to cream his jeans right there on the spot. He straight-up denies it, but I'm about ninety-nine percent certain our boy is a virgin."

A virgin baseball player. It's not completely unheard of, but it sure as shit ain't the norm. Lucky for Carter, he's only out in Seattle to sign contracts and meet the players. He'll be regulated down to one of the farm teams before the season starts. Though, from what I saw of the kid, it wouldn't surprise me if he got called up to the bigs sooner rather than later. Kid has an arm like I've never seen. But at least he'll be safe from Brandon's negative influence for a little while.

"Leave the poor kid alone, B. He's only twenty."

Brandon scoffs. "Please. He's way too damn green for a twenty-year-old. Shit, by the time I was twenty, I'd bagged at least a dozen chicks."

I roll my eyes. "Well, not everyone is as big a slut as you are, Jeffers. And nobody says *bagged* anymore. Get a new word."

"Boinked? Boned? Banged? Any of those tickle your fancy?"

"Anything involving you and your dick will *never* tickle my fancy. And you do realize there are other letters in the alphabet, right? Not everything starts with B."

"Yeah, but all the *best* things do. And, if they're lucky, they finish with B, too."

"Did you call me for a reason?" I groan.

The guy might be my best friend, but there is only so much of his ego I can take. Especially since I was up all night, thinking about a certain blonde who lives next door.

"My, my, aren't we touchy today? What crawled up your ass and died?"

I let out an exasperated breath. Brandon is a son of a bitch. But he is my best friend. There isn't anything I can't tell him. Besides, the guy knows me better than anyone. If I don't tell him what's bugging me, he'll probably show up on my doorstep—his doorstep. Whatever.

"So, there's this girl…" I start, letting my words trail off as I wait for Brandon to react.

He doesn't disappoint. "Yeah, buddy. Knew you wouldn't let that Angela bitch keep you out of the saddle for long. She hot?"

I shake my head even though he can't see it. Should've known his thoughts would go instantly to the sexual side of things.

"She is. But that's not the point."

"Bullshit, that's not the point. I know the bitch did a number on you, but that doesn't change the fact that you're Tag *fucking* Taggart. And Tag Taggart doesn't fuck ugly chicks."

"Dude," I blurt, cutting him off before he can continue. "Do you hear yourself right now? Do you enjoy being known as the douchiest douche who has ever played in the MLB?"

B is silent for a moment, as if my words have actually stunned him.

When he finally speaks, his tone is a mixture of remorse and fire. "Look, I'm sorry if I've pissed you off. But don't pile your bullshit on me. I'm sorry life sucks for you right now. But it's not my fault. So, stop being an asshole, and stop pawning it off on me."

A rush of guilt comes over me. B likes to act like a jerk, but deep down, he's one of the best guys I've ever met. I know he's just trying to get me to laugh. But I'm not in the mood.

"Sorry," I bite out. "Look, now's not a good time. I'll call you later."

He interjects before I can disconnect the call, "Hold up. You're not getting off that easy. I promise to be on my best behavior. Tell me about the girl."

I toss the options around in my head. On the one hand, I really would like to get B's advice on what to do about Lexi. The asshole knows me better than I know myself. But, on the other hand, do I really believe Brandon can be on his best behavior for longer than thirty seconds?

I sigh, knowing I need to talk to somebody. Guess I'd better talk fast.

"So, the morning after I got here, I decided to go for a swim—"

"Dude, it's fucking freezing up there this time of year," B interrupts.

"Are you going to listen or keep telling me shit I already know?"

"Sorry. Proceed."

"So, I jumped in and immediately knew it was the worst decision ever. But, while I was underwater, I somehow managed to float away from your dock and over toward the neighbor's."

"Which neighbor?"

"The one to the east."

B blows out a relieved breath. "Good. That house has been vacant for years. Now, if you'd drifted the other way, you might have managed to give sweet old Margie a heart attack. And then I'd have to kick your ass because she's just about my favorite person on the planet. Always cooks me dinner whenever I'm staying up there. You meet her yet?"

"Not yet. I haven't had a chance to get around and meet the neighbors. Except one. And I've got news for you, B. That house to the east…it's no longer unoccupied."

"No shit? Somebody finally bought that dump? I was actually considering it myself. Tear that piece of shit down, and put in a guesthouse or something. Or maybe a pool."

"Why do you need a pool when—" I stop, knowing this is Brandon we're talking about. Of course he wouldn't see the pointlessness of a pool when there's a lake mere feet away.

"Anyway, yes, a woman bought the house and has been fixing it up. She was out, enjoying a nice cup of coffee on her back porch, when I came running up, half-naked and thoroughly frozen."

B lets out a laugh. "I bet you were quite the pretty picture. Tell me, was there shrinkage?"

I roll my eyes. "So much for your best behavior."

"Oh, come on!" B retorts. "You can't tell me you jumped in a freezing cold lake and then went running up to some poor unassuming woman and not expect me to give you shit. That's in the manual. When one best friend embarrasses the fuck out of himself, the other best friend is required by law to laugh their ass off at him. You wouldn't want me to break the law now, would you, Tag?"

"Anyway," I say again, dragging out the word, so he knows I'm done with this subject, "since then, we bumped into each other once, and then, yesterday, I went over and offered to help her with a project she was working on. We ended up having dinner at her place."

"My man works fast. So, what's the problem?"

"The *problem* is, I'm supposed to be up here, keeping my nose clean and my dick in my pants. But I can't stop thinking about this girl."

"Are you worried she might be another Angela? Try to slap you with some ridiculous charges to get her fifteen minutes and some cash?"

I shake my head. "No, that's just it. She doesn't even know

who I am."

"Does she live under a rock? I mean, up until a few months ago, your face was practically plastered on every billboard and TV commercial in America." He leaves out the part where even *during* those few months, my face was everywhere. Just in a much less flattering light.

And this is why, even having to deal with all his shit, B will always be my best friend. He may be an asshole, but he's an asshole who's always got my back.

"I get the feeling she's not much of a sports fan. And I'm not sure why, but something also tells me she sort of *has* been living under a rock for a while. She's very closed off. Doesn't like to talk about herself. Hell, when I first went over there yesterday, she treated me like the scum of the earth."

"And you've recently developed a penchant for being treated like dirt?"

"Of course not. But, B, there's something about her. And, by the end of the evening, she dropped her guard and let me see *her* for a little while. And I like the real her a whole hell of a lot."

"But what's she hiding? What's the point of her acting like a bitch if that's not who she really is?"

"I dunno, B. But I want to find out."

Brandon blows out a long sigh. "I don't know, man. If this was about you getting your dick wet, I'd be all for it. And I am glad you're feeling better. But you sound different. You sound...*interested* in this girl. And I worry about that."

"You're worried that I might actually grow up at some point, want to stop fucking around, and settle down?"

"No, that's not what I meant. I know this player lifestyle isn't permanent for you. You've always been a bit more...committed than me. Even when you're playing the field. But you don't really know this chick. And you already sound like you're thinking more long-term."

I let out a laugh. "B, trust me, I'm not looking to marry her. Like you said, I barely know her. She intrigues me. She's someone I want to get to know. That doesn't mean I'm going to profess my undying love and start ring shopping anytime soon. Fuck, once I'm finally able to crack through her shell, she probably won't even be half of what I've built up in my head. But I feel like I'll regret it if I don't at least try."

"Well, it sounds like your mind is already made up then. Just promise me, you'll be careful. I'll vouch for you with Coach and Ray. I'll make sure they don't think anything is up, so they don't flip their shit. But only if you promise you'll watch your back. If there's any sign this girl might be trouble, you get your ass out of there, okay?"

"Promise. First sign of danger, and I'll be on the next flight home."

"Good. Don't make me regret doing this, asshole. Coach will string my ass up from the scoreboard if he finds out I helped you cover this up. She'd better be worth it."

I thank him again, not giving voice to the thought running through my head.

I'm one hundred percent certain she is.

chapter eight
lexi

There's a bite in the air today that wasn't here when I arrived last week, reminding me that fall is in full effect in Maple Lake. As if I could forget, the vibrant fall colors expand almost as far as my eye can see. Despite the bite to the air, it's a beautiful day to be outdoors, which is a good thing, considering I've got quite the walk ahead of me today.

The small hardware store in town—the one that acts as the town's grocery/convenience store as well—only has a limited selection of paint available. And none of the colors spoke to me for my living room. Fortunately, the town of Grover is only about fifteen miles away, and they have a full-blown Home Depot. Unfortunately, I don't have a car. Fifteen miles is a hell of a lot longer walk than drive.

Ella would be furious if she knew I was walking all this way.

But she's recently returned to work after having the twins, and as much as I know she'd be willing to drive me, I know she'd hate the idea of having to take off work. And I'm too damn impatient to wait for the weekend.

I figure I can grab a few gallons and get a decent start. Then, when Saturday rolls around, I'll have Ells drive me back, so I can get the rest.

Besides, the fresh air will do me good. I've been cooped up in that house for far too many hours.

Twenty minutes into my walk, however, and I'm already starting to rethink this decision. The sun might be shining, but that doesn't take away the chill that has settled into my nose and cheeks. I bury my hands deeper in my pockets, shrugging my shoulders up around my head to try to get some of the heat radiating off my midsection to my frozen face.

It doesn't work.

I'm too determined to turn around though. And, after a quick look around to ensure nobody is in my immediate vicinity, I do something I haven't done since I was probably eight years old.

I start skipping.

My arms swing wide as I try to warm up my body, my knees coming almost to my chest with every movement. I know I must look ridiculous, but it seems to be helping.

Deciding I might as well go all in, I start chanting my favorite nursery rhyme as I go.

"I'm a little teapot, short and stout,

"Here is my handle, here is my spout."

I put one hand on my hip for the handle and curl my other arm into my best impression of a spout, skipping along the street the entire time. *Hey, if I'm going to do this, I'm going to do it right.*

the Off-Season

"When I get all steamed up, hear me shout,
"Tip me over, and pour me out."

I stop for a moment, bending over to the right, spilling my imaginary tea all over the road.

I giggle at the absurdity of my actions. But it doesn't stop me from doing it again.

I'm in the middle of my third rotation when I hear it.

The sound of an engine.

Right. Behind. Me.

I was so caught up in my little song and dance, I didn't even hear the vehicle approaching.

And the fact that it's now slowly crawling along behind me instead of flying past me makes me think the person inside must know me.

That means, it's one of three people.

Charlie, Liv, or...

The sound of the horn causes me to turn around, coming face-to-bumper with a red Ford pickup. The glare from the sun off the windshield prevents me from seeing who's inside. But I'm pretty sure I already know.

The fancy red truck doesn't look like something Charlie or Liv would drive. At all.

That leaves...

The driver puts the truck in park and climbs down.

Ian.

Fuck my life.

"How much of that did you see?" I say by way of greeting.

The cheeky smile he gives me is all I need to know.

"Enough," he says simply, amusement alighting his eyes. "You're quite the little dancer," he teases.

I groan, dropping my eyes down to the ground, wishing it would open up and swallow me whole.

I grunt out an excuse about trying to keep warm, refusing to lift my gaze back to his.

"What are you doing all the way out here anyway?" he asks, as if it just now occurred to him that we're in the middle of nowhere.

"I was going to Grover."

He doesn't respond, and his silence has me curious enough that I finally lift my eyes. But the look I find on his face has me wishing I had kept up my staring contest with the ground.

"You were going to walk all the way to Grover? Isn't that, like, ten miles away?"

"Fifteen," I correct and realize that doesn't help me look any less foolish.

He shakes his head. "You'd never make it before dark. And how were you planning on getting back?"

I give him a sheepish look. "The same way I got there."

Ian mumbles something under his breath, his hand coming up to wipe across his eyebrow. He seems to debate on something for a moment, and then, without another word, he turns and walks back to his truck. But, instead of climbing into the driver's side, he moves around the passenger side and opens the door.

"Get in," he says, nodding his head toward the waiting seat.

My mouth falls open, his authoritative tone kicking my sassy side into full gear. "Excuse me? Who do you think you are? You can't order me into your vehicle."

His head falls forward on his neck, and I swear, I hear him mumble something about stubborn women. I'm about to show him how stubborn I can be when he lifts his eyes back to mine. They're softer now, though I can still see a little of the assertiveness I saw there when he told me to get in his truck.

"Lexi, will you please let me give you a ride into town? There's no way you'll make it before the sun goes down. And I'd rather not have the death of my new neighbor weighing on my conscience. Even if you don't freeze, who knows what sort of wild animals might be waiting in the wings."

A shiver rolls down my spine. I didn't even consider the animals before I set out. I've seen my share of deer and other benign forest creatures since I've been in Maple Lake. But it's never occurred to me that there might be something a little more…carnivorous out here.

"Fine," I say and stomp over toward the truck.

I might be appreciative of the ride so that I don't become something's dinner, but he doesn't need to know that.

The other night was a huge mistake. I let Ian get way too close for comfort and actually let myself think about the possibility of more. Maybe not with him. But I opened up a door I'd thought long since closed.

Deep down, I know I'm being irrational. I know that I paid the price for my mistake, and Lord knows, I've learned from it. But knowing something and actually forgiving yourself are two entirely different things.

I almost killed someone. Two someones.

In what world is it fair that I get to move on and live my life when someone else's is forever altered?

Not in mine.

So, despite the fact that Ian is charming and handsome and that I enjoy the hell out of his company, there's no way I can let what happened the other night become a regular occurrence. And the only way I can prevent that is by closing him off.

Completely.

I buckle my seat belt as he walks around the truck to the driver's side. He climbs inside, putting the car in drive without saying another word.

We ride in silence for about ten minutes. When we pass a sign indicating Grover is only a mile away, Ian finally glances at me and asks where I'm headed.

"The hardware store. I need to get some paint."

He quirks an eyebrow at me. "You were planning on hauling paint all the way back to Maple Lake on foot?"

I shrug. "I figured I'd grab what I could carry for now and have my sister bring me back this weekend."

He chuckles under his breath, the tension from earlier seemingly broken. "You are determined; I'll give you that."

The way he says it makes it sound like more of a compliment than a criticism, so I smile. "Damn straight. Never stand in the way of a woman and her home improvement projects."

He shoots me a dazzling grin, the dimples in his cheeks even more pronounced than usual. "I hope you don't take this the wrong way, but you're so different than the women I'm used to."

Before I can ask what that means, he pulls into the parking lot of Home Depot and kills the engine. "You need some help?"

I shake my head out of instinct. I've always been extremely independent, even back before the accident and I've never been one to readily accept help.

But, as I turn and look at him, I quickly find myself changing my mind. It would be nice to have a second opinion on colors. And, now that I don't have to walk back home, I might as well get all the paint I need so I don't have to inconvenience Ella this weekend.

"Sure," I say, giving him a small smile. "If you wouldn't mind, I'd appreciate another set of eyes and hands."

He quickly climbs out of the truck, like he doesn't want to give me the chance to change my mind.

Two hours later, the back of his truck is full of paint, brushes, drop cloths, and everything else I could possibly need to paint my entire house. Once I got started on choosing colors for the living room, I couldn't seem to stop. My bank account is now about a thousand dollars lighter, but I couldn't be happier with the choices I made for my new home.

Ian helps me unload it all when we get back to my place. I have to admit; the whole process goes a lot faster with someone who can lift more than one five-gallon drum at a time. It would've taken Ella and me at least twice as long to load and unload the truck.

Ian lingers for a moment after he finishes carrying in the last load, his hands coming to rest on his hips as he surveys my new mountain of paint supplies. "That ought to keep you busy for a while."

I smile at him from across the room. "Thanks for your help. You're a lifesaver. I'm sure Ella would thank you, too, if she were here. She hates going shopping with me."

The corners of his lips pull up into a sarcastic smile. "With you? I can't imagine why. I mean, it's totally normal to have to look at each and every single type of paintbrush—in detail, might I add—before finally purchasing the first one you picked up."

I giggle. "Hey, I want to make sure I'm getting the best bang for my buck. Besides, not all paintbrushes are created equal. Brush lines are a bitch."

His smile changes, a flash of something unreadable passing through his eyes. "You're not at all what I expected, Lexi."

Before his words register, he's in front of me, his body only inches from mine instead of the minimum five feet I've been trying to keep between us all evening.

I swallow hard, leaning back against the wall behind me to try to create a little space between us. He doesn't press, his eyes raking over my face before he gives me a crooked smile. He lifts his hand to my face, his index finger running softly down the line of my nose.

"See you tomorrow, Lexi."

He's out the door before I can even protest.

chapter nine
tag

I've always been a morning person.

I'm that annoying guy you see in movies who bounds out of bed before his alarm, ready to take on the day, a spring in his step as he sips his cup of coffee and gets ready for work. To tell you the truth, I've never understood people who hate mornings.

Until today.

I've been up since four, biding my time. I ran my three miles, had about six cups of coffee, read every stupid article I could find about me on my phone, and resorted to playing some ridiculous game with little pieces of candy I had to match. I've never been so bored in my life.

I have no idea what time Lexi normally gets up in the morning, but I don't want to give her a chance to get too far into painting without me. If I show up too late, she'll tell me she's got it covered and turn me away. But, if I show up too early, I risk pissing her off by waking her up.

I curse under my breath as the screen tells me I'm out of moves once again. Setting down the phone, I glance at the clock and see that it's finally eight. Thinking back to that morning on her back dock, I remember that she was up and having coffee well before eight. Surely, this is as good a time as any, right?

I grab my ball cap from the counter and make my way toward the front door. Straightening it over my messy hair, I briefly wonder if it's a bad idea to wear a Rampage hat when I'm trying to fly under the radar. *Will it tip her off?*

I stop in front of the mirror in the entryway, giving myself a final once-over. My ratty T-shirt and ripped jeans—I might have ripped a hole in the knee this morning just to give the appearance of owning work clothes—certainly don't scream baseball star. And, come on, I see more Rampage hats in the stands than I do on the field. It's not unusual for a man to wear swag for his favorite team. Mine happens to be the one I play for.

I shrug, deciding to go with it. If she somehow manages to put two and two together, then that's how it goes. I'm enjoying the anonymity, but I don't intend to lie to Lexi forever. Especially if things turn out the way I'm hoping.

After finding Lexi skipping down the highway and then watching her enthusiasm as she meticulously chose each and every item she purchased yesterday, I can't deny that the woman fascinates me. She is such an enigma, going from cold and closed off to open and bubbly, seemingly within minutes. The glimpses I've seen of the softer side of Lexi make me think there is more to her than she lets on. She tries to put up a hard front, but deep down, I can tell it's an act. One I desperately want to break through.

I step out onto the porch, pulling the door shut behind me. I don't bother locking it.

Striding across my lawn, I consider my options.

I can turn on the charm I'm famous for, hoping she'll eventually cave and let me in.

Or I can let her see the real me. The Ian Taggart I like to keep hidden from cameras and reporters. The Ian Taggart who's not quite as sure of himself as he pretends to be. The Ian Taggart who's a bit of a socially awkward dork when it boils down to it. The Ian Taggart I've buried so far down underneath the facade I present to the rest of the world that I'm not entirely sure he can rise back to the surface.

Something tells me Lexi would greatly prefer that Ian Taggart. The Ian who's not so full of himself and who constantly doubts everything he's ever done, just waiting for the day people realize he's not all he's cracked up to be.

Well, fuck. Now, I'm depressed.

But it's true. Underneath all the pomp and circumstance, I really am an average guy. And I want Lexi to get to know the real side of me before she gets to know the baseball player.

When my fist finally makes contact with her door, my mind is made up. I'm going to let this happen naturally. I'm not going to try to sweep her off her feet and lay it on so thick, she has to use a knife to cut through my bullshit.

Lexi is going to get the real Ian "Tag" Taggart. And, if she doesn't like what she sees, then…

Well, I'll think about that later.

The door swings wide only seconds after I knock, Lexi's brows pulling together when she finds me standing here. Her hair is pulled back into a neat ponytail, so at least that's a good sign that I haven't woken her.

"Ian. Do you need something?"

Just to see your pretty face.

The line comes to mind so easily, I almost spit it out. It's what I would say to any other woman whose door I was knocking on first thing in the morning. And, while it's true—I thought about her beautiful, full lips and sweet, kind eyes all last night—it's not the only reason I'm here. I decide to go for something a little less forthright.

"Came to offer up my services. Put me in, Coach. I'm ready to work."

She lifts a quizzical eyebrow at me. "What makes you think I need your help?"

I look past her, at the room behind her. "The fact that you bought enough paint to fill that lake out back *and* the fact that you only have two hands. Come on, Lex. I've got nothing else to do today. Keep me from dying of boredom."

She pulls her bottom lip between her teeth as she turns to the side and surveys the mess behind her, her eyes wide, as if the magnitude of her project is finally sinking in. My eyes narrow in on the corner of her lip, and I have to remind myself that I'm taking things slow. Because, right now? All I want is to find out exactly how that lip would taste between my own teeth.

When she turns back around, she surprises me as she says, "Okay. But only for today. I don't want you thinking I can't handle myself."

I expected a lot more of an argument. She's finally relenting, letting me help. And her words are almost laughable, her serious expression causing me to smile.

"Lex, the last thing I think of when it comes to you is someone who can't handle herself. In the short time we've known each other, you've shown me over and over how independent you are. This isn't me trying to take over. I know you've got this. This is simply a friend wanting to offer a helping hand."

She smirks. "A friend, huh? And who says we're friends?"

There's a hint of mischief in her eyes, as if she's enjoying teasing and toying with me. And, fuck, if that isn't the sexiest thing I've ever seen.

"Oh, we're friends. In fact, as far as I'm concerned, you're the best friend I've got right now. Though that might have more to do with me not having actually met anyone else in town yet. Other than the cashier at the grocery store."

"You really ought to get out more. Pretty sad when your best friend isn't even sure if she likes you."

I take a step back, covering my heart with both hands. "You wound me, woman. Straight through the heart with that one."

She chuckles, blowing a stray strand of hair from her eyes before turning and picking up a roller. "Get to work," she says, slapping the roller against my chest. "Don't make me fire you on the first day."

She must miss the implication behind her words, but I sure as hell don't. *First* day. That means, I'm coming back tomorrow.

Painting sucks ass.

I know I said I enjoyed helping my uncle during all those summers, but I forgot how much I absolutely *loathed* painting. It's so monotonous. Up and down, up and down—oh, but don't zone out because then you'll fuck up and have to do it over again. I'll never understand how people make a living out of this. I'd rather gouge my eyes out.

Lexi has been rather quiet the last few hours, working on one end of the room while I work on the other. We're getting close to meeting in the middle, however, and she's now only a few feet away from me.

An idea flashes through my mind.

Dipping my roller into the tray, I make sure it's nice and wet. Then, before I can change my mind on what's surely one of the dumbest ideas I've ever had, I turn and run the dripping roller right up the center of Lexi's back.

She lets out a little squeal, her back straightening as she stiffens. I gulp, wondering how this is going to go. The way I see it, I've got two possibilities. Either she kicks me in the balls and yells at me to never come back or…

She spins around, a wide smile brightening her entire face. "Oh, you're gonna get it."

I duck as she tries to hit me in the stomach with a splash of paint, which isn't the smartest move. I might have avoided ruining my already ratty T-shirt, but instead, I get a face full of gray.

Her eyes widen with shock, a surprised breath escaping her lips as she tries to stifle her laughter. When she finally decides it's safe and I'm not about to scream at her, she lets loose, her soft giggles quickly giving way to loud chortles.

"This means war," I say, playfully narrowing my eyes and lunging for her with the roller.

The next ten minutes pass in a flash of color, fits of laughter, and more paint on our clothes than on the actual walls. When she

the Off-Season

finally collapses and calls a truce, I fall down on my back next to her, my breathing hard from the workout I just got.

After my heart rate returns to a normal pace, I roll over onto my side, facing her. She does the same, her hand coming up to prop her head as she looks at me. There's a smudge of paint under her left eye, and her once sleek ponytail is now in wild disarray around her face.

She looks beautiful.

Without thinking, I reach over and tuck a stray strand of hair behind her ear. Her eyes fall down to the floor as her cheeks flame, a shy smile coming across her face.

"What?" I ask, surprised at her reaction.

"Nothing. It's just...I've always wanted a guy to do that. I always see it in movies. But that's the first time I've ever experienced it firsthand."

I want to follow up her words with a kiss, but I know that would be pushing my luck. So, instead, I settle for a smile before climbing to my feet.

"Come on, Disney," I say, referencing her hopelessly romantic comment, and extend a hand down to her. "We'd better get back to work."

Lexi smiles up at me as I set her plate down in front of her.

"This smells delicious," she says, her eyes ravenous as she takes in the steak, baked potato, and green beans before her.

We got so caught up in painting and our idle chatter today that neither of us had the thought to break for lunch. When my stomach grumbled so loud that even she couldn't ignore it, we looked at the clock and realized we'd spent the last ten hours painting.

Time flies when you're having fun.

After our paint war, Lexi and I fell into an easy conversation. Nothing profound, mind you. I still don't have any idea what makes this girl tick or what she might be running from. But she talked for hours about her sister and her new nieces. And how much she'd been enjoying fixing up her old house.

I threw in a few tidbits of information about myself—mostly related to my youth and growing up, helping out my uncle—just enough to keep the conversation flowing and not seem like I was hanging on her every word, which was exactly what I'd been doing.

Watching her talk about her family changed her entire demeanor. Her face didn't just brighten up when she spoke about Ella and her girls; her entire body also shifted. She used her hands more when she talked, acting out whatever story she was telling as best as she could. There was a lightness to her tone that wasn't present whenever she spoke about any other subject.

If there is one thing I'm able to surmise from today, it's that Lexi really, truly loves her family.

She doesn't love them for what they can do for her, which is something I've grown accustomed to over the years. It doesn't matter to her if her sister is the wealthiest or poorest person on the planet. She loves Ella for exactly who she is. And it's refreshing as hell.

When she realized the late hour, however, she immediately clammed up and thanked me for my help. She tried to offer me some money for my time, which I declined. Then, we had a few awkward moments before she excused herself to take a shower, which was my cue to leave.

Only I wasn't ready for the day to end. So, instead of saying my good-byes and walking home, I somehow managed to sweet-talk her into dinner at my place. It might have taken a bit of pouting and bribery on my part, but none of that matters now. Not with her sitting across from me.

When I went to the store a few days ago, I made sure to fill the fridge with plenty of nonalcoholic alternatives. I have no idea what she likes to drink, so I made sure to get a little bit of everything.

When I listed off her choices when she first arrived, she giggled and said, "Nothing like having a fully stocked bar at your fingertips, huh?"

Little did she know I'd done it for her.

Now, as she sips her sparkling lemonade, I'm glad I had the foresight to stock up. I didn't want a repeat of our first dinner date. I know there is more to the story other than her not drinking. I sensed it in the way she'd said the words. But I'm not going to push her. She'll tell me when she's ready.

It's my job to ensure that happens.

We eat in silence, both of us too hungry to bother with pleasant conversation while shoveling food in our mouths. She insists on rinsing the dishes when we're both done eating, and I catch her staring out at the dock as she stands at the sink.

I walk up behind her, stopping just shy of pressing against her back. "Would you like to go sit by the fire?" I ask, my voice soft and husky.

She slowly turns around, her eyes roving over my face that's mere inches from her own. She doesn't step back, however, and doesn't try to get around me. She stares into my eyes a moment longer before she finally drops her gaze and clears her throat. "I should go."

I nod, allowing her space to free herself from where she's trapped between my body and the counter. "I'll walk you."

I fall into step beside her as we make our way the short distance to her house.

When we reach her front porch and her newly finished stairs, she gives me a small smile and a nod. "Good night, Ian."

As her hand closes on the doorknob, I speak, "Come hiking with me tomorrow." I meant to phrase it as a question, but instead, it came out as more of a plea.

We managed to finish up most of the painting today, and I hate the possibility of not seeing her in the morning. So, I blurted out the first thing that came to my mind.

Lexi turns and looks at me over her shoulder, as if trying to gauge whether I'm serious or not.

"There are some great trails near here. I've been wanting to get out and give them a try before the weather turns." It's not a lie. I've seen several mountain trails while out on my morning runs. I've been dying to travel down them, but I figure I'd probably do better with some hiking boots and mountain gear rather than a pair of battered running shoes and some gym shorts. "I'd love it if you joined me."

Her face is unreadable as she takes me in at the bottom of her stairs. I start racking my brain for any other reasons why she should accompany me because I know she's going to say no.

So, I'm surprised when I hear her say, "Okay. I'll see you tomorrow, Ian."

I practically float back to my house. She said yes. I'm going to go hiking with Lexi tomorrow. We're going to be alone together all damn day—just her, me, and the trees. It's going to be fucking

amazing.
    Then, the thought hits me.
    I don't have any hiking boots.
    Fuck.

chapter ten

lexi

I'm not seeing the problem here, Lexi."

Liv toys with the wrapper on her blueberry muffin, pulling off a berry and popping it into her mouth before looking at me. It's only my third shift at Turn the Page, but Liv sort of makes it impossible for me not to spill my guts to her. First thing this morning, I told her all about my day with Ian yesterday and my agreement to go hiking with him today.

"You said he was a nice guy. You said you liked hanging out with him. What's the harm in a little hiking trip? Are you worried he's secretly a serial killer?"

I shake my head. "Of course not. It's just…it's complicated."

"Life is complicated, babe. Get used to it," she says, her eyes returning once again to the muffin.

Charlie interrupts, "What I think Livvy is trying to say is, things in life are never as easy as you hope they'll be. But that's the beauty of life. It's never easy, but it's always worthwhile."

I groan. My head hurts, and it's way too early in the morning for Charlie and his philosophical musings. I need at least three more cups of coffee before I'm up for this conversation.

Charlie smiles at me, and I instantly regret my ornery response.

"Sorry, Charlie," I say with a giggle. "I think that's the first time I've actually said that and meant it. Usually, it's more of a sorry-dude-but-suck-it-up type of response."

He grins. "Believe me, it's not the first time I've heard it. And I guarantee, it won't be the last. At least my mother didn't name me Jack. I can deal with, *Sorry, Charlie*, a lot easier than, *Hit the road, Jack*."

Liv grunts as she hops off her stool, stretching her back and cracking her neck from side to side. "Whatever. All I'm saying is, you need to live a little. You've been here two weeks now, and as far as I can tell, you've done nothing but fix up your house and spend time here."

"You truly should get out and see the beautiful leaves before they're gone," Charlie adds.

"Yeah, you never know when the first snow is gonna hit."

I stand. "Argh, all right. I'll go. Some friends you are. You're supposed to be on my side."

Charlie reaches out and pats my hand. "We are. That's why we're telling you to go."

The two of them exchange a knowing glance as I sigh and get to work.

"Are you…trying…to kill me?" I gasp, doubled over to try to ease the ache that's developed in my side.

When I agreed to a hike, I pictured a casual stroll through the woods. Not scaling the side of a mountain.

Okay, maybe that's a *slight* exaggeration. But, seriously, would it kill someone to level this shit out a little? I feel like I've gone a million rounds with the StairMaster.

Ian smiles at me as he grabs hold of my hand, pulling me up and over the next rock. "Trust me, it'll all be worth it once we get to the top."

"Yeah, because then I can push you over for trying to kill me."

He throws his head back in laughter, and even though I'm pretty sure my lungs are going to explode and my side is going to rip open, I can't help but chuckle with him.

"You think I'm kidding? You just wait, buddy."

"I'm not worried. I'm pretty sure I can take you."

He turns and leads the way down the path ahead of me, and I can't stop the perusal my eyes give his body. A fine sheen of sweat covers his arms and neck, causing the dark tan of his skin to almost glow. But that's the only indication he shows of any sort of exertion.

I knew Ian was in good shape—I mean, come on, *look* at the man—but he's in far better athletic shape than I ever realized.

"Are you Superman or something?" I huff as he hops deftly from one rock to the next.

He shoots me a crooked smile over his shoulder. "Superman? No way. I'm more like the Caped Crusader. Always dug that bat mask."

My face falls and I give him an exasperated sigh. "Seriously, how are you not dying right now?"

A confident grin spreads across his face. "I work out."

I snort. "Duh. I might be out of breath, but my vision works fine."

"There you go again, checking me out," he says with a smirk, reaching his hand down to me to help me up and over the next hurdle.

"Don't flatter yourself. It's not like I've had anything else to look at while trying to keep up with you." Except, you know, the leaves and the landscape—the entire reason I'm supposed to be out hiking with him today.

He laughs as he pulls me up to stand next to him. After I steady myself, I take a look around and realize we've finally reached the crest. My sharp intake of air must clue Ian in on my sudden awareness as well.

"Told you it would be worth it. Now, come on. The clerk at the grocery store told me there was a sweet little meadow over here where we could have lunch."

He turns and walks away without waiting for me to respond.

When his words register, I jog to catch up. "Lunch? I hope you don't expect me to trap and kill my own food. Because I sure as hell didn't bring anything to eat."

Just then, he holds back a few branches that were blocking our way. I step ahead of him, spinning around as I walk out into the clearing. It's small and private—not that anything this far up is a thriving metropolis—and absolutely stunning. The meadow is surrounded by a thick forest of trees and bushes, their vibrant fall colors breathtaking now that I have a moment to step back and enjoy them.

"Wow," is all I can say.

Ian steps out next to me, his hands coming to rest on his hips as he looks around. "Wow is an understatement. Can't believe I've been here for two weeks, and I haven't been out exploring yet. I've been missing out."

I nod. "Too bad we don't have much time left. They're saying we could get our first snowfall as early as next week."

I expect Ian to cringe, like most people do when they hear snow is on its way. But his eyes light up as he looks at me.

"Can you imagine how gorgeous this place will be, covered with a blanket of white?"

I look around me. "It'll be stunning. Too bad the trail will be impassable."

Ian continues to survey the scenery around us. "True. But I don't mean this meadow. I mean, all of Maple Lake. Sitting out on the back porch with a cup of cocoa and a blanket, watching the snow as it dances across the lake. I can't think of anything more heavenly."

I smirk. "Why, Ian, you sound like a bit of a romantic."

He puffs up his chest. "Me? No way. I'm manly. The manliest. To prove it, watch as I lug that big log over here, so we have somewhere to sit and eat."

He gestures to a fallen tree, the trunk of it at least a few feet around and fifteen feet long. There's no way in hell he'll be able to get that thing all the way across the meadow.

I smile as I watch him stride over to it, rolling up his sleeves as he nears. Spitting into his hands, he bends at the knees and works his fingers under the gigantic piece of wood.

"I can't carry you back down the mountain, so you'd better not hurt yourself!" I shout as I watch him strain to lift the log.

His face reddens with the exertion, and when I see a vein pop on his forehead, I decide enough is enough. I roll my eyes and walk over to him, grabbing the backpack he dropped when we first entered the meadow.

"How about we just sit here?"

Ian falls back on his ass, the breath coming out of him in a whoosh. "Oh, thank God. I didn't want to admit defeat, but that son of a bitch is heavy."

I laugh. "Well, it is a *tree*. Last time I checked, you weren't Paul Bunyan. Pretty sure mere mortals can't lift a full-sized tree."

I sit down on the log, leaning back so that I can lift my face up to the sun. It's a beautiful day outside, but the chill in the air has been stinging my cheeks. The warm sun is a welcome sensation.

Ian swings a leg over the log and sits next to me. "You hungry?"

I raise my eyes to his. "I meant what I said. I'm not killing anything."

He laughs. "Chicken. Lucky for you, I had enough insight to pack food," he says, unzipping the backpack at our feet. He pulls out a few wrapped sandwiches, two apples, some grapes, and a small box of crackers. Once he has that all arranged on the log between us, he reaches back inside and pulls out two bottles of water.

I raise an eyebrow. "This is quite the spread for an impromptu picnic."

He shrugs. "What can I say? I like to eat."

He tosses me a sandwich before promptly digging into his own. I unwrap it, not at all surprised to find PB & J. When I look back up at him, he smiles.

"It's tradition. We have lunch together, we have PB and J. Just the way it is."

I give him a playful roll of my eyes, smiling as I bite into the sandwich. It's surprisingly good.

I moan as I chew. "What did you put in this? Crack?"

Ian laughs as he watches me take another bite. "Nope. Just years of practice. I have the ratio of peanut butter and jelly perfected. I only use preserves, so there are those awesome little chunks of fruit. Plus, I'm convinced cutting it diagonally instead of horizontally makes it taste that much better."

His words make me giggle. "I've never heard someone speak so affectionately about PB and J."

"I'm a connoisseur, baby."

His tone is jovial and lighthearted, but the pet name still causes the bread to stick in my throat for a moment.

I turn and watch him as he finishes his first sandwich and starts in on his second, completely unaware of the internal panic attack I'm currently experiencing.

Because, despite how hard I've tried to keep my distance from this man, he's somehow managed to worm his way right into my life.

I know he wasn't using the word as a term of endearment. It was a flippant remark made in jest. If there's one thing I've learned about Ian over the past few weeks, it's that he's rarely serious. He's one of the happiest and most upbeat people I've ever met.

But, when he called me baby, I wasn't able to tamp down the butterflies that swarmed not only my stomach, but also my entire body. My tummy flipped, and my heart literally skipped a beat—something I'd thought was just a turn of phrase up until this point. Even now, as I watch him chug down half of his water, I can't help the giddiness flowing through my veins. It's everything I can do to keep from smiling at him like a freaking idiot.

the Off-Season

Or so I think.

When Ian turns to look at me, his own lips spreading into a goofy grin, I realize how horribly I've failed at hiding my feelings.

"What?" he asks, the smile not dropping from his face.

I shake my head. "Nothing. I'm just glad we're here."

And it's the truth. I'm glad I came out with him today. It's nice to know I'm not entirely broken. That the part of me I thought had died in the car that night is, in fact, still alive, just in a very, very deep coma. Ian has somehow managed to reach down to that part of me and pull it back from its eternal slumber.

But that still doesn't change the reality that I can't be with him. It wouldn't be fair to him.

Because, even if he's managed to reawaken the part of me I thought I'd lost, I'm still not the same person I used to be. Almost killing someone will do that. I got in the car that night as one person, and by the time I checked out of the hospital, I was someone entirely different.

Ian deserves better than someone just going through the motions, living her life day by day until the time finally comes for it to be her day.

Believe me when I say that I considered…the alternative…many, many times. The pain I felt after I was released from the hospital and during my days of rehab was almost too much to bear some days. But, deep down, I don't have it in me. I'm a coward. Besides, I deserve every moment of this hurt. Living with the knowledge of what I did is a fate far worse than death.

Or, at least, that's what I tell myself.

So, as much as I appreciate Ian for helping me achieve some small level of happiness, it can't continue. I don't deserve to be sitting here, in this gorgeous place with this gorgeous man, eating a delicious lunch and laughing.

If I let myself, I know I could fall for Ian. And he'd make me happier than I ever thought I could be. But that would be me destroying yet another life. Dragging Ian down into the depths of my despair and darkness.

I won't let that happen again.

After today, I need to work harder to keep him away. Buying the lake house has locked me into staying here. But Ian said he was only here for a short while. Soon, he'll go back to wherever he came from. I just need to keep my distance until then.

Ian packs all our garbage back into his pack. When he stands, he holds a hand out to me to help pull me to my feet. "You ready to head back?"

No, I think to myself. *Not in the slightest.*

I place my hand in his, knowing this will be the last time I feel his touch. "Yep, let's do this."

chapter eleven
tag

I bang on Lexi's door, blowing out a frustrated breath. I'm not sure what I did the other day up on the mountain, but it's been three days, and I haven't seen hide or hair of Lexi since she walked into her house and closed the door after we returned.

I know she's still in town. First, because she told me she bought the place, so it's not like she can cut and run. Second, because, despite the fact that I haven't actually seen her, subtle changes to the outside of the house let me know that she's still hard at work inside. A can of paint outside her front door that wasn't here yesterday. A toolbox propped up against the wall that was missing this morning when I stopped by the first time. She's still here. She's just avoiding me.

"Lexi!" I shout as I knock again. "Come on, Lex. I know you're in there. Can you at least talk to me?"

I press my ear to the door, listening for any signs of life on the other side. But I'm met only with silence. I bang my head against the wood, sighing once again.

I thought we'd finally turned a corner after our hike on Monday. She'd started off with her usual standoffish self when we first set out. But, after only a few minutes on the trail, she'd quickly dropped it and started ribbing me about trying to kill her and my "unusual energy" for someone my age.

I thought it was a good sign that it hadn't taken her hours to finally warm up to me, like it had on all our previous encounters. She'd continued laughing and joking with me all afternoon. I'd sensed a slight shift in her demeanor after lunch, but she still hadn't returned to her withdrawn disposition, so I'd simply chalked it up to weariness and enjoyed the scenery and her company.

But, when I'd tried to talk her into dinner as we neared her front porch, she'd said she had a headache and was going to go to bed. She'd given me a sad look as she closed the door on me, but again, I'd ignored it, thinking it was her headache.

But, now, I'm not so sure she even had a headache.

No shit, Sherlock. You're just not used to girls blowing you off. This is what rejection feels like, man.

For some reason, Brandon's voice is the one I hear in my head. Probably because I don't like telling myself I've failed at something.

I've never been one to easily accept defeat. When my junior high coach told me he didn't think I was cut out to be a shortstop, trying to relegate me to right field instead, I worked harder, improved my game, and proved the asshole wrong. When my dad told me I should finish school and not enter the draft right away, just in case something happened, I told him he was crazy and entered it anyway.

I'm not used to not getting what I want.

And I'll be damned if I start now.

"I'll be back later, Lex. Please talk to me. I'm not going to go away without an explanation, so you might as well get it over with."

I can picture her on the other side of the door, her bottom lip pulled between her teeth as she mulls over my words. Her hands are probably on her hips as she considers whether to open the door and yell at me for being so damn obnoxious or continue ignoring me in hopes that I'll eventually give in and go away.

Fat chance on that one, Lex. You might be the most stubborn woman I've ever met, but I put the ass in assertive. I don't give up.

I'll give her the time she needs. But she *will* talk to me. I need to set this right.

I step down off her porch, my shoulders sagging as I stomp over toward my house.

"Yoo-hoo." I hear a feminine voice call out.

I spin around on my heel, my eyes flying to Lexi's door, hoping she came to her senses even though I could tell right off the bat the voice wasn't hers.

And, like I expected, I find her door still firmly closed, not even the hint of movement in the curtains to show she might've been watching as I left.

Damn headstrong woman.

Remembering the voice, I turn my head from left to right, trying to find the source of the call. When my eyes land on the house next to Lexi's, I'm met by a waving woman.

"Over here!" she hollers, signaling me over to where she's standing.

She looks to be in her sixties, if I had to guess. Her dark hair is graying in areas, and her soft curves, now slightly weighed down by gravity, are indicative of years spent taking care of herself. I change my path, heading over toward her house instead of going back to mine.

"You must be Brandon's friend. I heard he had someone staying at his place but haven't had a chance to stop by and say hello. So, hello. I'm Margie."

"Ian," I say, reaching my hand up to shake hers over the railing.

She briefly takes it before dropping it and beckoning me up onto the porch. "Come on. Come sit for a spell. I've just finished baking a batch of cookies. Would you like one?"

I grin as I climb the stairs to join her. "Well, I've never been one to turn down free food. Especially of the cookie variety."

She ushers me over to a set of rocking chairs, gently patting me on the shoulder before turning to head back inside. "You make yourself comfortable. I'll be right back."

I watch her as she walks through the door, my eyes then falling back on Lexi's place. A sudden shift in the curtain upstairs—her bedroom, if I remember right—catches my attention, and I grin. So, she has been watching me after all.

I lean back in the chair, lacing my fingers behind my head, as I continue to watch for signs of Lexi. I'm so caught up in my study of her house that I don't even notice when Margie returns, a plate of cookies in hand. She clears her throat, and when my eyes lift to hers, she smiles warmly at me.

"I've seen you over there with her. You guys make a sweet couple." She sets the cookies down on the table between the two chairs, taking her seat beside me.

I rub my brow as I consider her words. "Thanks, but we're not a couple."

the Off-Season

Margie nods toward the plate of cookies. "Please, help yourself. And I've gathered as much from all the times I saw you over there the past few days, banging on that door and begging her to talk to you."

I pick up a cookie and take a bite, savoring the warm, gooey goodness for a moment as I think about how to respond. "I don't know what I did, but for some reason, she refuses to talk to me all of a sudden."

Margie watches me for a moment, her eyes scanning my face. I can practically see the wheels turning in her head as she thinks carefully on her next words.

"Care for some advice?"

I shove the rest of the cookie in my mouth, nodding as I dust the crumbs off my fingers. "Please," I say around a mouthful.

She smiles at my lack of manners. "Well, like I said, I've seen you over there quite a bit. But I've seen her over there on her own even more. And, when a person is alone, thinking nobody is watching, they tend to let their guard down. They drop the mask they put on for everyone else, and they're just themselves."

I nod, not sure where she's going with this.

"When she's with you, as I'm sure you've noticed, she tenses up. She doesn't let herself be."

I interrupt, "That's not true. Well, not all the time. She does start out tense, but normally, after a little while, she relaxes. She's dropped her mask around me several times."

Margie shakes her head. "I've seen what you mean. And while she does loosen up around you the more time she spends with you, she never completely lets loose. She's always on her guard. I'm not sure she even realizes it most of the time."

I pause, mulling over her words. "How can you tell?"

She smiles at me. "I've been around a while. Met a lot of people. I've developed quite a knack for reading them. Plus, I used to be a counselor. I can tell when someone is hiding something. Or *from* something."

"What is she hiding from?"

Margie shrugs. "I couldn't say for sure. My guess though? Herself."

My brows furrow. "How does one hide from oneself?"

Margie chuckles. "Oh, Ian. You'd be surprised how much people try to hide from themselves. Even people like you and me, who seemingly don't have anything to be afraid of, will try to keep secrets from themselves. Think about it. If you're truly honest with yourself, you'll realize there are things you're scared to even admit in your mind, let alone the outside world."

I want to brush off her words, to tell her that, if someone can't even be completely up-front with themselves, then they have more problems than they realize. But the more I think about her words, the more they ring true.

Like the fact that I'm terrified Angela's allegations have ruined me for good. The fact that I'm not sure I can ever come back from something like that.

I tell everyone I'll never let anything stop me, but deep down, I'm not nearly as confident as I try to put off. In every interview since the charges, I've made sure to present myself as self-assured and ready to get back in the game. But, underneath the facade, I'm terrified it will never happen.

Not wanting to admit that to a virtual stranger, however, I instead turn the attention back to Lexi. "So, how do I get through to her?"

Margie gives me a soft smile. "That is entirely up to her. My advice? Keep trying. Something happened to that girl. Something that causes her to cry alone on the deck at night. Something that makes her completely deflate when she thinks she's alone. Those times I said I've seen her completely drop her act? It's not a pretty picture, Ian. She's carrying something heavy. And my guess is, she's been carrying it on her own for a very, very long time. She needs someone to help offset the burden. So, keep that in mind. There's a possibility she'll never be completely healed. If you want to pursue a relationship with Lexi, you need to make sure that's something you're willing to accept. She's going to need someone who's in it for the long haul before she finally opens up."

I turn my gaze away from Margie, her words sinking in. There's something about Lexi that makes me want to try with her. Some part of me that recognizes itself in some part of her.

But, after the recent scandal and everything that went along with it—hell, that's still going along with it—am I ready to make that sort of commitment?

I'm not so sure.

"Thanks, Margie. You've given me a lot to think about."

She grins. "You're welcome. And I hope you won't give up on her because of what I said today. Because there's one thing I forgot to mention."

"What's that?"

She turns her attention over to Lexi's house. "The times I've seen her with you are the only times I've seen her smile."

My chest swells at her words, an intense satisfaction sweeping over me. And I know my decision is made. I might not know as much about Lexi as I want to. And, in the long run, things might not work out between us. But I'm not willing to walk away. Not without knowing I've done everything I can.

Lexi might need help discovering herself again.

But that makes two of us.

My soul recognizes itself in her; that much, I'm sure of.

And I won't give in until she sees it, too.

I stand up, an idea suddenly occurring to me. "I think I might know a way to get her attention. How would you feel about helping me plan a little neighborhood barbecue? We can get everyone in town to come. I'll provide all the food. It's about time I meet the people I've been living near anyway. And Lexi might like to give me the cold shoulder, but I know she'd never be able to ignore an invitation from her sweet neighbor."

Something mischievous glints in Margie's eye. "Why, Ian, I think you might be on to something," she says with a sly grin.

And, just like that, I'm going to have a party.

chapter twelve
lexi

"You're sure you don't need my help tomorrow?" Ella says into the phone.

To be honest, I need all the help I can get. A sudden rainstorm last night showed just how bad of shape my roof was in, and with weather reports calling for snow next week, I know I'm already on borrowed time to try to get the damn thing repaired. But Ella has just finished telling me about her long week at work; her boss was a complete douche nozzle to her all week, and she told me she's planning on spending tomorrow scouring the local classifieds for anything else that might pay nearly as well as her current position. I'm not about to add a day of hard labor to her plate after the week she's had. In fact, as soon as I get off the phone with her, I'm going to give my brother-in-law a call and make sure he knows she deserves a night of pampering tomorrow. Drew Garner won't let me down.

"I'll be fine, Ells. It's only a few patch-up jobs," I lie, knowing full well I need to replace nearly the entire roof.

My mind briefly flashes to Ian, knowing how willing he'd be to help and how much his skills would come in handy.

But I can't continue accepting his help—not when the more time I spend with him, the more I realize there's the potential for something more. Ian hasn't come right out and said it, but I can tell by the way he looks at me when he thinks I'm not looking that he's interested in me. And I'd be lying if I said there weren't feelings developing on my side as well.

That's exactly why every time he's come to my door over the past four days, I've hidden in my bedroom and pretended to be out. I don't trust myself to face him, to tell him exactly why this could never work between us. Looking into his honey-colored eyes would cause any reason and sense I'd managed to develop over the last few days to instantly evaporate. And if he unleashed that killer smile on me? I'd be a goner for sure.

No, it's safer to stay away. Safer for me and safer for him.

That is why I don't even bother bringing him up to Ella. I know she'd disagree with me. She'd tell me how stupid I was being and how I needed to learn to move on and forgive myself.

Yeah, well, I'm working on it. But how do you forgive yourself when you're not sure you even deserve forgiveness?

It's easier for both of us if I keep Ian to myself. Especially now that I'm not going to see him anymore.

I listen to Ella talk about the twins, making appropriate remarks and grunts when called for so that she knows I'm at least halfway paying attention. I focus the majority of my attention on the task at hand—painting my bathroom walls.

the Off-Season

Ian and I managed to get the big projects nearly completed the day before our hike, leaving me with only these small jobs. And, as I attempt to balance the phone between my ear and shoulder while I tape off the baseboards, I get a sudden desire for him to be here. I don't mind the actual *painting* part of painting. But this taping shit is for the birds. Ian took care of it with such ease the other day; it seemed like he'd been doing it for years.

I find myself wondering once again what he does for a living back in…wherever the hell he's from.

Stop thinking about him! I scold myself.

As if on cue, a knock sounds at my door. I duck down by the bathroom vanity, as if Ian will somehow be able to see through the door, the walls, and up the stairs from where he stands. I push myself back up, rolling my eyes at my own absurdity.

"What was that?" Ella asks on the other end of the line.

"Uh, nothing. I dropped something."

Just then, the knocking sounds again.

"Bullshit," Ella says. "Someone's at the door."

"Oh, maybe you're right," I say stupidly. I don't want to tell her why I'm avoiding answering the door.

"Well, aren't you going to see who it is?"

"I'm sort of busy right now, Ells."

"Lexi," she chides, sounding exactly like our mother before she passed. "How do you expect to meet any friends if you hide every time someone tries to introduce themselves? Besides, it's rude as hell to ignore your neighbors. Now, get your ass down there and answer the door. Don't make me come over there."

I let out an exasperated sigh. After our parents died in a car accident when I was nine, Ella sort of took on the role of my mother. We'd lived with our aunt and uncle until she'd turned eighteen, but even during those days, Ella was who I always turned to when I needed something. And she also took it upon herself to lecture me whenever I did something wrong—a habit that has followed us well past the days of when I snuck out to toilet paper the neighbor's house. "And what exactly would you do when you got here? Spank me for not listening?"

"Don't tempt me. Now, go."

I know she's not kidding when she says she'll drive all the way out here if I don't listen—though I'm pretty sure she *is* kidding about the spanking part; I hope—so I cross every body part capable of crossing that Ian will be gone by the time I get downstairs. I walk extra slow, dusting the banister as I descend, to buy myself some extra time.

"I know what you're doing, Lex," Ella admonishes when at least a full minute has passed. "Just open the damn door. I'm sure whoever's on the other side isn't going to bite."

He might, I think silently, knowing how upset Ian was the last few times he was here.

I admit, the way I left things was pretty shitty. But I keep reminding myself it's for his own good. He'd thank me if he knew.

I head to the window before the door, pulling back the corner of the curtains a fraction of an inch to see if he's still standing there.

All the tension drains from my body when I see it's not Ian on my front porch, but a woman. The woman who lives next door, if I remember correctly.

I move over to the door with ease now, smiling warmly as I pull it open.

The woman beams up at me. "Oh, good, you're home. I was starting to think I'd missed you."

"I'm so sorry for keeping you waiting," I say, pointing to the phone. "I didn't hear the door at first because I'm on the phone with my sister. And painting the bathroom on top of it."

"Liar," Ella says in my ear.

"Oh, I'm so sorry to bother you. I wanted to stop by and see if you'd like to join us for a little barbecue we're having. Sort of a last hurrah before the snow sets in. I know you're new in town, so I thought you might want a chance to get to know your neighbors."

I'm about to politely decline when Ella's voice sounds in my ear. "Go. Put the damn paintbrush down for one night, and go have some fun."

"Oh, um...that's awfully sweet of you. I'm a mess though," I tell the woman standing in front of me, ignoring my sister.

"You look wonderful, darling. But we'll be next door for a few hours. Feel free to swing by whenever you're available."

I nod. "Thank you..." I trail off, realizing she never told me her name.

"Oh, I'm sorry. I'm Margie. I live right next door. You must think I'm terribly rude for not getting over here and introducing myself before now."

"I'm Lexi," I tell her, extending the hand not holding my phone. "And I'm just as guilty as you. We've all been busy with trying to prep for the upcoming winter, I suppose."

Margie smiles. "Isn't that the truth? Some days, I'm not sure why I continue to stay here. But then I take one look at the lake, and it all comes back to me. Well, I'll leave you to it. I hope we'll see you soon."

I say good-bye and close the door after she leaves. It isn't even latched before Ella starts in, having heard the entire conversation.

"You'd better go, Lexi. You thought I was serious when I said I'd drive over there for not answering the door? Just try not going to that party. I will drag you over there, kicking and screaming, if I have to."

Meeting the neighbors does sound fun. And Ian hasn't been by all day today, so there's a good chance he's out of town. Maybe I can sneak down the dock and take a peek at who's in attendance. If Ian isn't there, then I'll make an appearance.

"Okay, Ella, you win. Let me go shower. I'll call you after."

"Yes," she praises. "I'm proud of you, Lex. It's time for you to put yourself back out there. A barbecue is the perfect place to start."

After making me triple-swear I'll call when it's over, she finally lets me go.

I look down at my clothes, my top smeared with paint and what I hope is dust and my shorts so short, you can practically see my ass when I bend over. Yeah, there's no way I'm meeting my new neighbors in this.

A half hour later, my hair is pulled back into a bun on my head, a red sweater and jeans replacing my stained and tattered painting clothes. It might not be the fanciest thing I own, but I figure it's suitable for a small-town barbecue. Margie was in a hoodie and sweatpants, so at least I won't be the most underdressed person there.

Stepping out my back door, I walk down the dock, peering over toward Margie's house to see if I can spot Ian. I'm surprised to find nobody in her backyard. *Did they move it indoors due to the cold?*

"Lexi!" a familiar voice calls from behind me.

the Off-Season

I turn, finding Liv waving at me from where she's sitting at Ian's fire pit.

"We're over here."

I briefly consider diving into the freezing water so I can avoid going over to his house. But, now that Liv has spotted me, several others are now waving me over, and I know there's no way I can go back inside and pretend none of this ever happened.

I walk along the shore until I reach Ian's yard. He's nowhere to be found, but I know he must be here somewhere. The lights inside are blazing, the grill up on the deck flaming in the dark. *There's no way he'd let everyone use his house if he weren't here, would he?*

I walk over to Liv, giving her a brief hug when I reach her. "What are you doing here?"

"Ian and Margie invited everyone. And, in a town this size, there's not exactly a lot to do on a Friday night. So, I figured, why not meet the new guy and get a free meal while I'm at it?"

"Is Charlie here, too?" I ask, looking around for his familiar cardigan.

"Yep. He's around here somewhere. He found your boyfriend shortly after we showed up and has been talking his ear off ever since."

"He's *not* my boyfriend," I bite out more harshly than I intended. I sound like a little kid trying to deny her first crush.

"Whatever you say. From what I hear, he put all this together to get a chance to talk to you."

My mouth drops open. "Are you serious?"

"Desperate times call for desperate measures," Ian's voice says from behind me.

I spin around, finding both him and Charlie standing there, smiling at me.

Charlie takes a step forward, giving me a quick kiss on the cheek. "I'm glad to see you out tonight, sweetie. You need it."

He walks past me and sits down next to Liv, putting his arm over her shoulders and hugging her to his side in a fatherly gesture.

"Come on," Ian says, tilting his head toward a group of people. "Let me introduce you around."

I follow him, meeting dozens of people in only a few minutes.

Margie smiles when I get to her, her bright eyes lighting up when she sees the two of us together. "I'm so glad you decided to join us," she says with a clap. "It's nice to see you two together again."

I give her a puzzled look, but Ian whisks me away to the next person before I can ask her what she means. Once he's done introducing me to everyone, he ushers me over to the grill and the giant table of food set up next to it.

"Get yourself something to eat. Then, come join us down by the fire pit."

He turns and walks down to where Liv, Charlie, and several others are now sitting. They make room for him as he strides over, all of them laughing and smiling as he takes his seat

The man is already the most popular guy in town, and he's been here for all of five minutes.

Well, that's about how long it took you to realize you liked him. Can you blame everyone else for falling for him, too?

I shove down the thought and pick up a paper plate, filling it with a various assortment of salads, pasta, and desserts before moving over and grabbing a burger from the grill. If I have my mouth full of food all night, I won't be forced to speak about things I don't want to talk about.

Problem solved.

the Off-Season

I walk down to the fire pit and try to take a seat next to Liv. But everyone shuffles around as I approach, leaving the space next to Ian the only spot available.

I just met these people, and already, they're trying to set me up.

I sit down, not wanting to appear rude. Just because I'm sitting next to him doesn't mean I have to talk to him.

"So, Lexi," a man says as soon as I'm situated. Frank, I think he said his name was. "You've been doing quite a lot of work on the old place next door. It's starting to look like it used to."

Pride rushes through me at his words, and I sit up a little straighter. "Thank you. I've still got a ways to go, but it's coming along."

"How'd the old roof fare during that storm the other night?" Charlie asks.

I groan. "Not so well. Starting tomorrow, everything else is being put on hold until I can get the roof patched."

Frank's eyebrows shoot up. "You know how to patch a roof?"

I shrug. "Well, it didn't look too hard on YouTube."

This causes Ian to laugh, his head falling back on his shoulders as loud guffaws escape his lips.

I shoot him a dirty look. "Excuse me, what exactly is so funny?"

He straightens his head, giving me an amused smile. "Nothing. Nothing at all. It just never occurred to me that that's how you've learned how to do all the stuff you're doing over there. I thought you were some carpentry prodigy. Turns out, you just know how to do your research."

I nod. "Damn straight I do. I'm not about to half-ass something like my roof. I spent hours online today making sure I had all the right equipment and supplies. There's nothing YouTube can't teach you."

Ian smiles at me, his eyes soft with what looks like affection. "If I heard those words from anybody else, I'd say they were crazy. But I've seen what you can do when you put your mind to it. If anybody can fix a roof based on what they found online, it's you."

His words are sincere, not a hint of mocking in them. And I can't help the smile that spreads across my face.

"Thank you."

Frank adds his impressed perspective. "You mean to tell me you've done all that by watching videos online? You've never fixed anything up before?"

"Well, I didn't say that. I did fix up a place back in Chicago."

"Is that where you're from?" Margie interjects.

I realize I've revealed a lot more about myself than I intended with one slip of the tongue. But I can't exactly rewind and take it back. "Um, yes."

"And what did you fix up back in Chicago? Another old house?" Margie pushes further.

I shake my head. "No. The project in Chicago was entirely different. It was a…business. My business."

"Oh, how lovely," Margie says, smiling at me. "What type of business was it?"

"Erm, it was sort of a craft store, I guess. We specialized in woodwork. We could cut pretty much any shape a customer requested and also sold the materials for them to be able to take it home and make it their own."

"Oh, like those cute family blocks that are all the rage right now?"

"Exactly," I say. "But we had all sorts of different options—Christmas decor, Halloween, names. If you could dream it up, we'd help make it a reality."

"And you were the owner, dear?" Margie asks.

I nod.

"Well, what happened? What caused you to close up shop and move out here?" Margie's voice softens, her concern over why I'd leave my business behind evident in her every word.

I stand suddenly, setting my half-eaten plate of food down on the seat behind me. "I'm sorry. I'm not feeling well. If you'll please excuse me."

I take off at a run, not slowing when I hear both Ian and Liv shouting after me.

I know I just gave all those people something to talk about for weeks, fleeing like that after being asked a seemingly simple question.

But I had to get out of there.

Because I refuse to let Ian see me cry.

chapter thirteen
tag

I know it's a risk. After Lexi took off like she did last night, the last thing she probably wants to see first thing this morning is my face.

But there's no way in hell I'm letting her fix that roof by herself.

Knowing she'll be outside today, I wait until I see her before I make my move. I'm not going to give her the chance to hide from me behind closed doors today.

I walk up behind her, watching as she gathers several packages of shingles and a box of nails.

"I come bearing coffee," I say, holding out the travel cup I filled at my place before heading over.

She spins around, her brows furrowing as she looks at me. When I keep my arm extended, she finally reaches out and takes the proffered cup.

"Thanks," is her only response.

She takes a small sip, cringing when the hot liquid hits her tongue.

"Sorry, I should've warned you it's still super hot. Just brewed it fresh."

She sets the mug down on the step, turning and looking back at the project before her. "Thanks for the coffee. I'll let it cool a bit while I'm getting stuff together."

She starts moving materials around. I set down my coffee mug next to hers and bend to help her.

"What are you doing?" she asks, her body going rigid as she sees me picking up a box of shingles.

"What does it look like I'm doing? I'm helping you fix your roof."

Lexi shakes her head. "No, you don't have to do that. I've got it covered, I promise."

I go back to what I was doing. "I'm sure you do. But that doesn't mean I'm going to sit over there on my ass while you're over here, busting yours to beat this storm. Now, you can sit here and waste time arguing with me if you want, but it's not going to change my mind. I think it'd be in everyone's best interests if we just got to work."

I pick up a tool belt that's sitting among the roofing materials and buckle it around my waist. "Where's your ladder?"

Her jaw is clenched tight, her eyes hard as she looks at me. I can tell she doesn't like being told what to do, but like I said, I'm not going to let her do this on her own. My mother would skin me alive if she knew I let anyone, let alone a single woman, climb up onto a roof by themselves when I was perfectly capable of helping.

"Ladder, Lexi?" I say, letting her know her pissed off expression isn't going to intimidate me.

"In the garage," she clips, her arm flinging out and pointing toward the detached garage to the side of her house.

Now, that wasn't so hard, was it?

I know better than to say the words aloud, but it still doesn't stop me from gloating a little on the inside.

I walk over to the small garage, sliding open the ancient door and stepping into the dusty space.

There's so much shit in here; I know it can't possibly all be hers. Besides, some of it is covered in dust so thick, it looks as if it hasn't been touched in decades. I quickly locate the ladder, hoisting it up onto my shoulder and walking back over to where Lexi is standing.

"The original owners leave you all that crap?" I ask once I reach her.

She sighs. "Yep. It's such a mess. But I guess there was nobody to go through it after the old couple who lived here died. They didn't have any children. So, I sort of inherited it. One of these days, I'll have to get out there and go through it all."

"Some of it looks pretty old. Might find something valuable among all the garbage."

She smiles softly. "Hopefully. Antiques are sort of a hobby of mine. I'd love to find something amazing out there that I could restore and use inside."

"If anyone can make that junk beautiful again, it's you, Lex."

She blushes at my words. "Did you come here to bullshit me, or did you come here to help?"

the Off-Season

Ah, so we're back to stubborn, obstinate Lexi.
It's going to be a long afternoon.

lexi

I should've never said anything about the damn roof last night. I basically opened myself up for this. I should've known, the second Ian heard I was going to be working on the roof, he wouldn't let it go until I let him help.

That's what you really wanted all along, isn't it?

"Shut up," I murmur under my breath at my subconscious thought. I wanted no such thing.

Uh-huh. And the sky is purple.

I turn my attention back to the task at hand, holding a few shingles in place while Ian reloads the nail gun. I take a look at the areas we've already finished. Thanks to Ian, I might actually have this thing done before the storm hits.

Once again, this man is saving my ass.

After he secures the shingles in place, he heads back down the ladder to grab another box. I was nervous the first time he insisted doing that alone. Those suckers are heavy, and I had no clue how he'd get back up the ladder with the box in tow. But he simply lifted it up onto one shoulder, holding it in place with the same arm while using the other arm to climb. He made the whole process look entirely too simple, reminding me of the exceptional strength he possessed. He'd denied being Superman, but I'm not so sure he was telling the truth.

When he heaves the box up onto the roof, quickly following behind it, he gestures back down over his shoulder with his thumb. "We might need a few more boxes if we want to get this done. I can keep working here if you want to head to the hardware store and grab a few. You can take my truck."

I pull my bottom lip in between my teeth, his words causing an unease to creep up my spine. "Um, I don't drive."

He turns and looks at me, his surprise evident in his eyes. "Oh," is all he says.

I know I should probably expand on that. I don't want him to think I'm some idiot who doesn't know how to drive. But then again, is the truth really a better alternative?

I'm warring with myself on what to say next when he speaks, "Well, we still have a few days until the snow hits. Let's finish up with what we have here, and then tomorrow, we can head into town to grab the rest."

I nod, grateful he doesn't hound me for the reason I don't drive. Though, if he's half as smart as I think he is, he's surely already connected the dots. A twenty-seven-year-old who doesn't drink and doesn't drive? It doesn't take a genius to figure out why. The whole situation reeks of a DUI.

If only that's all it was.

Ian opens the box and starts removing the shingles when a car door slams from down below. I turn, finding Ella opening the door to the backseat before unbuckling one of the twins. Drew climbs out of the driver's seat and goes to get the other.

"Shit," I mutter, turning back and closing my eyes as I scramble for an idea.

Ian's eyes burn into me as he asks, "What is it?"

"Uh, well, my sister is here," I say, opening my eyes to gauge his expression.

He cranes his neck to look over my head, taking in the two people with tiny bundles in their arms. A white plastic bag is hanging from Drew's wrist, and even from up here, I can make out the shape of the Styrofoam food containers inside.

"Looks like she brought lunch," he says, standing up and wiping his hands on his pants.

I grab hold of his wrist, pulling him back down. "I haven't...well, I haven't exactly told her about you yet."

He raises an eyebrow. "What are you planning on telling her?"

Well, I'd hoped I wouldn't have to tell her anything. Guess that's off the table.

"I'm not sure. It hasn't come up yet."

"So, what you're saying is, there's no food for me in those boxes?"

I sputter out a laugh. Of course, the first thing his mind went to was the food.

He stands again, pulling me to my feet. "Don't worry, Lex. I won't do anything to embarrass you. As far as your sister is concerned, I'm a friendly neighbor helping you out. There can't be any harm in that."

I skeptically look at him. "Were you just a friendly neighbor last night? Is that why it seemed like everyone was in on some inside plot to get me near you?"

He holds his hands up, feigning innocence. "Hey, I can't help the actions of others. Maybe they see something in me that you don't," he adds with a wink.

Oh, believe me, I see it. I just don't want to.

He holds out his hand, his pinkie extended. "I pinkie swear. I won't say or do anything to give your sister the wrong idea about us."

I look down at his finger and then back up at his face. "You pinkie swear? What are you—a seven-year-old girl?"

He puts on an air of offense. "Excuse me? There's nothing more sacred than a pinkie swear. I don't offer them up to anyone, you know. Consider yourself inside my secret circle of trust."

I roll my eyes, linking my pinkie with his. "Okay, Robert De Niro."

"I've got my eye on you, Focker."

He insists on climbing down the ladder first so he'll be there to catch me if I fall. I wage an internal battle over whether to argue and tell him to stop being a chauvinistic pig or smile and thank him for being so thoughtful of my safety. In the end, I decide silence is the best answer, and I wait for him to climb down the ladder before I follow. When we both reach the bottom, I'm met with the very surprised eyes of my sister.

"Hey, Ells," I say, heading over to give her a half-hug around the baby.

I still can't tell my nieces apart, especially considering Ella is one of those obnoxious mothers who dresses them exactly the same.

I once asked her how she could tell them apart herself.

Her response was, "A mother knows."

I call bullshit. I don't think she knows which is which either. When they get old enough to understand, she'll have to decide which one is Ava and which one is Amelia. Until then, they're "the twins."

"Hi, Lex. We thought we'd swing by and bring lunch, see if you needed any help. But I can see now you've got it covered," she adds, her tone pointed.

Ian takes a step forward, extending his hand to my sister and then her husband. "Hi there. I'm Ian, Lexi's neighbor. I saw her out here this morning and couldn't let her do this all on her own. My mother raised me better."

Ella smiles as she studies him. "Well, I'm glad my stubborn sister actually allowed you to help. Since she moved in, I've been trying to come out to give her a hand, but she always keeps me away. Now, I see why."

I choke on a breath. "Ells, he's just helping me for the day. That's it."

"Mmhmm," she says, studying Ian once again.

"Who's hungry?" Drew asks. "There's plenty here for everyone."

I want to lunge over and hug my brother-in-law for breaking some of the tension in the air.

Ian grins, raising his hand. "I'm always up for food. Especially when it smells as good as that. What is it?"

"Chinese. Lexi has always had a soft spot for Chinese, ever since we were kids," Ella responds, turning to walk inside the house. She ushers Ian along with her, linking her arm through his. "So, Ian, tell me about yourself."

I turn to Drew for help, but he just smiles. "Don't look at me. You know how she is."

That's the problem. I have a feeling Ella is going to know a hell of a lot more about Ian than I do by the time she leaves here.

chapter fourteen
tag

J've often wondered how weathermen are consistently so wrong yet somehow able to maintain their jobs. In any other career field, if you failed so spectacularly at your job over and over again, you'd be out on your ass without so much as a, *Don't let the door hit you where the good Lord split you.* But, if you're a weatherman…well, you can predict the blizzard of a lifetime, telling everyone to batten down the hatches and prepare for the next ice age, and when only a few flurries fly, you can shrug and say, *Whoops. Guess Mother Nature had other plans.*

I mean, by now, the technology must surely be there. I think these assholes like seeing the mass hysteria of a big storm. Or the mad scramble to get things done when a small snowstorm expected at the end of the week suddenly turns into Snowpocalypse and will be here before the day is through.

the Off-Season

That is exactly what Lexi and I are doing out here, in the blistering cold. My hands and face are so numb, I'm not entirely sure they're even still attached to my body.

When we went into town yesterday to grab the rest of the supplies, there was chatter about the fast-approaching storm. Where we'd thought we had at least two or three more days before the snow hit, it turned out we had less than twenty-four hours. We worked well into the dark last night and have been back at it since the crack of dawn this morning.

Lexi's roof ended up needing almost a total re-shingling. Luckily, the deck of the roof was in pretty decent shape; otherwise, this two-day job would've turned out to be a lot longer, and Lexi would've been out of a place to stay.

I had a feeling, now that her sister knew I lived next door, she wouldn't be so quick to offer Lexi her couch.

I smile as I pound in another nail—Lexi has the nail gun on the other end of the roof, so I'm back to doing it the old-fashioned way—and recall the conversation I had with Ella the day before yesterday.

She certainly didn't suffer from the same reservations her sister did.

"Have you lived in Maple Lake long, Ian?" she asked before I even had a chance to shovel my first forkful of food into my mouth.

"Bout the same amount of time as Lexi actually. I got here a few weeks ago."

"Interesting," she said, pursing her lips together as she eyed me. "And you own the house next door?"

I shook my head. "No, ma'am. That monstrosity belongs to my buddy Brandon. He's letting me borrow it for a bit."

"So, what brings you all the way out to this small town?"

I cleared my throat. "Well, I guess I needed a break. And B has been trying to get me to come up here for years. I figured now was as good a time as any."

"And what do you do back in...where did you say you were from?"

I didn't, I thought sarcastically.

The woman was starting to get a bit too pushy for my liking.

"Washington."

"State? Which part?"

"Ella!" Lexi interrupted. "Knock it off. The man was kind enough to offer to help me with my roof today. That doesn't mean he's required to subject himself to your third degree."

Ella looked at her sister, her eyes narrowed slightly, as if thinking. "You're right. I apologize, Ian."

I waved off her apology, telling her not to worry about it.

And, after that, we all fell into a comfortable companionship. Ella stopped asking me personal questions, instead changing the topic to the approaching storm.

Once she dropped the fierce-protector act, I decided I actually really liked Ella. She had a wonderful sense of humor, much like Lexi. Very dry and sarcastic but sweet underneath the surface. She laughed easily, and it was evident how much she and Drew cared for each other in the way they interacted. Drew seemed to know what she needed before even she did, handing her a glass of water just as she went to reach for it, shifting in his seat so that she'd have more room to move her arms as she animatedly mocked something her boss had done to her during the week.

It was also clear how much he hated that she was stuck in a job she so clearly despised, their two girls spending their days with a

the Off-Season

sitter because she needed the job in order for them to make ends meet.

My eyes flashed to Lexi. I was glad to know that, no matter what happened with my career, I'd always be able to support her if the need ever arose. She'd never have to feel stuck.

And then I all but needed the Heimlich maneuver as I tried not to choke to death on the food in my mouth.

Where in the hell did that thought come from?

I filed it away for later, not wanting to have a nervous breakdown in front of Lexi and her family. But, before Ella and Drew left, Ella only further solidified that there was something between Lexi and me despite how hard she might be trying to fight it.

Ella pulled me aside in the kitchen, Lexi and Drew preoccupied with the twins in the living room.

"I know she's difficult. She's going to try her damnedest to push you away. But I also know she's worth it," Ella said, her voice barely above a whisper.

I leaned down, my eyes briefly darting over to where Lexi sat on the floor of the living room with one of the babies in her arms.

"I think you know that, too," Ella added, as if reading something in my eyes.

I gave her a stiff nod. "But why? Why does she want to keep me out?"

Ella's eyes softened. "That's her story to tell. Just...don't give up on her. Not yet. She's different with you."

I'd taken Margie's words the other day at face value. She'd said the only time she saw Lexi smile were the times she was with me. But Margie didn't know Lexi, so it was hard to put much stock in her observations.

But Ella…Ella knew Lexi better than anyone. And, if she was able to detect a change in Lexi in only a half hour of her being in my company…well, it made me pretty damn happy, to say the least.

I wasn't sure where my sudden feelings had come from. But there was no longer any doubt in my mind. I was falling for this woman.

This stubborn, frustrating, soul-consuming woman.

She laughed at something her niece had done then, drawing my attention back to her. And I had my answer.

I'd said I wasn't sure where my feelings had come from. But that wasn't true.

They were sitting cross-legged on a wood floor desperately in need of refinishing, smiling at a tiny baby.

I hadn't suddenly developed some weird need to settle down and find *the one*, mistakenly falling for the first woman I'd found after Angela in search of trying to fix something she'd broken.

No, the changes I felt were all Lexi.

She makes me want things I haven't wanted before. She makes me feel things I haven't felt before. And she makes me be someone I've been scared to be before.

Me.

I'm no longer all about baseball. I'm not Tag Taggart, shortstop for the Washington Rampage. I'm Ian, part-time handyman and full-time average Joe. There's no pressure to always be at my very best, constantly improving and finding new ways to impress fans and sponsors. It's not about making next year's all-star team or winning a World Series. Though let's be real; I'll always want that last one. But it suddenly isn't my entire reason for existing.

Breaking through to Lexi, getting her to open up to me, has become my primary goal in life.

the Off-Season

That's hard though with her currently on the opposite end of the roof, doing her best to ignore me.

Since the day with her sister, she's been different. Not exactly back to her usual standoffish self, but not the Lexi I've caught glimpses of here and there over the past few weeks. The Lexi I know I'm falling for. No, she's been…contemplative. I've caught her staring off into space several times in the past few days, her thoughts clearly taking her somewhere far away from here. And, instead of giving me her typical spitfire response when I've asked her about it, she smiles and shrugs, telling me she's thinking.

Yeah, I got that, Lex. Care to fill me in on what you're thinking about? I'm dying over here.

But I've been so happy she hasn't immediately shut me out whenever I've called her on her zone-outs that I've dropped it, letting her have her time to get lost in her thoughts and hoping, if I stick around long enough, maybe she'll eventually give me a break.

My phone rings, startling me out of my own thoughts. I laugh under my breath, realizing I was doing the exact thing I'd just been thinking about Lexi doing. I stand up from my crouched position, pulling my phone out of my pocket.

Ray's name appears on the screen.

I look over at Lexi. She doesn't seem to be paying attention, but I still don't want to take the chance on her overhearing.

I call over to her, "Hey, I've gotta take this. Be right back."

She waves, not looking up from the row of shingles she's currently nailing in place.

I marvel once again at the independence and resilience of this woman—*how many women would even climb up onto the roof, let alone actually nail shingles?*—but quickly shake it off and climb down the ladder.

Ray's call goes to voice mail by the time I reach the bottom, but instead of waiting to listen to the message, I immediately dial him back.

"Tag, when you didn't answer, I got worried. Thought maybe you'd drowned in that lake. It's not like you not to answer my calls."

I take a cue from Lexi and roll my eyes. "I was busy. Believe it or not, I'm not waiting around by the phone for you to call."

"Well, you should be. The fate of your career is in my hands. What could be more important than that?"

You don't want to hear the answer to that, I think to myself. I keep quiet though and wait.

"Well, while you've been up in Bumfuck, Egypt, I've been working my ass off, trying to make sure you've still got a future in this business."

He lets those words sink in, and I know he's not going to continue until I respond.

"And you know I appreciate everything you do for me, Ray. So, tell me, what's the word?"

I can hear the whoosh of air he intakes and can already tell it's good news. He's excited.

"You'd better be prepared to kiss my ass for the rest of your fucking life, kid. Because I not only got three of your sponsors back, but I also managed to book you a commercial with Nike."

A rush of adrenaline floods through my veins, and I can't stop the little whoop of excitement that escapes my lips. "Are you fucking kidding me right now, Ray? I swear to God, if you're joking, I'm catching the first plane out of here and coming to kick your ass."

"Dead serious. Angela has dropped off the face of the earth, and we've had a long parade of character witnesses doing interviews on your behalf. Mostly women who have attested to the fact that you were a perfect gentleman with them and how you'd never do the things Angela accused you of. Haven't you been following the news?"

I reach up and run my hand over my head. "Uh, not in a few days. Internet connection up here is pretty shitty." Not entirely true, but he doesn't need to know that.

"Fucking boonies. Anyway, so it's been nothing but good press for you during the last week or so. And, even before that, there was speculation that Angela was full of it. I guess this isn't the first sexual assault charge she's tried. She's filed a few others against previous employers. All men with a lot of money and a lot to lose. All of them settled outside of court. Once word got out about that, people really started doubting her credibility."

I fucking hate that Angela has done this. Not just to me, but to women everywhere. You always read these reports of women who don't come forward after they've been actually assaulted—especially by a recognizable name—because they're afraid nobody will believe them. Seeing women like Angela—women who try to use something as awful as sexual assault to their advantage—adds a little doubt to everyone's mind. Now, instead of believing a woman when she says she was raped, they think, *Well, that one girl accused so and so, and she was just trying to get money. I bet this is the same thing.*

It's a fucking disgrace.

I listen to Ray spout off the rest of the details, my excitement about the commercial growing with every word. Until he gets to the last part.

"And the best news is, your sabbatical is officially over. They want to start shooting next week. So, that means, you need to get your ass on a plane, so we can get you ready."

My heart drops. As excited as I am about the prospect of a

commercial, it doesn't change anything about the way I feel about Lexi. And, if I leave her now, there's no way in hell I'll ever break through her walls.

"Uh, Ray, we need to see if we can push that out."

He sputters, "W-what? It's fucking *Nike,* Tag. You don't try to push out Nike."

"Well, we're going to have to. There's no way I can be in Seattle by next week."

"You care to run that by me one more time?"

I sigh. "You heard what I said, Ray. I can't be in Seattle next week. See if we can push it out until after Thanksgiving."

Ray doesn't say anything for several moments, instead breathing heavily into the phone. I can practically see him standing there, mouth hanging open at what I just said.

"Thanksgiving?" he finally shouts over the phone. "You're lucky I even got you this gig, and now, you want me to reschedule until after Thanksgiving? That's a month away. They'll drop you faster than you can say *finished.*"

"Then, they'll drop me," I say, hating the sound of the words even as they leave my tongue. But that doesn't mean I regret them. "And I know you. You won't let one little deal gone south ruin me. Not after everything we've been through. There will be other opportunities."

"I still can't believe what I'm hearing. Care to tell me *why* you think you need to stay there in the bushlands of Fuck If I Know?"

I laugh. "Maple Lake. And it's really not so bad, Ray. You'd like it here. The scenery is beautiful."

"Oh, God. You've met a girl, haven't you?"

My eyes flick up to the rooftop. I need to get back up there and help Lexi. The wind has already started to pick up, and I know we're only a matter of hours away from the storm hitting.

Ray has been my agent since the day I signed my first contract. He knows me inside and out, so it doesn't really surprise me that he's able to see through my non-answers and surmise what is really keeping me in Maple Lake. But I'm not in the mood to listen to him tell me how stupid I'm being.

"Bye, Ray. Let me know what Nike says."

I hang up and stuff my phone back in my pocket, climbing back up the ladder.

Lexi looks over at me when I reach the top. "I thought you were never coming back."

I smile, not giving voice to my thoughts.

If I have it my way, I'll never leave.

chapter fifteen
lexi

I bust through my front door, shaking off the layer of snow covering the entire top half of my body. Ian follows closely behind, mirroring my actions almost exactly.

The snow started about an hour ago, just a few flurries at first but quickly picking up into heavy flakes. We were so close to finishing the roof that we decided to suffer through the cold and finish. I might have hypothermia now, but at least I won't have to worry about the roof collapsing this winter.

My hair is wet, and my sweatshirt is completely soaked through. I look over at my coat on the hook by the door, wondering why in the hell I hadn't thought to put it on. I twist my long locks, trying to wring as much water from the strands as I can. When I'm done, I glance over my shoulder at Ian and find him running his fingers through his own wet hair.

the Off-Season

"Let me get you a towel," I say, reminded of the first time we met on the dock.

He was freezing cold and soaking wet then, too. Only this time, it's my fault.

I shuffle into the bathroom, grabbing a fluffy towel from the linen closet before returning to the living room and handing it to Ian. "Feel free to stay and thaw out a bit. Or, if you'd rather get home and into a hot shower, I understand that, too."

Ian looks up at me, his teeth chattering as he tries to smile. "I'm not ready to go back out there yet. If it's okay with you, I think I'll hang out for a little while. See if I can get some feeling back in these toes."

"Let me see if I can find some clothes that might fit you. I've got some old baggy T-shirts around here somewhere. You need to get out of those wet clothes."

He looks down at his wet jeans and long-sleeved shirt. He hadn't brought a coat over with him this morning either "If you've got something, that'd be great. If not, I'll make do. You go get changed though. Don't worry about me."

I hustle off to my bedroom, shucking my clothes as soon as I'm out of Ian's line of sight. Wrapping a large towel around me, I shudder, instantly feeling a million times better. Being cold sucks ass.

I revel in the warmth for a minute before kicking into action. If I leave Ian out there much longer, he'll probably develop pneumonia and then I'll have to live with the guilt of potentially killing my neighbor. I've got to have something around here that'll fit.

I find a large pink sweatshirt I purchased several years ago for a Halloween costume. I wore it with a pair of pink leggings, sprayed my hair pink, and went as cotton candy. It was at least two sizes too big for me, which means it might fit Ian.

I smile at the idea of Ian pulling on the pink monstrosity. I can't wait to see his face when I show it to him.

I dress swiftly, pulling on my favorite chunky sweater and a pair of wool leggings. Shoving my feet into my slippers, I scurry down the hall.

When I step into the living room, Ian's back is to me, his arm bending over his head and pulling his shirt off. I inhale sharply, the sight of his bare skin causing the air to catch in my throat. I take a step back behind the wall of the hallway so that he won't catch me watching him and slowly peer out.

The muscles of Ian's shoulders ripple with each movement, his hand running the towel up and down each of his arms as he tries to get dry. The strong curve of his spine arches as he bends forward, giving me the perfect view of his lower back and ass, the soaked denim of his jeans leaving nothing to the imagination. I gulp as he straightens, marveling in the sinewy tension of each and every inch of his skin. The man is one hundred percent solid muscle.

And that's just from behind.

I desperately want him to turn around, so I can see the show from the front. There's no doubt in my mind that his abs and chest are even more impressive than the back. I've brushed past him a time or two over the last few weeks. I've felt how solid he is under those clothes. And, now, I want to see it.

A pang of guilt jolts through me at the fact that I'm standing here, ogling him without his knowledge. But the heat burning deep within my belly rapidly overshadows it. It's been a long time since I've seen a man like this. And, certainly, none of them were ever as impressive as Ian.

the Off-Season

My breathing picks up as he unbuttons the clasp on his jeans, tucking the towel into the waistband. I slowly reach my hand out to the wall, pressing myself against it, needing the support of *something* in order to remain on my feet.

My mind flashes to the conversation I had with Ella yesterday. She called at the crack of dawn, saying she needed to talk to me before I got to work on the roof. And she sure as hell didn't beat around the bush.

"So...Ian..."

"What about him?" I asked, not liking where the conversation was already going. It was too damn early for this. I hadn't even had my coffee yet.

"I like him," she said simply. "And I think you do, too."

I tried to play it off. "Well, he's a nice guy for helping me with the roof. Of course I like him."

"Cut the bullshit. That's not what I mean, and you know it."

I sighed. "Look, Ells, I don't know what you want me to say."

"I want you to admit that you like him. You're different with him. And I want you to admit that this has been going on for far longer than since yesterday. I saw you, Lex. I know you. You were more familiar with him than someone you just met yesterday."

I groaned. "Ugh, fine. He's been helping me out around the house for the past couple of weeks. But that's all it is, Ella. He's a nice guy who happens to know his way around a hammer and a paintbrush."

"If that were all it was, then why couldn't you take your eyes off him every time he spoke? When he left the room, why did your eyes follow him, the sad pout on your face like a kid whose puppy had been kicked?"

Laughter bubbled up from my chest, and I snorted. "Oh, please, Ells. You were here for five minutes. There's no way you saw what you think you saw in the short time you were here."

"It was half an hour, and it was long enough to see plenty. You forget how well I know you, Lexi. Even after the accident, when you fell into this weird funk, I was still able to read you like an open book. You think you do such a great job at closing yourself off. But you can't hide from me. I'm your sister."

Her words caused a tremble in my lower lip, and I pulled it in between my teeth in an attempt to stave off the tears.

And, as if driving home her previous point, Ella sighed, her voice softening when she spoke again, "I'm sorry, Lex, I didn't mean to upset you. I just want to say that it's okay. It's okay for you to let go and move on. It's okay for you to be happy. Yesterday was the first time I saw a genuine smile on your face in over eighteen months. It looked good on you."

"It's not fair to him though. He doesn't know. And there's no way I can tell him."

Ella sighed deeply. "One of these days, you're going to realize that you're better than you think you are. You're worth so much more than you allow yourself to feel. And the right man will see that. He'll realize that, no matter how hard things might be at times or how dark your past is, you *are worth it. You're a treasure, Lex. And you can't keep punishing yourself forever."*

She hung up shortly after, and I've been thinking about her words ever since.

Can I let myself be with Ian? Can I open up to him, tell him everything about my past, and hope he accepts me, scars and all? Can I allow myself to fall for the man who's so obviously changed my life?

I still don't know the answer to those questions, but as I watch him, half-clothed and completely unaware of my presence, I let myself imagine. I let myself picture it—what it would be like to actually *be* with him instead of constantly trying to push him away.

I picture myself walking over to him, my fingers trailing along the width of his back as I come around to his front. I imagine his smile, his dimples deep as he stares down at me, heat flaring in his eyes with every breath. I envision his strong hands cupping my face, tilting it back to give himself better access. And I imagine the warmth of his lips as they crash down on mine.

The sound of the towel hitting the floor pulls me out of my fantasy, and I quickly dart back down the hallway before he can turn and see me.

Ducking into the bathroom, I splash some cold water on my face, trying to cool the flush that has settled in my cheeks.

What in the hell was that, Lexi? You're lucky he didn't catch you standing there, watching him like a freaking Thanksgiving turkey being pulled out of the oven, the drool practically hanging from your chin. Get yourself together.

Knowing I can't hide in here forever, I muster all the courage I have and open the bathroom door, mentally preparing to face the man who just unwittingly starred in my naughty daydream.

tag

A loud cough from the hallway precedes Lexi's reappearance. Her cheeks are slightly pink when I turn to face her, and she won't look me in the eye as she hands me a giant pink sweatshirt and points down the hallway.

"The guest bathroom is right down there if you want to get changed. There are fresh towels under the sink. You can wrap one of those around your waist. We can toss your clothes in the dryer for a bit, so you don't freeze to death on your way home."

I smile at her awkwardness. I want to tease her about telling me where the bathroom is. I was in here for most of the day not too long ago, so I know my way around. But I hold off. I'm not sure why she's suddenly so embarrassed, but I have to say, I like it. The way her eyes flick up to mine when she thinks I'm not looking, her shy smile when I catch her…if I didn't know better, I might think she was…*flirting*.

I grab the pink eyesore and move to leave the room. Just before I step behind the wall leading down the hallway, I turn and look at Lexi over my shoulder. Her bottom lip is pulled between her teeth—a gesture I'm very familiar with at this point—but the look in her eyes is definitely new. Hidden behind hooded lids, the flash that ignites as she takes in my form…it almost looks like desire.

Surely, the cold from being outside has gone to my head. My brain must be frozen solid, causing me to see things that aren't really there.

I head into the bathroom, making quick work of my wet clothes and tugging on the ugly sweatshirt before wrapping a towel around my hips. Anything I might've seen in Lexi's face as I left the room will definitely vanish the minute she sees me in this getup.

And, to think, I was listed as one of People's *Sexiest Men Alive last year. If only they could see me now.*

Sure enough, whatever I thought I saw before I left the room is nowhere to be found when I reenter it. Lexi is sitting on the corner of her couch, her chin resting gently on her fist as she stares off into space. When she hears the creak of the floorboard, her eyes dart up to mine, the thoughtful look in her eye disappearing as soon as she looks at me. It takes all of two seconds before she dissolves into a fit of laughter.

"Laugh it up, chuckles," I say, striding across the room and sitting down next to her. I make sure to keep a safe distance between us, not wanting to make her uncomfortable and ruin the lighthearted mood that's enveloped the room. "Need I remind you, *you're* the one who actually owns this hideous thing?"

"Yes, but it was for a Halloween costume," she says in between gasps of air. "Besides, I'm positive it didn't look nearly as ridiculous on me as it does on you."

I look down at my pink chest, the material stretched tight across my pecs. She might be right about that.

"Fine. I'm sure you looked cute as hell as a bottle of Pepto-Bismol. But can we please get those clothes in the dryer before what's left of my manhood shrivels up and dies?"

"Real men wear pink," she tosses out over her shoulder as she moves to the bathroom to gather my wet clothes. After she slams the dryer door, she walks into the kitchen. "Do you want any coffee?" she shouts over the din of the dryer.

I get to my feet, rounding the corner of the living room and entering the kitchen behind her. She must not have heard me come in because she starts a little when I speak, "You got any cocoa? When I was a kid, my mom would always make hot cocoa whenever I came in from playing in the snow. Seems fitting for this situation."

"I wouldn't call re-shingling a roof in a freaking blizzard 'playing in the snow.' But, yeah, I think I've got some around here. I'm afraid I'm fresh out of marshmallows though."

I stick out my lower lip, giving her the saddest look I can manage. "No marshmallows? But that's the best part."

She shakes her head, a wide grin spreading across her face. "You'll live, I promise."

I bat my eyelashes. "Will you at least add extra chocolate?"

"Oh my God, you're like a child. Yes, Ian. If you go sit on the couch like a big boy, I'll bring over your extra-chocolaty hot chocolate when it's ready."

I pump my fist in the air, heading back into the living room. I look around as I sit down, wondering what in the hell we're going to do for an hour while my clothes dry. Lexi doesn't have a TV set up yet. Can't say I blame her, as she's got plenty around here to keep her occupied. Normally, I have no problem finding something to talk about. But, considering Lexi doesn't like to talk…

The house is quiet, the whir of the dryer and the humming of the microwave the only sources of sound. So, when the power goes out, the sudden silence is almost deafening.

Lexi steps out of the kitchen, stopping just inside the living room. The room is dim, the faded daylight from the setting sun the only light available now that the electricity is out. I can just barely make out the incredulous look on her face as she gapes at me from across the room.

I stand up, clapping my hands together. "Well, I guess we'd better start a fire."

chapter sixteen

lexi

*I*f God does exist, I'm convinced he hates me.

Not only for all the mistakes I've made in the past, but also because there's no other explanation for why he's stranded Ian in my living room, clad in only my giant pink sweatshirt and a towel.

Fuck my life.

I can't send him home. His clothes are in my dryer, which is now dead, thanks to the powers that be. Why, when all I want is to be alone with my thoughts and inappropriate desires, does this happen?

I'll tell you why.

Because God hates me.

I watch as Ian leans into the fireplace, arranging a small pile of logs he pulled from my back patio. Thankfully, I'd had the foresight to cover them with a tarp; otherwise, we might have frozen to death in the safety of my own home.

When I bought the place, I found it quaint that a wood-burning fireplace was its only source of heat. But, now, as my fingers have already started to stiffen in the chill, I realize how stupid I was. I mean, it's the twenty-first century. Things like a gas furnace should be a given.

Ian gets the fire started almost immediately though, sitting down cross-legged in front of it as it roars to life. He turns and smiles at me over his shoulder, patting the floor next to him. "Come sit. I promise I won't bite."

I choke on a breath, my thoughts returning to my earlier fantasy. I can't say I would mind if he *did* bite.

I spin back into the kitchen, yanking open the microwave, and pull out the lukewarm mugs of cocoa. I hand him his when I reach him, taking a seat at least five feet away instead of the spot directly next to him where he indicated.

He doesn't seem fazed though, taking a swig of the cocoa as I arrange myself.

Once I'm settled, I apologize for the crappy drink. "Sorry it's not very hot. I'm sure we can find something to put over the flames if you want to heat it a little more."

He smiles at me. "It's perfect. I've always liked it a little better once it's not scalding. Easier to drink."

I take a gulp of mine, relishing in the silky smoothness of the chocolate. It's been a long time since I've enjoyed a cup of cocoa, and as the liquid runs down my throat, I realize he's right. It's so much better when you don't have to worry about scorching off all your taste buds.

We sit in silence for a while, watching the flames as we finish our drinks. When his mug is empty, he sets it on the hearth of the fireplace. He turns his face to mine and scoots himself a little bit closer.

I see a flash of something I can't quite place in his eyes as he looks at me, and I swear, it looks as if he's clenching his teeth.

Taking a deep breath, as if steeling himself for what's to come, he speaks, "I know you don't like to talk about yourself, Lexi. But it seems as if I might be stuck here for a bit. We're going to need to do something to pass the time."

A dozen scenarios flash through my mind—most of them definitely not PG—and my eyes fall to the floor before he can sense where my thoughts have traveled.

"So," he continues, as if he didn't even notice my indiscretion, "if you won't talk about you, I think it's about time you find out about me."

His words surprise me. Not only because I'm not sure what made him suddenly want to tell me about himself, but also because it's just now occurred to me that, despite how hard he's tried to get to know me, I haven't done the same. Sure, I know the basics—name, where he's from, and...well, I guess that's about it. I've spent so much time trying to keep myself guarded and closed off from him that I haven't even thought to ask much about him.

And I suddenly want to know it all.

I nod, letting him know I want him to continue.

"My name is Ian Taggart." It's all he says, his voice serious and steady, as if this statement is supposed to mean something.

I shoot him a confused look. "I know..." I trail off, letting him know I'm not getting what he's trying to say. I mean, I guess I didn't know his last name. But what exactly does that have to do with anything?

"You haven't heard of me?"

I shrug. "Should I have?"

He laughs. "No. Though I'd say you're probably one of only a handful of people who don't recognize my name."

I raise my eyebrows. "You've got a pretty high opinion of yourself, don't ya?" I tease.

He gives me a sad smile. "Until recently? Yeah, I did."

I don't like the upset look on his face, so I try to turn the conversation back around. "So then, tell me, Ian Taggart, who are you?"

"Ian Taggart, better known as Tag Taggart, shortstop for the Washington Rampage."

I might not be a huge sports aficionado, but even I know who the Rampage is. I remember seeing all the headlines when they missed the playoffs this last season. Everyone said it was because of…

Wait.

"*Tag* Taggart. Not the same Tag Taggart who was accused of…" I cut myself off before I say the word aloud.

"One and the same," he says, giving me a weary look.

I know I should be getting up and fleeing the room, considering I'm sitting mere feet away from an accused rapist. But…I know Ian…*Tag*. Whatever. I've spent countless hours with him over the past few weeks, most of the time alone, and not once has he ever made me feel uncomfortable. Okay, that's not completely true. I was pretty damn uncomfortable a half hour ago when I was watching him towel off. But that was something else entirely.

So, even though I know I should be scared to be alone with a man who's been accused of such a heinous act, I'm not. Because I know, even more than I know how guilty I am, that he's innocent. There's no way in hell he hurt that girl.

"I didn't do it," he says after I don't speak for a few moments, his voice soft and pleading.

I realize he must think I'm scared. He doesn't want me to run, to push him even further away than I already have.

I scoot toward him, closing the majority of the space left between us, and place my hand on his. "I know you didn't."

His eyes snap up to mine, shock evident in every line of his face. And, in the dim firelight, I can see how much just speaking about it seems to age him. There's a hollowness under his eyes that wasn't there only minutes ago. I hate seeing the smiling, happy man I've come to care for look so run-down.

And I realize then how true those words are. I didn't want to admit it, but I do care about him. He's shown me a different side of humanity that I didn't even know existed. Someone who can accept you and be there for you, no matter what. And not because they have to—because they're your sister, like Ella—but because he genuinely *wants* me around. Don't ask me why. I've been nothing but horrible to him. But, for some reason, he sees something in me that has kept him coming back. And I'm suddenly incredibly grateful he has.

"How can you be so sure?" he asks, his eyes boring into mine.

I squeeze his hand, turning his palm over and lacing my fingers with his.

"Because, if there's one thing you've shown me these past few weeks, it's how *good* of a person you really are. There's not a single part of me that doubts you for a minute. And, quite frankly, I'm surprised anybody did. They only need to be in your presence for five minutes to realize there's no way you could ever do such a thing."

He swallows hard, his Adam's apple rising and falling with the effort. "Not everyone would agree with you. I haven't always been the best guy."

I shake my head, careful not to break eye contact. "I remember reading about your…personal life…in a few of the articles after the news first broke. They were quick to judge you on your extracurricular activities. But just because you enjoy sex doesn't mean you're a rapist, Ian. And fuck them for implying otherwise."

He pulls my hand into his lap, his thumb tracing small circles around one of my knuckles. "I'd give anything to go back and live that night over again. To not drink quite so much. To not go back with Angela—that's her name. She had such a magnetic pull to her. I couldn't look away from her as she moved out there on the dance floor. I should've known nothing good could come from someone like that."

A sharp pang of envy flashes through me as he talks about how he couldn't take his eyes off another woman, but I squash it down before it has a chance to fully ignite. Ian is a professional baseball player, and if the stories are to be believed, he has been with hundreds of women. Of course he found them attractive. Now is not the time to act like a stupid, jealous girlfriend.

Besides, I can understand the feeling he's describing all too well. I can't even begin to count the number of times I've wished I could go back to that night and not get in the car. How many times I've wished I'd stayed home that night instead of joining my friends for a drink. How many times I've wished I'd had the willpower to have one drink like everyone else instead of quickly falling victim to my vice. And the one I've wished most of all: that it was me who was injured in the accident instead of the mother and daughter who were simply on their way home, the little girl still in her pink leotard and skirt, her hair smoothed back in a perfect bun, her cheeks pinked with blush from her first ever dance recital.

I know how bad it feels to realize that one split-second decision completely altered not only your life, but also the lives of those around you. And I know the pain that comes with knowing you can never, ever do anything to change it.

I decide in that moment that I want Ian to know more of me. I want him to know how much I can relate to his words.

I turn my face away from his, my eyes falling to the floor as I speak, "A year and a half ago, I did something that changed my life forever. Something I've regretted with every fiber of my being since the day it happened. Something that, like you, I wish I could go back and do over. But, believe me when I say, no amount of wishing will ever make it go away. All you can do is move forward and hope to hell that, someday, you can be forgiven."

Ian's fingers trail along my cheek as his hand cups my chin, bringing my eyes back to his. The corners of his lips lift into the tiniest hint of a smile when our eyes lock. "You said, over the past few weeks, I've shown you the goodness inside me. But, Lexi, anything you might have seen in me pales in comparison to the light I see in you. You do a good job of trying to keep it hidden. I see the change in you when you realize you're feeling something you don't think you should be allowed to feel. It's as if a switch flips, and then the light pouring out of you vanishes, plunging you into darkness. You don't deserve to live in the dark, Lex. You shine brighter than the brightest star in the sky when you let yourself. It's why I haven't been able to stay away from you despite how hard you've tried to keep me away. You're my sun, Lexi."

I don't think. I don't let myself ponder his words or what they mean or how inaccurate they might be. I only act.

I lean forward and press my lips against his.

chapter seventeen
tag

Lexi's lips are soft as they lightly graze over mine. Her movement is so unexpected, it takes me a moment to catch on to what's happening. My mind is reeling over the fact that, after weeks of pushing me away, she's now about as close as she can get. When I don't respond, there's no mistaking the embarrassment that rolls off her as she goes to pull away, and the realization suddenly spurs me into action.

I lift my hands, closing them around her face, locking her into place. I pull back just enough that I can feel her breath against my lips, my nose nuzzling against hers as I relish the sensation. Her hot breaths come fast and short, and in place of the embarrassment I felt a moment ago are nerves.

My tongue flicks out, licking along the edge of her lower lip before tenderly sucking it in between my teeth. I give it a soft nip, which earns me a breathy moan from the back of Lexi's throat.

Pulling back again, I press my forehead to hers and smile against her lips. "You have no idea how long I've wanted to do that."

"Do what?" she breathes out, her eyes still closed, as she continues to press her face into mine.

I bite her lip again before answering, "That. You drive me crazy with that every time I see you. Each time you pulled your lip in between your teeth, I couldn't resist imagining what it would feel like. Taste like."

"And?" she asks, finally opening her eyes and looking at me through her lowered lashes.

"Better than I could have possibly imagined."

I completely capture her mouth with my own, my tongue pressing against the seam of her lips until she opens for me. She doesn't take long to comply, her soft whimper going straight to my dick as she accepts me into her mouth.

I softly lean her back, rolling us so that I'm positioned over her, cradling her body with my arms while bracing myself up so that I don't crush her with my weight. When I lean back down to kiss her, the hood of the stupid pink sweatshirt falls down over my head, and much to my horror, she giggles.

I push myself up, grabbing the hoodie with one hand and pulling it over my head. Her giggles are cut short when she sees me above her, completely naked from the waist up.

Her eyes dance over the muscles of my chest, her lip once again tormenting me as it slides between her teeth. She tentatively lifts a hand, her fingers twitching slightly as she raises her eyes to mine. I can see the question in them before she even has to ask.

"You can touch me," I manage to rasp out when I really want

to scream, *God yes, please touch me before I combust!*

Her fingers are gentle, the pads barely brushing along the heated skin of my pecs. And, if I thought I was about to ignite before, it's nothing compared to the sensation building in my cock now that her hands are on me.

She slowly spreads her hands out across my chest, her fingers exploring every inch of bare flesh. When one of them dips lower, running down the rigid landscape of my abs, I nearly collapse on top of her.

I lower my head back to hers, taking her mouth with my own once again. She doesn't hold back this time, her tongue tangling with mine as her hands continue their exploration of my body. I grind my erection into her hip, letting her know just what her touch is doing to me.

When she reaches the edge of the towel, her fingers toying with where it meets the V of my lower abdomen, I pause, my spine stiffening as I realize her fingers are trying to loosen the towel tucked around my waist.

I place my hand on hers, stopping her efforts. "We don't have to do that, Lexi. That doesn't have to be what tonight is about."

She pushes my hand away, her fingers quickly resuming their work with the knotted towel. "I want you, Ian. I want to feel you. I want to feel beautiful and normal and..." She trails off, her eyes glistening as they dart away from mine.

I drop my lips back down, pressing a soft kiss to her lips. "You've always been beautiful. From the moment I saw you, I knew there was something special about you. You're the most gorgeous creature I've ever seen, Lexi. And, as far as normal goes...fuck normal. You're the most spectacular woman I've ever met. There might not be a single thing about you that's normal. But that's only because everything about you is extraordinary."

I melt back into her, pressing my body against hers as my mouth continues its assault on her lips. When she frees the towel from my waist, I inhale sharply at the feel of my bare skin against her clothed body. Her arms wind around me, her hands finding their way to my ass as she tosses the towel out of the way.

She presses her nails into the skin of my ass, pulling me hard and close against her. I grind my rigid cock against her warm body, the soft fabric of her leggings heightening the sensation. I drop my face from hers, my mouth on her neck, sucking and licking as I continue to rock against her.

"Touch me, Ian," she gasps between moans, her fingers tracing lines up and down my back and ass.

She doesn't have to ask me twice. Pulling back for a moment, I lift the thick sweater over her head, flinging it behind me, not giving a shit where it lands.

Her soft, smooth breasts strain against the fabric of her bra, her erect nipples evident through the thin lace. I freeze for a moment, marveling at the sight of her lying beneath me, her long blonde hair splayed around her head, her cheeks flushed, her lips red and swollen from my kisses. And her supple, flawless skin on display, just waiting for me to claim it.

I run my finger along her collarbone, taking my time as I slowly trail my hand down from the base of her neck to the swell of her breasts. She presses up into me when my hand closes around her still-covered breast, her body rolling against my touch.

"Please, Ian. I need to feel you."

Returning my mouth to her neck, I nip and tease at her skin with my teeth as I rub my thumb against the rosy bud of her nipple. The feel of her moan vibrates against my lips, and I pull the thin fabric of her bra to the side, closing my hand around her bare flesh.

"Ian," she whimpers as my finger and thumb roll around her nipple.

I fucking love the sound of my name on her lips. And I'm determined to hear it again and again and again, as many times as I can make her pant it before she finally screams it in ecstasy.

My lips replace my fingers on her breast as I maneuver us into a sitting position, her legs straddling mine, her head rolling back on her neck as my mouth works her nipple. I make quick work of her bra, unhooking the clasp and baring her exquisite chest to me completely. I take turns lavishing her breasts, making sure each nipple gets the attention it deserves, my hand toying with the other at the same time. Lexi lies slack in my arms, completely giving herself over to me, my arm the only thing keeping her from slithering to the floor.

I feel like a fucking god.

After a few minutes of me worshipping her perfect tits, she starts to rub against me in earnest. From our new position, her core is pressed firmly against my cock, her wet heat radiating through the fabric of her leggings.

She rocks against my cock, groaning as her clit comes in contact with my stiff length.

"You like that?" I ask, sliding my hips forward to give her better access.

She nods, pulling her lip between her teeth once more.

"Then, use me, baby. Use me to get yourself off. I want to see you when you come."

She picks up speed, rubbing and grinding herself against me, and I meet her inch for inch. I don't take my mouth or hands from her body, teasing her nipples as she chases her orgasm.

"That's it," I say, grazing my teeth over one sweet bud. "That's it, baby. Let me see you come."

I look up at her face from my position at her breasts, and I see the exact moment when she goes over the edge. Her eyes squeeze shut, her head thrown back, as she screams out my name, her entire body curling around mine in the frenzy of her orgasm.

It's the most beautiful thing I've ever seen.

I grab hold of her hips, moving her against me when the sensation becomes too much for her to continue, letting her ride out her orgasm for as long as possible. When she finally collapses into my arms, her eyes hooded and her smile sated, I kiss her.

"You're fucking gorgeous."

She smiles against my mouth, her hands trailing down to the space between my legs.

"We don't—" I start, but she quickly cuts me off, nipping my bottom lip.

"Shut up, Ian. I know you want this as much as I do."

I can't argue with that—not with the evidence so obviously raging from my body. The second her fingers close around my length, I hiss. The feel of her body against mine through her clothes was almost too much to bear. The feel of her bare skin on mine is…

Fucking unreal.

She lets go of my cock for a moment, leaning back to shimmy out of her leggings. I watch her breasts sway as she moves, still a little in shock that this stunning woman is naked in front of me.

When she comes forward, my cock poised right at her entrance, she breaks the trance I fell into. "I don't have any condoms."

Fuck. I wasn't even thinking about protection.

I pull back, my mind spinning as I try to come up with an alternative. *Saran wrap is pretty much the same thing, right?*

"I've been on the pill for years though. And I've been tested. I'm clean."

When I realize what she's suggesting, it's all I can do to keep from flipping her over and pounding into her right then and there. "I've never been with anyone without one. And I get tested regularly. I'm good."

She presses her core down onto me, the tip of my cock barely breaching her entrance. "Then, make love to me, Ian."

I surge upward, my head falling forward against her shoulder at the feeling of her wet heat. She's so tight, the walls of her pussy clenching around my cock like a vise.

"Oh, God," she groans as I fill her, stretching her hungry little pussy to the breaking point.

I've definitely been blessed in the dick region, and I'm incredibly grateful. Because the sight of this woman as my cock stretches and fills her…it's enough to wreck me.

It doesn't take long until I'm at the brink of my own orgasm, but I refuse to let go until I've gotten her off at least one more time. I slow down and think of baseball—ha-ha—and bring my thumb to her clit. I use my hand to stroke her on the outside as my cock slowly caresses her on the inside, and before I know it, she's gasping against me, her body clenching around mine in the most delicious way possible.

I let go at the same time I feel her come, tripling the speed of my thrusts as I drive myself toward orgasm, using my body to extend hers. She screams out my name as I collapse against her, completely spent.

I grab the towel I was wearing earlier, cleaning up the mess I made between her legs. We don't talk, just smile and touch as I arrange her in my arms in front of the fire. Pulling the blanket from the back of the couch, I drape it over both of us as I pull her against my body. She nestles her head into the crook of my shoulder, and within minutes, she's asleep.

It takes me a little longer to finally give in to my exhaustion. Because I know, no matter what might lie ahead of me in my dreams, nothing could possibly be as good as the reality I just experienced.

chapter eighteen

lexi

I awake the next morning with a smile on my face. My lids flutter open, wonder filling me as I realize I actually slept through the night. It isn't until I move to stretch that reality sets in.

A large arm is wrapped around my waist, pulling me against a warm chest as I begin to move. It's then I realize I'm lying on the floor of my living room, a few dying embers in the fireplace still glowing before me.

Ian.

Ian spent the night last night.

And we...

I bring my hands to my face, scrubbing my palms down my cheeks as I wonder how in the hell I let this happen. I'd been so good, sitting down on the floor away from him, keeping as much distance between us as possible. But then he'd told me who he was…told me about his struggles. And my resolve had completely melted away.

I look back over my shoulder, only able to catch a glimpse of his profile from the position we're lying in. I still can't believe I've been spending so much time with a Major League Baseball player. How stupid he must think I am, not knowing who he was this whole time. I mean, I'd followed the news stories when they first broke a few months ago. I just hadn't paid much attention to the man himself. Like so many others, I'd heard about the allegations and assumed he was guilty as sin.

But that was before I knew him. Watching the man sleeping peacefully beside me, I know there's no way in hell he'd hurt anyone. I meant what I said to him last night. And I've never felt safer in the last eighteen months than I do when I'm with him.

But that's the problem, isn't it? I can no longer deny the attraction and feelings I have for Ian. They came to fruition—several times—last night. *But is it fair to him to drag him down with me?* I've had my reservations already, and that was before finding out he's a major sports star who's already facing a world of rumors and hurt. *Can I add more to that, knowing that, if word got out about my past, it would surely deepen the blow to his career?*

No, I can't do that to him. And what's more, I don't deserve to even be considering the possibility. People like me don't end up with people like Ian. Ian deserves the absolute best, not the lowest of the low.

I squeeze my eyes shut tight, trying to figure out how I'm going to get myself out of this one without hurting him. When I've half-convinced myself to get up and flee, never setting foot in Maple Lake again, he stirs behind me.

the Off-Season

"You look like you're thinking entirely too hard for this early in the morning."

My eyes pop open, finding Ian gazing down at me from where he's propped himself up on his elbow.

"Morning," he adds, his dimpled smile greeting me.

I want to groan because it's a sight I could definitely get used to seeing every morning.

And I know that'll never happen.

"Listen, Ian, about last night..."

He presses his finger to my lips, cutting off what I was about to say. It's probably a good thing, considering I don't have a freaking clue what that was going to be.

"Don't, Lex. Don't you dare say anything that happened between us was a mistake. Last night was incredible. And today is going to be even more so. So, get out of your head, and go get your cute butt dressed."

My eyebrows pull together, the argument I was preparing as he spoke rushing out of me with a whoosh. "Get dressed? Where are we going?"

Ian sits up, tossing another log onto the fire to warm the cool house. I snuggle deeper into the blanket, not wanting the chill in the air to permeate my cozy haven.

"*You're* going to get dressed while I make a mad dash over to my place and grab some clothes. I'm going to have to borrow that awful pink sweatshirt. Don't worry; you'll get it back," he adds with a wink. "You're crazy if you think I'm putting that thing in my closet. Even if it does smell like you."

I can't help the smile that spreads across my face. In less than thirty seconds, he's completely turned my thoughts away from the negative path they were traveling, reminding me again why he's so impossible to resist.

"You didn't answer my question," I point out, watching as he stands to get dressed, my eyes instantly falling on his bare ass.

After he pulls on the sweatshirt, he flicks the power switch a few times, double-checking that the power is indeed still out. It's a pointless task, considering the switch was already in the on position and there was no light.

He moves down the hall, his lower half still completely bare to my perusal. It really isn't fair for a man to have such a fantastic ass, the round curve a perfect half-orb.

When he returns, I smile up at him from where I'm lying on the floor. "You have a bubble butt; you know that, right?"

He shoots me another dazzling smile. "Is that a good thing?"

"Well, considering I used to go to yoga five days a week, trying to get one, yeah, I'd say it's a good thing. It looks much better on you than it ever would on me though."

He throws his head back, his hearty laughter ringing through the room. "I highly doubt that. But I'll take the compliment. Must be all those squats the trainers make us do."

"There's a reason women are such big baseball fans. I can assure you, it has nothing to do with the game. Baseball players are renowned for their bubble butts. It's those tight white pants. They get us every time."

He raises a brow. "Is that so? Well, I'm pretty sure I can scrounge some up. Brandon has to have a pair or two hanging around next door somewhere. I wouldn't want to disappoint."

I wonder if Brandon is one of his team members, the huge lake house suddenly making sense. Surely, nobody who didn't make at least seven figures could afford a vacation home like that.

the Off-Season

Ian shoves his feet into his boots before bending down to kiss me on the forehead. "I'll be back in a few minutes. Dress warm."

He turns and heads out the front door without another word.

"You can't be serious," I say as I watch Ian kneel down in the snow in my front yard.

He rolls a tiny ball of snow in his hands before dropping it down in the rest of the snow before him. "What? You don't want to build a snowman?"

"No, Anna, I don't. Or ride my bike in the halls."

He shoots me a puzzled look. Apparently, he's never seen *Frozen*.

"Never mind," I mutter, trudging through the snow to his side. "It's freezing out here, Ian. Wouldn't you rather go back inside? Sit by the fire?"

"Are you kidding? Do you know how long it's been since I've seen snow like this? It hardly ever snows in Seattle, and when it does, it's only an inch or two. Nothing like this. This is ideal snowman snow."

I roll my eyes but can't help but smile at his excitement. "Fine, let's build a stupid snowman."

Rolling around and playing in the snow ends up being a lot more fun than I anticipated. As I kneel and watch Ian, I'm struck with the memory of a certain paint roller running up my back a few weeks ago, and I decide now is the perfect time to seek my revenge. Ian is working on propping the middle part of the snowman up onto the base, so while his back is turned, I grab a handful of snow, forming it into an oddly shaped snowball.

"Hey, Ian," I say when I'm satisfied with the size of my ball.

I launch it at him as soon as he turns around. He falls back, momentarily thrown off-balance. I laugh as I watch him stammer around in the snow, trying not to go down.

When he finally rights himself, he narrows his eyes at me, a playful smile coming to his lips. "Oh, you asked for it, woman."

He rushes me, circling his arms around my waist when he reaches me and pulling me down to the ground with him. He twists us just before we land so that I come down on top of him instead of the other way around. But, as soon as we're down, he flips us, pinning me down with one arm while he grabs a handful of snow with the other.

"No!" I shout through a giggle. "Ian, don't. I'm sorry!"

He tickles my middle as he pins me with his legs, never dropping the threatening handful of snow. "I don't think you are. You'd better show me how sorry you are."

I gasp out the word, "How?" between sharp intakes of air, my stomach starting to ache from the depth of my laughter.

And, still, he doesn't relent.

"Say uncle!" he shouts as he continues his torment.

"Uncle! Uncle!" The words are broken and completely incoherent. I'm sure, if any of the neighbors are outside, they're wondering what in the hell we're doing and why I am screeching like a maniac.

Ian drops the snow next to my head, his cold hands dropping to cradle my face. "You look like an angel, lying here in the snow. A beautiful, unmarred angel."

He lowers his face to mine, capturing my lips with his own.

The cold from the snow is instantly replaced with heat as his mouth works over mine, every single part of my body lighting up at his touch.

He kisses me in the snow for what feels like hours and seconds all at once. All I know is, when he pulls back, it's entirely too soon.

"We'd better get inside. If we stay out here much longer, we're liable to get frostbite. And I happen to like all your body parts exactly where they are."

I smile as he pulls me to my feet, letting him tuck me under his arm.

"How about we head over to my place for a bit? B has a generator. It's not enough to heat the whole house, but we could at least take a shower."

I grin at him. I like the sound of that—*we*.

chapter nineteen
tag

I've never seen so much snow in my life. The morning after I spent the night at Lexi's—a night that quickly went on my list of top five best nights *ever*—we woke to at least a foot of the fluffy white stuff. And, in the three days since then, it's piled up even more. I used to be able to make out the shape of Lexi's house from my kitchen window, but now? Now, it's a never-ending spread of white.

It's hard to believe it's Halloween day. It looks more like Christmas.

Lucky for us, the power came back up shortly after Lexi and I made the trek over to Brandon's place. Because I've promised her a night full of terror and fright. It's a good thing B has an Apple TV in this place. First up is my all-time favorite Halloween movie ever—*Hocus Pocus*.

What? I figured I should ease her into it. We'll start there and work our way into Freddy versus Jason.

I hear the shower turn off in the master bathroom upstairs. I smile up at the sound before turning back to the coffeemaker in front of me. I pour two mugs, adding sugar and cream to Lexi's until it's exactly how she likes it.

I've carefully watched her over the last few days. And I want to surprise her with breakfast in bed this morning. Good thing my girl fell in love with B's shower the second she saw it. She's been in there long enough that I've had plenty of time to make coffee, scramble some eggs, and fry up some bacon. It's nothing special, but I hope she appreciates the gesture anyhow.

She's walking out of the bathroom, rubbing a towel through her hair as I step into the bedroom.

She smiles at me when she sees the tray. "What's this?"

"Scary Halloween breakfast," I say, nodding toward the bed.

She sits, propping herself up with some pillows and swinging her legs out before her. I place the tray over her lap, and she looks at the food.

"Looks like a normal breakfast to me. What's so scary about it?"

"I made it," I say with a wink.

She shoots me a bemused grin, rolling her eyes in what I've come to call her trademark look. On anybody else, it'd look bitchy as shit. But, on Lexi, it's cute as hell.

Maybe I'm a little biased.

She dives into her food, and I sit on the edge of the bed, watching her eat.

When she realizes I'm not joining her, she sets down her fork.

"You're not eating?" she asks around a mouthful of food, her hand coming up to shield the offending morsels from sight.

I shake my head. "I snatched a couple bites downstairs while I was cooking. You go ahead."

She scrunches her nose as she looks away from me to the food in her lap. I know she doesn't like my answer, but I also know Lexi isn't going to turn down breakfast.

In the past three days, I've seen this girl wolf down more food than half of the guys on my team. I have no idea where she puts it all, considering how tiny she is, but I have to say, it's refreshing to watch a girl actually eat. Not pick at her food and claim she's full after eating a crouton. Lexi can put it away like nobody's business.

And, as expected, she shrugs after a moment, picking up her fork again and shoveling a large amount of eggs into her mouth.

I laugh as she struggles to close her mouth around it. "Calm down there, turbo. It isn't gonna run away, you know. You don't have to try to eat it all in one bite."

She finishes chewing, giving me an embarrassed smile as she swallows. "Sorry. I haven't been eating much lately. I forgot how good food could be."

My brows furrow. "Um, what? How does one forget good food? You sort of need it to survive."

She shrugs again. "I guess I haven't had much of an appetite for a while. I eat what I need and sort of leave it at that. But, God, how I've missed bacon."

I want to push further, find out why she hasn't been eating. *What happened to this girl to make her want to ignore such a basic human need as food?*

the Off-Season

I'll admit, when things were first going down with Angela, my appetite fell by the wayside for a bit. But I quickly realized that wasn't getting me anywhere. Starving myself hadn't made Angela's accusations go away. It'd just made me hangry.

But, despite the progress Lexi and I have made over the last couple days, I know that, if I push, she'll shut down. I've made the mistake a few times already, thinking a question is innocent enough, only to see the walls slamming down behind her eyes as soon as the words are out of my mouth.

I've learned which topics are safe and which aren't during all the hours we've spent together. And talking about her past is definitely off-limits.

That's not to say it's all been bad. Far from it actually. Aside from the occasional awkward silence and tense moment, the past three days have been amazing. I've seen Lexi smile and laugh more than I ever thought possible.

And the sex? Don't even get me started on the sex.

Let's just say, I'm surprised *I* can still walk after all the time we've spent in bed.

And in the kitchen…

The shower…

The hallway…

You get the picture.

Watching Lexi open herself up to me in that way is even more than I could have ever dreamed of. She might not trust me with her secrets yet, but she trusts me with her body. With the delicate part of herself that she's so obviously kept hidden for far too long. And that almost means more to me than all the rest.

Almost.

I stand and clear the dishes after Lexi finishes up, smiling at her and letting her know I'll be right back. I walk downstairs and rinse off the plate, my eyes going to the vast whiteness again as I let my thoughts consume me.

Last night, after we finished making love for the hundredth time, I rolled to the side and tucked her into my body.

Her voice was so gentle, barely above a whisper, as she spoke, "What's it like?"

"Hmm?" I murmured against her ear.

"What's it like?" she repeated. "Having all your dreams come true?"

Earlier in the day, I'd told her all about growing up with only one goal in mind. From the moment I'd picked up my first bat, I had known I was destined for the major leagues. There wasn't any other option. Baseball was in my blood. And I wasn't going to quit until it became my life.

Normally, when someone asked this question, I would play it off. I would try to be humble, telling the person that I was lucky and still wanted for plenty. But I'd dropped the pretense when I was around Lexi. Lexi didn't know Tag, the professional baseball player. She knew Ian, the man who was grateful for everything he'd earned but wasn't willing to brush off the sacrifice it'd taken to get there.

"I'd be lying if I said that I don't wake up every morning, amazed that this is what my life has become. As a kid, I wanted nothing more than to play in the big leagues. And not a day goes by that I don't thank my lucky stars that I am where I am."

I felt her lips spread into a smile against my arm.

"I'm glad you have everything you've ever wanted."

I propped myself up on my elbow, using my other hand to turn her face toward me. I looked down at her, the sadness in her eyes telling me her question was more than a flippant topic of conversation.

"My dreams came true, yes. But, Lexi, it took a hell of a lot of hard work

and sacrifice on my end. While all my friends were hanging out and going to the prom, I was at the batting cages and in the field. Instead of spending my summers goofing off and mowing lawns, I spent my time fielding balls and strengthening my arm. I didn't have many friends. And I certainly didn't have time for girlfriends. My teen years and my time at college were spent studying and playing. There was nothing else."

Her brow lifted, her mouth opening to say something but immediately snapping shut. It occurred to me that she didn't know how to respond, and I realized how silly I must've sounded, complaining about things like missing prom and sleepovers when I had no idea what the woman beside me had gone through.

"I'm not telling you this because I want you to feel bad for me. I'm very aware that I've lived a blessed life. My parents never forced baseball on me. It was my choice, and I've never regretted it for a second. I don't feel like I've missed out on anything, not really. I just wanted you to know that good things can happen to those who are willing to work for it. If you're ready to put in the time and the effort, then you can accomplish anything, Lex. You're bigger than this small town; I could tell that within minutes of meeting you. But there's something holding you back, something you're afraid of maybe. But you can't be scared. Life is going to throw you curveballs. And there will be times you strike out. But, when the next curveball comes, all you can do is tighten your grip and swing for the fences. If you wait for the perfect pitch, you'll find yourself back on the bench, sad and disappointed you didn't take the risk. You'll miss your chance for a grand slam."

I expected her to rib me for my shoddy baseball analogies—I mean, how stereotypical can I be, professional baseball player talking about life as if it were a game?—but she didn't. She simply closed her eyes and rolled away, facing the wall.

She'd been the one to bring up dreams, but when I'd tried to press her, telling her I knew she was destined for more than Maple Lake could offer, she'd shut down again.

But not before I had seen a flicker in her eye, telling me that, deep down, she did have dreams.

She has hopes for the future that she doesn't dare give voice to. Out of fear, defeat, or simply because she doesn't think she deserves them, I don't know.

But, God, do I want to find out.

I want to see this girl, who's completely taken over my life, happy in every single aspect of hers. I want to see her thrive, flourish, and blossom into the amazing woman I know she can be. The amazing woman I know she *was* before whatever happened to make her close herself off from the world.

A creak on the stairs pulls me from my thoughts, and the smile that greets me makes me forget all about the maudlin conversation we had last night.

"You took so long, I started to worry. Thought maybe someone had come and stolen you away from me."

She smiles coyly as she crosses the room, her legs bare, the only article of clothing on her body the button-down shirt that was tossed over the chair back in my bedroom. Only the bottom three buttons are buttoned, her breasts almost on full display, their weight swaying slightly with every step she takes. By the time she reaches me, my cock is rock hard in my shorts, the painful throbbing almost too much to bear with her nearly naked body right before me.

She doesn't waste any time when she reaches me, her arms circling my neck as she pulls my face down to hers. Her mouth takes mine in a possessive kiss, her lips hard and firm against mine. I whirl her around, lifting her up onto the counter and wrapping her legs around my waist.

Her wet heat presses into me, and I surge forward at the knowledge she's not wearing any panties. I bury my left hand in her hair, locking her face against my own as my right hand trails down her stomach to the sweet spot I've come to love so much.

The moan that rumbles against my lips when I find her center is the only sound I need to know that I've got her exactly where I want her.

Until a crash sounds from the living room, a loud voice causing me to spring away from Lexi like I was just caught with my hand in the cookie jar.

The world's sweetest cookie jar.

"Ho, ho, ho, motherfucker. Santa's come early. The fucking *Nightmare Before Christmas* has arrived."

My head falls forward on my neck, the loud groan I felt since first hearing his voice escaping my lips.

Lexi hops off the counter, rushing to my side, panic wide in her eyes. "Who is it? Should I call the cops?"

I'm half-tempted to tell her yes. I mean, it has to be illegal to bust in and interrupt your buddy as he's about to get some, right? The Cockblocker law. That's a thing, isn't it?

But I shake my head, pushing her behind me to keep her from view. "No. It's just Brandon."

And, as if summoning the devil himself, the second his name leaves my lips, the asshole appears. He stops short when he sees us in the kitchen, my bare chest on full display, my erection still half-evident in my gym shorts. And, when his eyes dart to Lexi hidden behind me, the shit-eating grin that spreads across his face is too much.

Before he can speak, I throw my arm out, pointing to the room behind him. "Out. Give me a minute to get Lexi upstairs."

He stands there, as if my words don't compute, smile widening further.

"Get. Out. I mean it, B. Get your ass out of this kitchen before I physically *kick* your ass out of it."

He snaps out of his trance then, shooting me a knowing look before turning and walking back into the living room. "I'll wait here. Hurry back, honey!" he shouts over his shoulder.

I roll my eyes, turning to Lexi and closing my hands around her arms. "Head upstairs, and get dressed. I'll keep him busy for a bit. Then, come on down and meet the dumbass I like to call my best friend."

She looks over my shoulder, toward the living room. "That's the guy who owns this house?"

I nod. "Yep. And, trust me, he's as stupid as he looks. Now, go put some clothes on. I don't want to have to kill my best friend for thinking dirty thoughts about my girl."

I ignore the flash of unease behind her eyes at my words, giving her a gentle shove toward the stairs and patting her on the ass.

She yelps, turning to shoot daggers at me. "Don't do that with company in the house!"

I grin, giving her the full-on dimple effect. "It's Brandon. He hardly counts as company. More like an unwelcome uncle you can't wait to get rid of. Now, hurry up. If I have to come looking for you, who knows what might happen?"

I lean forward, giving her a quick peck on the lips. Hers stretch into a smile beneath mine, and she grins up at me before turning and skipping up the stairs.

Now, to deal with the cockblocker in the living room.

the Off-Season

Brandon plops down on the couch next to Lexi, throwing his arm over her shoulders and pulling her into his side. "Now, tell me, Lexi, what does a gorgeous girl like you see in a fuckwad like Tag here?" he asks, gesturing to me with his beer bottle.

He takes a swig as I walk into the living room, having just cleared the dinner dishes from the table.

Margie and Charlie are sitting on the couch across from the two of them, the impromptu dinner party coming together after Lexi and Brandon started talking and B realized he'd yet to meet Charlie and Liv. And, being the social butterfly that he is, B couldn't stand the idea of someone having friends that he didn't.

Liv is supposed to stop by after she closes up the bookstore. I can't wait to see the look on Brandon's face when he meets her. Small, spritely, and cute as hell, she's everything B would be attracted to at first sight. But, despite the way she looks, Liv can give a tongue-lashing like nobody's business. And, if anybody deserves to be on the receiving end of one of her tirades, it's Brandon Jeffers.

I walk across the room and hold my hand out to Lexi. She takes it without a word, letting me pull her to her feet. Brandon mocks offense, making an exaggerated gasping noise as he watches Lexi and me move to the chair between the two couches, her taking up residence on my knee.

"You wound me, woman. Taggart's okay, I guess, when there's no other option. But when you've got all this right in front of you?" He stops, waving his hand up and down his body. "There's no contest."

Lexi leans back against my chest, settling herself in my arms as she nuzzles her head against my neck. "I agree. There's no contest."

I shoot a smug grin at Brandon. "Why would she settle for ground beef when she's got prime rib right here, man?"

Brandon rolls his eyes. "Fuck that. If you're prime rib, then I'm fucking Kobe beef. Your girl just doesn't know quality meat when she sees it."

Charlie clears his throat. "Your prime rib, he's Kobe beef, and I'm dried up old jerky. Now that we've got that settled, can we talk about something other than cuts of meat?"

Margie giggles, taking a sip from her wine glass. "And, unlike man meat, women are like fine wine. They only get better with age." She lifts her glass in Lexi's direction, who raises her water glass in response.

"Hear, hear."

Charlie starts talking to Lexi about the new shipment of books they're expecting tomorrow, and Margie joins in, asking about new releases and planning out her next week's reading material. I zone out, not really a part of the conversation but not wanting to appear rude. B catches my attention with a wave, crooking his head toward the kitchen when my eyes meet his.

I nudge Lexi. "I'm gonna go clean up the kitchen with Brandon," I tell her when she turns to look at me. I press a quick kiss to her forehead as I scoot her off my lap and join my friend in the kitchen.

Brandon turns the faucet on as soon as we're within reach. After looking back over his shoulder to ensure nobody else is paying attention, he turns back to face me, his eyes lit with amusement. "Dude, you're so whipped."

I roll my eyes. "You've been here for, like, three seconds. You can't say that."

Brandon gives me a stupid smirk. "Oh, please. I've known you longer than anybody. You think I can't tell when my best friend has it bad?"

I try to think of something to say, some way to tell him he's wrong. But I can't. Because he's absolutely right. I've got it bad. So, so bad.

B gives my shoulder a brief squeeze. "It's all good, man. I can't say I blame you. I've only known her a few hours, but she seems like a cool-ass chick."

"She is," I agree.

"She seems to make you happy," B observes, his light tone deepening momentarily. "I haven't seen you laugh this much in ages. Even before Angela."

"She does."

"But..." He trails off.

"But what?" I ask, already knowing where he's going with this.

"But I haven't forgotten our conversation a few weeks ago. And, judging from the delicate way you watch her, your eyes flying to her face every time somebody asks her a question, I'm guessing she still hasn't told you what brought her here."

I blow out a breath, bringing my hand to my brow and rubbing at the tension that's been building there since Brandon showed up hours ago. "I don't know what to do, man. On the one hand, I feel like I need to know. I need to know what it is she's hiding because I can't take another hit. If she's hiding something that could potentially destroy my career after all we've done to get it back on track, then I feel like I should know."

"But?" he says again, knowing I'm not finished.

"But, on the other hand, I don't give a fuck. Whatever it is, it's in the past. It's obvious she's remorseful. And it's definitely something she's ashamed of. Why drag up the past when it doesn't matter? Nothing she says will change the way I feel for her."

B's mouth drops open, his eyebrows shooting up in a shocked expression. "Holy fuck. You love her."

"I…no…you don't…" I stammer over my words, trying to come up with some response to that observation.

But I can't.

Because I fucking love her.

I'm not sure exactly when it happened. Hell, it might've been that first day when I crawled out of the freezing water and watched her assess me as I strode up her dock, looking like the biggest idiot on the planet. Or maybe it was when I caught her skipping down the street, singing a nursery rhyme at the top of her lungs. Or maybe it was a few days ago when she finally let me in and gave herself to me in the most beautiful way possible.

Whenever it was doesn't matter. It doesn't make it any less true.

I'm in love with Lexi Barnes.

And it's fucking amazing.

B claps me on the shoulder, and I realize a wide grin has spread across my face. I can only imagine the stupid look he must be seeing because I feel like I'm two seconds away from floating right out of the damn kitchen. My heart flutters—fucking *flutters*—in my chest, and a tremor quakes through my body at the realization.

God, I'm becoming a chick.

"I'm happy for you, dude. Really. And, if the stupid-ass look on your face is any indication, I'd say you're pretty happy with your sudden epiphany, too. But can I offer some advice?"

I shoot him a wary look, and he laughs.

"I know, I know. I'm the last person who should be offering

up relationship advice. But this is important. You said it doesn't matter, that whatever happened is in the past. And that might be true. But you still need to find out what it is." He holds up a hand when I open my mouth to speak. "Now, I'm not saying it has to change anything. You just need to know what you're dealing with. If it's something major, then we need to get to work on it. We need to get ahold of the story before the press does. Give Ray a chance to work his magic and make it seem like a lesser deal than it is. Because, if the press gets ahold of it first, it won't only destroy you; it'll destroy her."

I turn, leaning my hands against the counter and lowering my head. He's right. I know he's right. But it still doesn't make the task any easier.

"You can't ignore it forever, dude. You know I'm right. Sit her down. Explain everything."

"But what if she ends it? What if she decides I'm not worth the risk? Not worth dredging up the past she so clearly wants to forget?"

B shakes his head. "Won't happen. I've watched you with her. But I've also watched her with you. That girl's as head over heels as you are. But, in the off chance it does, wouldn't you rather find out now? Wouldn't you rather end it before you got in even deeper?"

No. I'd rather things stay the way they are than risk losing her. But, again, I know he's right. If Lexi isn't willing to open herself to me in every way possible, then there's always the risk that, one day, she'll wake up and realize we're living a lie. And then I'll lose her anyway.

I sigh, turning around and crossing my arms over my chest as I lean back against the counter. B shoots me a grin.

"You're annoying as fuck; you know that, right?" I say, giving him the best irritated expression I can muster.

He throws his head back and laughs, coming to my side and throwing his arm around my neck. I bend as he pulls me down into a headlock, his knuckles rubbing against my scalp.

"Yeah, but you love me anyway," he says as he gives me a noogie.

I pull away, straightening and running a hand through my messed up hair. "Dude, what are you—twelve?"

"Twelve and a half, thank you very much," B says with a pompous grin. "Now, let's get back out there before that old geezer runs off with your date."

chapter twenty

lexi

I step through my front door, alone for the first time in almost four days.

Brandon tumbled through the front door as Ian and I were finishing breakfast this morning. The rumpled state of his hair and the fact that he was still wearing the same clothes he'd left in last night—with Liv, I might add—told both Ian and me that, whatever he'd gotten up to, he certainly hadn't gotten much sleep.

I took the chance to excuse myself, telling them I'd leave them to catch up for a bit and go home and clean up. Ian tried to argue against me leaving, but I insisted, telling him some guy time was needed between the two of them.

Besides, I need to call Liv. And find out what in the hell happened last night.

When she'd shown up late for dinner, I'd expected Brandon to flirt with her and try to pick her up. What I *hadn't* expected was Liv reciprocating. Instead of telling him off and calling him on his bullshit lines, she'd laughed and flirted back. I'd barely caught sight of the two of them as they rushed out the door, giggling like two kids who had almost gotten caught doing something they shouldn't have been doing.

I rush upstairs and turn on the shower, pulling my cell out of my pocket while I wait for the water to heat. No calls or texts from Liv. She's probably still sleeping it off.

Fuck it, I think, pulling up her number and pressing Send.

It rings once and then goes to voice mail. The bitch must've turned her phone off. She knew I'd want details.

Well, she's not getting off that easy. I'll have to stop by the bookstore after I get ready for the day. I'm not scheduled until this evening, but I can't wait that long. And it'll give Ian and Brandon a little more time to talk.

I'm not sure what went down between the two of them in the kitchen last night, but Ian was different the rest of the night after they reappeared. He held me a little tighter, his hands in almost constant contact with some part of my body. Every time his gaze caught mine, he would smile, the gesture reaching all the way to his eyes. And, after everyone left, he took my hand and led me to the bedroom where he made love to me over and over, his whispered words and soft caresses carrying me even further than the frantic and frenzied ones from before.

I never really understood the term *making love* before last night. I'd used it plenty of times in the past because it seemed a little more intimate than saying I fucked someone. But, until last night…until Ian, I never quite grasped the concept.

There is a vast difference between fucking and making love.

the Off-Season

They might look the same to an outsider. And, Lord knows, the end goal is basically the same. But, when you're with someone you truly care for, someone who understands you on a deeper level, who might even understand you better than you understand yourself…

It's downright magical.

I can now say I truly understand the meaning of becoming one. We weren't Ian and Lexi last night. We were…us. And I like us a hell of a lot.

And that is a problem.

I jump in the shower, rushing through the motions so that I can get out and clear my head. And there's only one way I know how to do that.

I need to call my sister.

I don't even dry off, wrapping my puffy robe around my wet body and walking out to my bedroom. I collapse on the bed, both dreading and looking forward to this conversation.

"Hello?" Ella's voice comes over the line after a few rings. When I don't respond, her natural instinct kicks in—or, as I like to call it, mom mode engages—and the words tumble out. "Lexi? Are you okay? What's wrong? Where are you?"

I let out a soft laugh. "Hi, Ells. I'm fine. I'm at home."

She blows out a loud breath. "Don't scare me like that. You know I worry about you living all on your own. Even with the buff guy living next door."

The sound that escapes my lips at the mention of Ian must carry through the phone because Ella stops short.

"What is it, Lexi? Did something happen with him?"

I bury my face in the pillow, reminded of the times we were kids and she'd come home and throw herself on her twin bed next to mine, sighing into her pillow over her latest crush.

"You could say that," I mumble into the pillow, knowing full well Ella can't understand me.

But, to my surprise, she gasps. "Alexis Marie Barnes, you tell me what happened right now. Don't make me come over there."

I laugh at her usual threat. "He's…Ella, he's so amazing. Like the stuff-of-fairy-tales amazing. I'm half-expecting him to bust out his shining armor and his horse to ride us off into the sunset. He can't be real."

Ella laughs at my dreamy tone. "I was wondering why you hadn't called lately. I figured you were busy with all this damn snow. Drew and I were actually going to drive out there this afternoon and see if you needed help digging out. He just finished our house. Poor guy has been out there for hours."

I shake my head and then realize she can't see me. "No, I'm okay. You guys stay home and stay warm. We'll take care of things over here."

"We, huh? You're already a *we*?" she asks, amusement evident in her tone.

"Well, considering I've spent every waking moment—and sleeping moments, too, I guess—with him for the past four days, I think it's safe to say we're a *we*."

"Lexi!" she shrieks into the phone. "*Four. Days*? Can you even walk?"

I groan. "Dude, I love you, Ells. But can we *not* go there?"

"Sorry, sorry. But, damn…four days. I can't even fathom…"

"Ella Garner! Enough!" I giggle. "Let's just say, it's true what they say about athletes. They have great…stamina."

"Oh, he's an athlete?" she asks, her interest piqued and finally off my sex life. "That's not surprising. He's got one hell of a physique."

the Off-Season

"Hey." I hear Drew bark in the background.

"Don't worry, sweetie. I still like yours better!" she shouts to him before turning her attention back to me. "So, what does he do?"

"Well, erm...he's a baseball player."

"Oh, baseball. I've always liked baseball. Does he play for a rec team?"

I laugh. "Not exactly. He's from Seattle, remember? Where he plays for the, um...Rampage."

Ella is silent for so long, I pull the phone back and check the connection to make sure the call didn't drop. When I see she's still on the other end of the line, I prod, "Ells? You still there?"

"Did you just say the Rampage? As in the *Washington* Rampage? Like the professional baseball team?"

My tongue swells, and I worry that Ella might disapprove of me dating a professional sports star. Especially when she realizes who he is.

"Yes," is all I get out before the phone clatters to the floor, and I hear her footsteps bounding across the room.

"Drew! Lexi is dating a professional baseball player! You know that guy at the house the other day? He plays for the Washington. Fucking. Rampage!"

"I knew I'd heard that name! I can't believe I didn't recognize him. Tag fucking Taggart. I was standing in front of Tag Taggart and didn't even get his autograph. He's the greatest shortstop the league's ever seen."

I listen to them freak out for a few minutes before Ella returns and picks up the phone.

"Lexi? Are you still there?"

I cough. "Thanks for dropping me to go fangirl with your husband."

"Dude, it's not every day your little sister calls with news that she's banging a sports star. It had to be celebrated."

We laugh for a few more minutes, joking about the long ball and tight baseball pants, Drew throwing out an occasional smart-ass remark before the mood shifts.

"Wait a minute." I hear the trepidation in Ella's voice as soon as the words are out. "Lex, I'm looking at my laptop. Tag Taggart…he's the player who was—"

"Yes," I interrupt, not wanting to hear the words come out of her mouth. "But he didn't do it. Come on, Ella. You met him. Did he seem like that type of guy?"

"Well, no," she says tenuously. "But then again, everybody said Ted Bundy was charming as hell. And look how he turned out."

I roll my eyes. "Ian is *not* Ted Bundy. He told me all about it. How he went home with the girl. They fooled around. And, the next thing he knew, he was being hit with a rape charge and slandered all over the news."

"But, Lexi—"

"No, Ella. I know he didn't do it. I *know* he didn't. It's not even up for discussion. The dumb bitch was after money and thought destroying a good man's career was the best way to go about it. From what Ian's told me, he's not the first one she's gone after. Apparently, she's made a living out of extorting money from wealthy men."

That's all it takes to get Ella on my side. "That bitch. I hate women like her. They make all women seem like gold-digging whores, and when something bad really does happen to a woman, it takes a freaking act of Congress to get anyone to believe them."

"Oh, I get it. And so does Ian. He told me all about how much it pisses him off that women like Angela get away with shit like this when other women have legitimate cases and can't do anything about them. He's quite the little feminist."

"I like him already," Ella says, the jovial tone returning to her voice.

She asks a few more questions about Ian's story, and I readily answer them to the best of my ability. I'm glad to hear her mind is at ease. But talking to her has only further deepened the realization that, while I know his deep, dark secret, he still has no clue about mine.

"When are you going to bring him over? Officially introduce him to the family?" she asks during a lull in the conversation.

"Actually, Ells...that's sort of the reason I'm calling. I need my big sister."

I picture her sitting up straighter, her ears perked at the sudden change in my voice.

"Hold on, let me go into the bedroom. Drew, can you keep an eye on the girls? I need to talk to Lexi in private for a minute."

I hear Drew grunt in response and then the sound of Ella moving down the hall.

As soon as the door latches behind her, she starts, "Okay, tell me what's wrong."

I can't help the tears that instantly spring to my eyes. After our parents died in that car crash, Ella had been the only source of comfort I'd had. She held me while I cried, laughed with me as I smiled, cheered when I accomplished something I'd set my mind to. We might have lived with our aunt and uncle, but really, Ella has been the only family I've had in a long, long time.

"He doesn't know," I say through my tears, my voice wavering slightly as I choke back a sob.

Ella doesn't have to ask what I mean. She knows. "You haven't told him?"

I sniffle. "I'm too scared. Too frightened of bringing up the past and letting that darkness back inside."

Ella exhales slowly. "I can understand that. Let me ask you this. Do you think it would change things between you two?"

I let out a shaky breath. "Well, of course it would. How could it not? I almost killed someone, Ella. *Two* someones. All because I was a stupid, careless asshole. What would happen if word of that got out? He's finally rebuilding his life after the charges were dropped. How could I let myself ruin his career if reporters got hold of this?"

Ella's silent for a moment, and I can practically hear the words turning in her head. "Don't you think you might be making a bigger deal out of this than it is? I mean, yes, the mistake you made was awful. Nobody is downplaying that. But do you honestly think reporters are going to dig so far as to find that out and then spread it all over the tabloids?"

When she says it like that, I realize it does sound a bit outlandish. I mean, there are plenty of people actively committing crimes every day. *Who's going to care about a DUI from almost two years ago? But then again, am I willing to take that chance?* I've seen drug charges from decades before come back to haunt celebrities and athletes. *Who's to say this will be swept under the rug?*

I voice these concerns to Ella, and she clicks her tongue.

"I don't know, Lexi. I still think you're making this into something it's not. I think you need to sit him down, tell him what happened, and let him make his own decision. If he decides it's something he can't deal with, well, then he doesn't deserve you anyway."

I laugh at her protective tone. Ella Garner, big-sister

extraordinaire.

"Thanks, Ells. Thanks for talking me through it. I feel a lot better now."

"Good," she says, her smile evident from her tone. "I'm glad you feel better. But, Lexi, I meant what I said. You can't start a relationship with someone when you're hiding so much of yourself. It might be in the past, but it still actively affects who you are. He deserves to know."

"I know," I say, giving myself a stern nod. "I'm going to tell him. Tonight."

Ian's alone by the time I make my way back over to his house.

"Where's Brandon?" I ask as Ian leans in to kiss me on the cheek.

"Out with Liv. And then he's got a late flight back to Seattle. He asked me to tell you good-bye for him. And make you promise you'll visit him when you fly out to see me," he says matter-of-factly, like there's not even the slightest possibility that I might not visit him once he returns to Seattle.

It only enhances the importance of the topic I need to broach, and I wring my hands, moving around him as I head straight to the couch.

He joins me, perching himself next to me and nervously running his hands up and down my arms. "Lexi? What is it? What's wrong?"

I bite back the tears, determined to get through this

conversation without crying. "We need to talk."

Ian lets out a loud sigh. "We do. I was hoping we could put it off a little longer, but I guess sooner is better than later."

I'm a little shocked that he has something he needs to say to me, too. And I grasp at it, desperate to put off the conversation I've been stewing over all day. "You go first."

Ian rubs his hands over his face. "Okay, here goes nothing." He takes a deep breath, and then the words pour out of him. "I realized something last night. While I was in the kitchen with Brandon. And then again while we were in bed. And I know you're going to think I'm crazy. You're going to tell me it's too soon. And you might even run from me. But I'm done lying to myself. I'm done trying to pretend like I don't feel the things I feel for you simply because I've been hurt before."

I gulp, my thoughts spinning over where this might be heading, when he takes my hands in his, turning so that he's looking me straight in the eye.

"So, here it is, Lexi Barnes. I'm in love with you. I'm in love with your smart mouth and your shrewd comments. I'm in love with your kind eyes and your beautiful smile. I'm in love with your gorgeous body and your insanely perfect mouth. But, most of all, I'm in love with *you*. The you I get to see when nobody else is around. The you I see when you drop your guard, letting the world—letting *me*—inside those barricades you've so carefully constructed. I'm in love with every single part of you, Lexi. Even the less than perfect ones."

I choke out a sob, the plan to make it through the evening without tears dissolving before it ever really began. Because, despite the facts that it *is* too soon and he *is* probably crazy, everything he just put into words…I feel for him, too. Every single thing.

But it isn't fair of me to tell him that yet. It isn't fair of me to accept his words and his love when there is still so much hanging between us.

I pull my hands from his, dropping my eyes to the floor at my feet. "Ian, I need to tell you something."

He lets out a broken laugh. "Well, that's not what I was hoping to hear after I said all that. But, okay, tell me."

I bite my lip, trying to decide on how to start. *Should I come right out and say it? Or ease him into it? Maybe tell him how sorry I am and how I wish every day that I could do it over again?*

But he already knows that. That night in front of the fireplace, I told him how familiar I was with what he was feeling. And, surely, if he loves me like he says he does, then he already knows how sorry I am for what I did. He might not know the details, but I know that my sorrow and remorse permeate my every movement and decision. If he thinks he knows me well enough to love me, then he must see that, too.

Fuck it, I think.

And I spill all my deepest, darkest secrets.

"A year and a half ago, I almost killed a mother and her daughter. They were on their way home from her dance recital. I crossed the centerline and hit them head-on. I was speeding—more than twenty miles per hour over the limit. And my blood alcohol level was more than twice the legal limit."

Ian's mouth falls open, his eyes instantly saddening as he looks at me. His gaze travels over my face before settling on a spot over my shoulder. I shrink back.

He can't even look at me.

Without returning his eyes to my face, he tells me to go on.

"I had known my drinking was getting a little out of control.

My friends had been giving me subtle hints for months that maybe I was taking things a bit too far. But I didn't care. I knew I was fine. I could stop whenever I wanted. I just didn't want to.

"That night at the bar, I cut myself off after a few drinks. I knew I had to drive home, and I wanted to be *responsible*. I thought I was fine. I didn't even feel buzzed. I slid behind the wheel of that car, turned the ignition, and told myself, if I drove slow enough, I'd be fine."

Ian's throat bobs, his expression blank as he listens to me recount the worst night of my life. It hurts, seeing him so completely…vacant.

I expected him to get angry. Or tell me how disappointed he was in me. Ask me how I could possibly keep something like this from him. *Something*. But, instead, all I'm met with is stony silence.

"The next thing I knew, I was coming to in a hospital bed. I was all alone with no recollection of how I'd ended up there. Until I sat up and felt the blinding pain stabbing through my head. Then, I remembered. I remembered getting in the car. And I remembered the lights—the bright shock of white as my attention turned from my phone to the car careening toward me."

"They're okay?" His voice is gravelly.

I nod. "They're okay. But okay is a far cry from good. The little girl's femoral artery in her left leg was damaged on impact. It was either amputate or risk death while they tried to repair it. So, of course, her parents chose the former option."

Ian's an athlete, and I can see the pain at the thought of losing a limb roll through him. I can't imagine losing a part of my body. But losing one when it has such a large bearing on who you are…

"The little girl still has big dreams of becoming a professional dancer though. She's only seven, but she's already been fit with a prosthetic. And she practices nearly every day. Despite the fact that I nearly took her life, she hasn't let me take her dream."

"You talk to them?" he asks, his tone laced with shock.

I shake my head. "No. I haven't been able to face them in person. I follow her Facebook page. After the accident, they set up an account, so people could get updates on her progress. They post pictures of her in her little dance costumes. She's adorable."

Ian nods. "And the mother?"

"She was pretty banged up but nothing serious. Broken collarbone and a bunch of stitches. I think her damage is more of the emotional variety."

He's quiet for a little longer, mulling over the story I told him. I sit next to him, watching as he debates his next move, waiting for him to kick me out.

So, I'm surprised when he finally lifts his eyes to mine. There's a hint of something in them that I can't quite read. Betrayal maybe? Anger? Whatever it is, I'm not sure. But, beyond that, there's a hell of a lot of questioning. And, dare I say, concern.

"Why did you get in the car, Lexi? What led up to that night?"

I cringe. Thinking back on what drove me to such a dark place seems so ridiculous in the grand scheme of things. Businesses fail every day…yet when mine did, I couldn't take it.

"Right after I graduated from college, I used the little bit of money I had left from my parents' inheritance to open a small store. A craft store of sorts. We specialized in wood crafts, but we also refinished furniture, sold antiques…I loved bringing new life to old items. For as long as I could remember, I'd always been creating. So, as soon as I had my business degree, I took every penny I had and invested it in my business.

"And it was good for a while. Business wasn't exactly booming, but it was steady. I was able to pay my two employees a decent wage and still had enough to pay my bills and the needs of the shop every month. But, unfortunately, the novelty began to wear off, and people stopped coming. I set up craft nights, put on boutiques, did everything I could to get people in the door. But none of it worked. Just before the second anniversary of our grand opening, I filed for bankruptcy. We were finished. *I* was finished. And it broke my heart."

Ian's eyes soften, and the heat from his hand as it rests over the top of mine on the couch sends shivers up my spine. I didn't realize how worried I had been that I would never know his touch again until that moment.

"Needless to say, I didn't handle it very well," I continue. "I started drinking to numb myself from the sting of my failure. A drink or two a night turned into three or four. One night at the bar turned into *every* night. And, before I knew it, I was sliding down the slippery slope of addiction. Only I was too blind to see it."

Ian rubs his thumb against the back of my hand, the gesture almost as comforting as an actual embrace, considering, two minutes ago, I was certain he'd want me out of his life for good.

"Instead of getting the help I needed, I denied that anything was wrong. Ella was here, more than a thousand miles away, and even she could tell something was seriously off with me. My friends tried to warn me. At first, they indulged with me. They would take me out, buying me drink after drink, telling me I deserved it after all I had done for my failing business. But the pity party only lasted so long. After a few weeks, it wasn't fun anymore. Not for them. But it was the only way I could get through the day without feeling like absolute scum."

I think back on those days, about how depressed I was. How

the Off-Season

I'd go days without leaving my apartment. And, when I did, it was only to go out drinking. There were times when I couldn't even drag myself out of bed. But I'd never been the type to succumb to addiction or temptation before. I'd always been so strong. So hardworking. I told myself it was a rough patch. Just a phase I was going through. I would come out of it soon enough. What was the harm in having a little fun? Lord knows, I hadn't had enough of it in college. I'd worked my ass off to keep my scholarship and graduate early. I was simply making up for lost time.

It all sounds so stupid now. How could I not see how far off the deep end I'd gone? Those first few weeks in rehab were, without a doubt, the worst of my life. I was so young when my parents had died, I didn't really remember the pain of their death. But coming off a yearlong bender?

There were days when I was certain death would be preferable.

I look back at Ian, ashamed of myself. "I know you're probably thinking how ridiculous that sounds. I lost a business. And, as a result of my poor decisions, a little girl lost her leg. Her mother lost her easygoing, carefree attitude. Everything in their lives is so much harder than it was before they turned down that road. Lily should be dancing like a normal little girl, having fun and forming lifelong friendships. Not having to learn how to move again."

"Lily? That's her name."

I nod. "Lily James."

He pulls out his phone, his fingers moving around the screen for a few moments until a smile spreads across his face. He holds the phone out to me, showing me what's on the screen.

It's a picture of Lily, her hair pulled back into a tight bun, her lips painted bright red, and the apples of her cheeks a rosy pink. She's in a purple dance costume, the sun glinting off the sequins in the photo. Her prosthetic leg is on full display as she cocks her hip out to the side, hands on her hips, mouth pursed into a sassy smirk.

She looks…happy.

The sight of the little girl in the photo causes my breath to catch. I reach out, taking the phone in my hand and bring it closer. I study every detail of her face, trying to determine if the happiness shining in her eyes is real or forced.

But, no matter how hard I scrutinize the picture, I can't find a hint of deception. The light in her eyes is too bright to be faked for the sake of a photo.

Ian gives me a moment, but his eyes bore into me as I study the picture. When I finally look up and hand his phone back, he gives me a timid smile, the corners pulling up ever so slightly.

"She looks like a pretty happy little girl," he observes.

I nod. "She's adorable."

"Do you think she's sitting at home right now, cursing the very ground you walk on?"

I sputter out a laugh. "Lily? You think that sweet little girl has a malicious bone in her body?"

He looks back down at the photo. "No, you're probably right. She's way too damn cute to be a bitch."

I laugh again. *He did not just insinuate a seven-year-old could be a bitch, did he?*

"But, Lexi, she's moving on with her life. She's putting the past behind her, not letting what happened stand in the way of what she wants most in the world. So, why can't you?"

His words cause me to come up short, my response jamming in my throat.

"Be-because I…she didn't…it was me…"

His hand rests on mine, and while I'm stumbling over my

words, he takes the opportunity to turn his palm over and take my hand in his. "You made a mistake. A horrible mistake. But that doesn't mean you don't deserve to live your life. You've paid the price…" He trails off, quirking an eyebrow up at me in question.

I nod. "Since there were no fatalities and it was my first offense, I got off easy. Too easy if you ask me. Six months probation—following rehab, of course. I was ordered into a program, though after the accident, I would've gone voluntarily."

Ian smiles. "See? You've done your time. You might think you got off easy, but I can assure you, Lexi, you didn't. I'm pretty sure you've punished yourself far more than the court ever could have."

"You don't get it though. Because of me, that poor girl will never walk normally again."

Ian scrolls through his phone another second before turning and showing me a video of Lily doing a pirouette. Her left leg—the prosthetic—gracefully cuts through the air as she spins on her right.

I've seen the video dozens of times, but it still brings a tear to my eye.

"You see this? She might never be normal again. But, like I said before, who wants to be normal when you can be extraordinary? She won't 'walk normally' again," he says, putting air quotes around the words, "but you can be damn sure she's going to dance phenomenally for the rest of her life."

"But—"

He presses his finger against my lips, cutting off my words. "No. It's time for you to move on, Lexi. I'm not saying you should pretend it never happened. You'll never forget the way that night changed you. It's ingrained in you. So, don't forget. But you need to forgive. You need to forgive *yourself.*"

I have to smile at his words. "Ella has been telling me that for months. Long before I moved out here."

Ian reaches out and brushes a single tear from my cheek. "I knew she was a smart girl."

"You're not mad?" I ask when my eyes meet his again.

"Mad? No. Upset you didn't think you could tell me before now? A little. But, Lexi, none of what you told me changes a single thing about what I said to you earlier. I loved you then. And I love you even more now, knowing what you went through and coming out stronger for it."

I shoot him a puzzled look. "Stronger? Are you crazy? I'm a mess."

He chuckles. "Okay, you are sort of a mess sometimes. But you've been through hell. Despite your flippancy now at losing your business, I know how much that must've hurt. It's not stupid. It's not silly to mourn the loss of something so near and dear to your heart. You could have chosen a better way, yes. But you've learned from your mistakes. You're here, building a new life for yourself. Do you know how many people would've shut down after going through what you did?"

"Well, I sort of did. And I was a total bitch to you for weeks, trying to keep you at arm's length."

He smiles again. "Don't I know it? But that wasn't you shutting down. That was you trying to protect yourself. You've been hurt. Maybe not by love. Maybe not even by another person. Life hurt you big time. She knocked you down and kicked you while you were in the dirt. It takes time to come back from something like that. But you're getting there," he adds with a wink.

"But what if people find out? What would they say if they found out you were with a drunk who almost killed two people?"

He shrugs. "We'll cross that bridge when we come to it. But

know this, Lexi. *Nothing* is more important to me than you. *Nothing*. Not baseball, not money, not fame. The moment you walked into my life, I was a goner. You're it for me."

A flutter moves through my entire body, stopping when it reaches my chest and staying there.

I lean forward, pressing a soft kiss to his lips. "You *must* be crazy. But I'm glad you are. Because I love you, too."

chapter twenty-one
tag

"If this keeps up, we might not get out of here again before spring," Lexi observes, watching the fat white flakes fall outside the living room window.

Another day, another snowstorm. It's a good thing I have a gorgeous woman here to keep me occupied; otherwise, I might have started developing cabin fever. I've never been one to enjoy sitting still, my childhood consisting of constant baseball practice and my adult life not turning out much different. But, for some reason, with Lexi sitting next to me, hanging out on the couch while bingeing shit TV shows doesn't seem so bad anymore.

I turn and look out the window, twisting my head to see over the top of hers. She's tucked into the crook of my arm, her legs curled up on the couch beneath her. Until she spoke, I thought her attention had been solely on the two brothers fighting demons on

TV in front of us. But, apparently, the impending ice age is more worrisome than the fate of Sam and Dean Winchester.

"That's fine with me," I respond, tugging her in a little tighter. "Though Coach might be pissed if I'm late to spring training."

"When is that?" she asks, her attention swinging back around to me.

"Mid-February."

"February?" she exclaims. "That's hardly spring."

"It is down in Arizona. It's usually in the seventies. Perfect baseball weather."

She purses her lips as she thinks. "So, we have only a few more months until it's back to reality?"

I press a kiss to the top of her head, rubbing her arm to try to soothe away her worries. "As far as I'm concerned, *this* is my reality. I will have to go back to Seattle. But that doesn't make *this* any less real."

She smiles, letting out a content sigh. Seemingly satisfied with my answer, she scoots down the couch, stretching out her legs and laying her head in my lap.

She's out within minutes, her tiny snores absolutely adorable in the quiet room. I grab the remote and turn off the TV, not wanting to risk a loud noise from the show waking her.

I kept her awake all night last night, determined to prove to her that, even after our talk, she still meant the world to me. I spent hours worshipping her body, kissing and licking every square inch until she begged me to end the torture. And then I made sure she came so many times, there wasn't a single orgasm left in her spent body. It was glorious.

But, looking down at her now as she sleeps, I can't deny that it's a lot harder to stay up all night, having sex, than it was even five years ago. Despite my best efforts to the contrary, I seem to be getting old.

Age. The athlete's worst enemy.

Lucky for me, baseball is a lower-impact sport, so provided I don't blow out my knee or my arm, I should still have another ten good years left in me. Maybe even fifteen, if I'm lucky.

I think back to my and Lexi's conversation last night and her worry over what her past could mean for my career. I wasn't surprised by the DUI. I'd figured as much after finding out she didn't drink and no longer drove. But I hadn't expected the part about the accident. Hearing the pain in her voice as she spoke about the woman and child she'd hurt was devastating. But not as much as it had been for her. I couldn't bring myself to be concerned about me after hearing how much it hurt her talking about the accident. And then seeing that little girl…

Let's just say, there will be a substantial donation made to her medical expenses as soon as I can get a moment to myself. It won't make up for the things she's lost, but maybe it'll help make them a little easier. And maybe, by making things easier for Lily, Lexi will be able to start forgiving herself.

I'll be honest, if word got out, there's no doubt in my mind some dumb-ass reporter would grab hold and not let go until I was finished. God knows, plenty of them tried after this shit with Angela. My only saving grace was the fact that she recanted. Still…I'm sure there are people who still want to see me ruined.

Jealousy is a fickle bitch. Something I've learned all too well in the past decade.

Pulling out my phone, I decide to do a quick search of my name. Last time I talked to Ray, he said things were starting to die down. I haven't bothered to check the headlines since then. One,

the Off-Season

because I've been too busy with Lexi to check. And, two, because I've been too preoccupied with Lexi to give a shit.

I type my name into the search bar, cringing when the first article that comes up is a negative one.

Tag Taggart—Hero or Villain?

There's a picture of Angela in the thumbnail, so I don't even bother to click the link. I'm already certain which option the author chose.

I scroll a little longer, keeping a mental tally of the good versus the bad. Surprisingly, the majority seems to be in my favor. There are even a few attacking Angela. I click on one out of curiosity and almost feel sorry for her after reading the first few paragraphs.

Almost.

I see a particular name pop up in the byline over and over again, so I click on one of his articles, dated shortly after Angela dropped the charges.

America's Dirty Sweetheart

By Paul Sharp

By now, you've surely heard the good news.

Tag Taggart is innocent.

Tag Taggart isn't a rapist.

Tag Taggart is everyone's favorite guy again.

Angela Hancock, the woman who formerly charged Taggart with sexual assault, dropped the charges on Thursday afternoon, following a lengthy meeting between her attorneys and Taggart's. Sources say Taggart paid Hancock something in the vicinity of three million dollars, and in return, she recanted her previous statements. Hancock has fallen off the radar since the meeting, a fact that's causing many to wonder if she fabricated the whole thing in order to extort money from Taggart.

Based on this new evidence, it would certainly seem so, wouldn't it?

However, in this reporter's humble opinion, Tag Taggart isn't nearly the man he tries to convey. His humble, boy-next-door attitude is all well and good—until the truth comes out. And, ladies and gentlemen, the lens doesn't lie.

Case in point, the week prior to the supposed rape, Taggart and the Rampage were in California for the first round of the playoffs. After every game, Taggart and the team would frequent a local bar. And, each night, Taggart would be seen leaving the bar with a different woman, most of them heavily intoxicated. As the photos below suggest, Taggart had to, quite literally, hold some of these women up as they made their way to his car.

My eyes flash over the pictures, each of them taken at such an angle that it would appear the woman present couldn't stand, let alone agree to any sort of sexual activity. They're total bullshit, of course, as anyone with half a brain can see. A woman's head thrown back as she laughs is hardly the same thing as her being so drunk, she can't hold her head up. But, to someone who already thinks I did it, they definitely look incriminating.

I scroll past the scores of pictures to find the rest of the story. *I mean, seriously, was this guy stalking me? How does he have so many?*

As you can see, the evidence is there. Tag Taggart might have gotten away with rape, but there's one thing that's for sure.

He's hardly innocent.

the Off-Season

I stop there, not wanting to see any more about all the ways I'm guilty of being the worst person on the planet. My nostrils flare as I seethe over the words I just read. My gut reaction is to call Ray and find out exactly what in the hell is being done about this asshole. But I know that conversation won't be quiet. And I don't want to wake Lexi. Besides, this article was written *before* I last spoke with Ray. He assured me things were good.

I lock my phone and toss it on the floor beside me. There's no way I'm going to be able to nap now, but I scoot down next to Lexi anyway, spooning her warm back to my front. Just the feel of her lying next to me is enough to lessen some of the anger and anxiety currently coursing through my body.

I close my eyes, reveling in the scent of Lexi's sweet shampoo. There's nothing I can do about this Paul dickwad today. It's obvious from the entire tone of his article that the douche has some sort of vendetta against me. And the thought of him catching wind of Lexi's past…exposing it for the entire world to see…

It's the sort of thing that would give a fucker like that a chubby. He'd get his rocks off from destroying not only my life, but also the life of the woman I love.

And that won't fucking happen. Not when she's finally starting to get some of it back.

First thing tomorrow, I'm going to call Ray, and I'll tell him everything. He won't be happy with this turn of events. But he's going to have to deal with it. We'll come up with some sort of plan, something we can put into place in the event of Lexi's past coming to light.

I don't care what they say about me.

But if they try to fuck with her?

It's war.

chapter twenty-two

lexi

The sound of "Thunder" by Imagine Dragons blaring from my phone is what rouses me from sleep. I blindly fling my arm out, hitting the button on the side to shut it up and send the call to voice mail. Whoever is calling me this early in the morning can go straight to hell.

When Dan Reynolds's voice immediately starts up again, I groan, rolling over and looking at the screen. The sight of Ella's name causes me to jackknife out of bed.

There's only one reason Ella would be calling me before eight a.m.

Something is wrong.

"Ells," I say, my voice coming out in a panicked whisper. "What is it?"

I look back at Ian over my shoulder as I slide out of the bed, careful not to disturb him.

After I crashed on the couch yesterday, he finally woke me up around ten and carried me upstairs to the bedroom where I promptly passed the hell out again.

Ian seems to be resting peacefully, which is more than I can say for my sister. Her voice is a rush of words and emotions, worry and tears making it almost impossible to make out what she's saying.

I close the door behind me, padding down the hallway and the stairs. Once I'm sure I'm out of Ian's earshot, I speak, "Whoa, whoa, whoa, Ella. Calm down. Take a deep breath. I can't understand a word coming out of your mouth. Calm down, count to ten, and tell me what's wrong."

I hear her suck in a rush of air and mentally count to ten right along with her.

When she finally speaks, her tears are still evident, though her tone is much less frantic, "Oh, Lexi. I'm so, so sorry. We're going to figure this out. We're not going to let this set you back. You hear me?"

I shake my head, still struggling to blink away the sleep in my eyes. I rub my thumb and forefinger over my brow and into the corners of my eyes. "Ells, it's way too damn early for me to make sense of what you're saying. Care to explain? Are the girls okay? Drew?"

Ella lets out a deep breath. "I take it, you haven't seen the news."

I collapse on the couch, huffing out my annoyance. Now that I know she and her family are fine, I'm a little irritated she woke me up. *This couldn't have waited until after ten?*

"You know I haven't. I've been sleeping, which is what normal, sane people do at seven thirty on a Sunday."

"It's all over the news, Lex. All over the internet. Everybody is talking about it."

I roll my eyes, letting my head fall back against the back of the couch. "What is *it*, Ella? Stop beating around the damn bush and tell me already."

"You. They're talking about you."

My blood runs cold.

"Wh-what do you mean?" I ask stupidly. I know what she means.

"Someone found out. Someone found out Ian Taggart was dating you. And it didn't take long for them to go digging into your past."

"I-I-I…" I stammer, trailing off, unsure of what to say.

"What they're saying is terrible, Lexi. And one hundred percent not true. I don't even know where they're getting some of their statements from."

I reach for Ian's laptop, grateful he told me the password a few days ago when I needed to use it to order some curtains for my house. I type it in, pulling up the first news site I can think of.

And there it is.

The main headline alongside the mug shot that was snapped after I was released from the hospital and taken down to the station. My eyes are puffy, my mascara smeared, a dark, swollen gash stitched across my left cheek.

TAGGART'S NEW SQUEEZE—DRUNKEN PARTY GIRL

As soon as I click the link, I'm assaulted by images of me out at clubs. In the bar. Dancing with strangers. Images that could have only come from my friends—or at least, those people I thought were my friends.

There's also an image of Ian and me outside his lake house. I remember the moment it must've been taken.

We were walking back from my place, and I nearly slipped on some ice. Ian swept me up into his arms, telling me I couldn't be trusted not to fall and bust my ass in my cute, furry boots. I protested, of course, going limp in his arms in an effort to make myself harder to hold on to. I didn't need to be carried like a damn toddler. No matter how good his arms felt wrapped around me.

But seeing the picture now, my arms hanging loosely and my head bobbing back on my neck, I look like I passed out. Whoever took the picture snapped it right when my eyes were closed, my mouth open in what's surely me trying to berate Ian for thinking he could swoop in and save me whenever he felt like it. But, in still life, it looks much worse, head rolled back on my shoulders, as I'm being carried up the stairs. I look exactly like the headline suggests. Like a drunk.

I skim through the article, skipping over the parts about Ian's rape charge and landing on the bits about my past.

> *Taggart's recently been seen with Alexis Barnes, pictured right and below, in the small town of Maple Lake, Colorado. That would explain why he's been flying under the radar the last few weeks. Barnes recently moved to the town after a stint in rehab and six months probation, following a car accident that nearly killed a woman and her then six-year-old daughter. Barnes was charged with a DUI and sentenced to rehab and community service, and the child lost her left leg.*
>
> *"Lexi has always been a bit of a partier," an anonymous source told us. "We've known each other for years, and she's*

always been the one who takes things a step too far. She likes to drink. There were times when she was at the bar every night. Nothing anybody said to her did anything. She just didn't care."

"Lexi knew she was drunk that night," said another source. "She knew she shouldn't drive home. When we tried to take her keys, she laughed in our faces and told us to back off. She acted like we were daring her to drive home drunk."

"That isn't true!" I shout to nobody, rage flooding through me as I read these so-called statements from people who supposedly know me.

It's not until Ella speaks that I even remember I'm on the phone with her. "None of it is true, sweetie. Stop reading it. It'll only hurt you more. Whoever said those awful things deserves every bit of Karma that comes their way. And I'm going to personally find out who they are and ensure said Karma finds their sorry asses."

My eyes continue to scan the words before me despite Ella's urges to do otherwise. Certain phrases jump out at me, and each one is like a stab straight through my heart.

"…selfish person…"

"…only cares about herself…"

"…didn't even show any remorse."

Tears flood my eyes, blurring the words on the screen until I'm unable to make them out. I slide the laptop off my lap and curl into myself, rounding my back so that my forehead is resting on my knees. As soon as my face is hidden, I crumple.

A loud sob breaks free from my chest, taking all the air in my lungs with it. I can't breathe. I can't think. I can't do anything but try to stave off the pain coursing through my body.

the Off-Season

It hurts. It hurts so goddamn bad.

I'm vacantly aware of Ella's soothing voice in the background, but I can't make out any of what she's saying. I'm grateful for her though. Her soft tone and loving words are the only things preventing me from shattering completely.

When a large hand closes over my shoulder, I jump, choking on my tears and sputtering out a horrendous cough. I swing around, finding Ian standing behind the couch, worry etched into his every feature.

"Lexi?" His voice is tentative, scared. "What's wrong?"

I sniff loudly and turn around, my eyes falling to the carpet in front of me. I don't want to look at him. I don't want to see him right now, not after I've ruined everything between us. But I also know I owe him an explanation. He deserves to know that I've destroyed him. And he deserves to hear it from me, no matter how much it will hurt to say the words.

"Ella, I'm going to have to call you back," I say through my tears, my voice wobbly and cracking. "Ian just woke up."

"Fuck," she mutters under her breath. "Okay. But promise me you'll call me back as soon as you're done talking to him. I mean it, Lexi. If I don't hear from you in the next hour, I'm coming over there."

I can't even muster the strength to squeeze out a soft laugh at her threat, like I usually do.

"Bye, Ella."

I pull the phone from my ear, pressing the End button and setting it on the coffee table. Ian steps around the sofa, taking a seat next to me and grabbing my arms, turning me to face him.

"What is it, Lex? Is Ella okay? The twins?"

I nod, the tears rushing back to my eyes as I look at him. Taking in the handsome lines of his face, the golden honey brown of his eyes, the scruff along his jaw. My eyes pause on his lips—those soft, amazing lips that have become so acquainted with every part of me. I'm going to miss every single part of him. But I think I'll miss those lips the most.

I open my mouth, and I begin to speak.

chapter twenty-three
tag

"How in the *fuck* did this happen?" I roar into the phone the second Ray answers.

"I could ask you the same question," he bites back. "What the fuck were you thinking, Tag? A fucking drunk? Really? After everything I've done to restore your career?"

"Don't you fucking dare. You don't even know her. You don't get to make those assumptions based on what some dumb-ass reporter thinks he knows."

"I wouldn't fucking have to if my *client* had told me what the fuck was going on in his life. You haven't been answering any of my calls, Tag. What the fuck am I supposed to think?"

I exhale loudly, trying to rein in my anger. It obviously isn't getting me anywhere. And it's only pissing Ray off even more.

"Look, I'm sorry, okay? I should've called. I should've

explained what's been going on. But, believe me when I say, it was the first thing on my list to do today. I just found out about Lexi's past the night before last. I was going to call you today, find out how we should handle it."

"You mean to tell me you didn't know until two days ago? How is that possible, Tag? And, even still, even if you didn't know about the accident, you couldn't have thought dating a drunk was a good idea. Not after everything you've been through."

"Stop. Fucking. Calling. Her. That," I seethe. "She's not a drunk. In fact, in the entire time I've known her, she hasn't had so much as a sip of alcohol."

He lets out a sardonic laugh. "You expect me to believe that? I saw the picture, Ian. I saw you carrying her into the house while she was stone-cold drunk."

I cringe a little when he uses my real name. I don't think he's called me that since the first day I met him. The turning it causes in the pit of my stomach reminds me of when I was a kid and my mother would use my full name whenever I was in trouble.

I shake it off though, my need to defend Lexi eclipsing my need to please Ray.

"You saw what a reporter wanted you to see. I was carrying her inside because she'd almost slipped on the ice. I didn't want her to hurt herself. The picture was simply taken at the perfect moment to make it appear how the photographer wanted."

Ray sighs loudly. "Be that as it may, it looks bad, Tag. This is bad. Not only are people up in arms about the fact that you're dating a woman who almost killed someone—a fucking kid, no less—but now, they're all turning their backs on you. People who, yesterday, were singing your praises are now convinced you'd paid Angela off to keep her quiet. And they're wondering if she wasn't the first."

the Off-Season

I put the phone on speaker, tossing it onto the table and running my hands over my face. "Of course they fucking are. Because, naturally, if I'm dating someone who made a mistake, that must mean I'm a fucking rapist, too."

Ray kicks into gear at the defeat in my voice. "We'll fix this, Tag. We just need to get you home. We need to get you away from that girl and show everyone that what they think they saw isn't true. They don't have to know you knew about her past. We'll spin it, so you look like the victim here."

"No!" I howl, springing to my feet and grabbing the phone again. "That's not a fucking option, Ray. I won't leave her. And I sure as shit won't drag her through the mud to make myself look better."

"What the fuck, Tag? Do you realize what's at stake here? What's the harm? People will forget about her as soon as you drop her. I don't see the problem here."

"The problem, *Ray*, is that I'm in love with her. So, no, I'm not going to fucking *drop* her, as you so eloquently put it. She's not going anywhere. And neither am I."

"You're *what*? You've been there all of a month, and you think you're in love with her?" The shock in his voice rolls through me, only deepening my anger.

"I don't *think* anything. I fucking *know* it. So, tell me what we're going to do to fix this."

Ray lets out an exasperated sigh. "Fine. I hope you realize what you're doing. I knew how to fix this when I thought you'd use your damn brain instead of your dick and *listen* to me. But, obviously, that's not going to happen. Let me think."

I let the insult slide through because, as much as he's pissing me off at the moment, I know Ray has my best interests at heart.

He's not only my agent; he's also one of my best friends. And I know this hurts him almost as much as it does me. Not just his income, considering whatever sponsors he managed to reel back in are no doubt going to bail. But it hurts him on a personal level, too. He doesn't like seeing his friends in pain.

"First things first," I say before he can get too much into defense mode. "We need to find out how this even came out."

"Already ahead of you there," Ray tells me, some of his usual confidence coming back into his voice. "As soon as the news broke, I tracked down the little fucker and made him talk. It sure as hell wasn't easy. I had to get pretty creative to get him to spill it."

I don't even want to know what sort of threats Ray made to get the asshole to speak. Not right now at least. Right now, all I'm concerned about is who and why.

"Name is Paul Sharp. He's some small-time sports writer for a local paper. His stories have been gaining a little more traction lately though. After Angela dropped the charges, he wrote a series of articles that didn't exactly paint you in a positive light."

"I saw," I say, my tone devoid of the anger that's taken up residence in my chest. It shouldn't surprise me that the dickwad whose articles I'd been reading the other day was the one to do this. "How did he find out?"

"Followed Jeffers when he came to visit you. Asshole had been watching Brandon's every move, waiting for him to give some sort of hint as to where you were. When Brandon had unexpectedly jumped on a plane, Sharp said he knew there was only one place he could be going. To you. So, armed with only his camera and his cell phone, he'd bought a ticket and followed. Son of a bitch didn't even have an overnight bag. Just jumped on the plane and left."

I shake my head. "So, he followed B, found out where I'd been hiding, and then what? Thought it would be a good idea to try to ruin the life of an innocent woman?"

Ray is silent for a second, as if he's thinking over his next words. When he finally speaks, I wish he had stayed quiet.

"She's not exactly innocent, Tag. Even if what you say is true, she *did* drive under the influence and nearly killed a little girl."

I bristle at the surety in his voice. Reminding myself he doesn't know Lexi and has no idea what she's put herself through, and that I'd probably have the same reaction if I were in his shoes, I explain her to him, "I'm not debating that, Ray. She fucked up. Big time. But nobody knows that more than Lexi. If you met her, knew exactly how much guilt has hindered every single moment of her life since then…you wouldn't be saying the things you are. She's guilty of making a stupid decision. But who among us can say we haven't? Hell, I can name a handful of times when you got behind the wheel when you probably shouldn't have. The only difference between you and her is, you were fortunate enough to make it home. One split second, and you could've been exactly where Lexi is right now."

Ray doesn't say anything, but if the change in his breathing is any indication, he's definitely affected by my words. He knows damn well he's driven under the influence. Maybe, now, he'll think twice.

"So, yes, she's guilty. But nobody can say she's not sorry. Whoever the fuck said that in that article is a goddamn liar. I've seen her guilt firsthand. I've seen the half-life she's been living since that night. And, when she was finally starting to make a little progress, *this* happens."

The look on Lexi's face when she told me about the article will haunt me for the rest of my life. It might have only been an hour ago, but I already know it's a memory that will be forever etched into my brain.

And, when she told me about the remarks from her friends, the person who'd said she didn't feel any remorse, her face crumpled in such a way that I instantly wanted to hurt the person who'd caused that pain. I wanted to track them down and make sure they felt every ounce of the pain they'd put her through.

I'm not a violent person by nature. But I'm finding that, when it comes to Lexi, I'll do all sorts of things I've never imagined. Starting with cruel and unusual punishment.

Ray apologizes for his remarks, his words sounding sincere, even to my enraged ears. He tells me to keep my phone nearby, so he can get in contact with me whenever he needs me.

"We're going to make this better, Tag. I promise. I just need some time to get it all sorted out. We'll find a way to make this work. Stay by your phone, and get things squared away, so you can come home. I need you back here soon. Laying low after Angela dropped the charges was good. But I think, if you stay hidden after this, it's only going to make things worse."

"I'm not leaving Lexi. Not after all this."

"Then, bring her with you. Let's show them that the two of you are serious about each other, and despite her past mistakes, this girl is good for you. Show them she's changed, and she's changed you. For the better."

I hesitate, certain Lexi isn't going to like the idea. "I'm not sure I can convince her of that. She's pretty shaken up."

"Make her see reason. I'll give you a few days. We'll make a statement this evening, but by the end of the week, I need the two of you here, in Seattle. I'll call you when I have more details."

I promise him I'll do my best and disconnect the call.

My spirits have lifted a little after talking to Ray, but I'm still pissed as hell. If Paul Sharp happens to cross my path anytime in the

the Off-Season

near future, he'd better hope I'm feeling particularly charitable that day. Because, right now, I want nothing more than to pummel his ass into the ground with my bare hands.

But, knowing Ray is on my side and that he's confident we can get this to all blow over, it gives me hope that this might not be the catastrophe I originally thought. Maybe we can spin this in a positive light. I like the idea of letting people know Lexi is mine. That I'm hers. And that the two of us together is not a bad thing. It's as good and pure as they come.

Now, if I can just convince Lexi to tag along.

I walk into the bathroom and splash some cool water on my face. Once I'm positive that the flushed anger is washed from my cheeks, I head over to Lexi's.

After we talked, she asked for a few minutes alone to think while I called Ray. I didn't like the idea, hated the thought of her being alone while she was so visibly shaken. But I needed to talk to Ray, and despite my hesitance, I agreed it might be good for her to clear her head.

I knock softly as I open the front door. "Lex? Where are you?" I call out as I step inside.

I'm met with silence.

I check the kitchen, but she's not there. Returning to the living room, I climb the stairs to her room. Maybe she went to lie down. Crying can really take it out of you. And she certainly did her fair share of that this morning.

I step into her bedroom, and my stomach drops. The drawers of her dresser are open, clothes strewed across the floor. It's obvious she was in a hurry.

I don't even have to check the closet to see if her suitcase is missing. I already know.

I rush down the stairs, sprinting across the snow as fast as humanly possible to Margie's house. I bang on the door, and she answers, looking at me like I've lost my damn mind.

"Is Lexi here?" I ask frantically before she can speak.

She gives me a puzzled look. "N-no. What—"

I don't wait for her to finish. I can't. Lexi couldn't have gotten far yet. I was on the phone with Ray for only a half hour, tops. And she doesn't have a car.

At the thought, I run back to my house. As I round the side, I can't say I'm surprised by what I find.

An empty space where my truck should be.

Seems that, in her desperation to get away, Lexi was willing to overlook that whole no-license thing. I wonder how it felt for her to slip back behind the wheel. I wonder if she's okay.

And then I realize, it doesn't really matter at the moment.

Because she's gone.

And *I'm* not okay.

chapter twenty-four

lexi

*M*y hands are trembling as I slide down from the driver's seat of the truck.

The *stolen* truck.

The truck I had no business driving, given that I don't have a license. Not to mention the fact that I was in no emotional state to be behind the wheel. In the five minutes it took to get to the bookstore, I almost ran off the road twice because of the tears blurring my vision.

Add to that the anxiety of being behind the wheel of a car for the first time since the accident, and it's a miracle I made it here in one piece. Lucky for me, I hadn't passed a single car coming in the opposite direction. That might've been too much for me to handle.

I know I won't be so fortunate if I try to make the trek to Ella's all on my own though. Thus the reason for the pit stop. Besides, I need to say good-bye anyway. And it's not like I can keep Ian's truck forever. Sooner or later, he'll report it stolen, if only to try to track me down. This plan works better for everyone.

Now, I just need to convince Liv to drive me.

I walk into the bookstore, the small bells chiming on the door as it closes behind me.

Charlie steps out from the back, the smile on his face dropping as soon as he sees me. "Lexi? What's the matter?"

He steps around the counter, coming to my side faster than I would've thought possible, considering his age. He puts his arm around my shoulder and leads me over to the chair in the corner of the room. He guides me down until I'm seated and then shouts for Liv as he perches on the ottoman.

Liv appears, blowing her overgrown bangs from her face as she sets down a stack of books. When she sees my tearstained cheeks, she forgets the books, leaving them to topple over as she rushes across the room to my side.

"Liv, the books," I point out, hating the sound of them clattering to the floor.

She shoots a brief glance over her shoulder before turning back to me with a wave of her hand. "They'll be fine. You, on the other hand…what's wrong, Lex?"

I take a deep breath, wanting to delay the inevitable. I've done my best to avoid talking about that awful night for the past nineteen months. Yet here I am, having to explain it all for the second time in as many days.

"There's something I need to tell you," I say.

Then, I launch into the story. I tell both of them the details about my business and how losing it sent me into a downward spiral. I tell them about the drinking and the constant state of denial I lived in for months before that fateful night. And then I tell them about Lily and her mother. I watch as their faces fill with shock when they hear what I did. And I'm reminded once again why I've avoided the subject entirely. It hurts too damn much to see those I care about disappointed in me.

Charlie recovers first, closing his hand over mine and giving it a gentle squeeze. "Oh, honey, I'm so sorry you've had to live through all that. That's a lot for someone as young as you."

Liv snaps out of her thoughts, placing her hand on my shoulder and nodding. "I'm sorry, too, Lex. I can't even imagine. I'm glad you told us though. It helps me understand you better. Some of your reactions and emotions make a lot more sense now."

I sniffle, grateful that I have such wonderful people in my life. Even if I am completely undeserving of them.

They spend the next several minutes asking me questions, which I answer as best I can.

After they feel like they've gotten the whole story, Charlie gives me a puzzled look. "That doesn't explain why you showed up here today, looking like you'd lost everything though. What haven't you told us?"

My hands begin to tremble again as I think about leaving Ian. "You both know who Ian is." It's not a question.

Once he told me, he saw no sense in trying to hide it from the rest of the town. Charlie was quite excited to know we had a professional baseball player living right here in Maple Lake. He was a big fan of the Babe, he added after Ian told him who he was. And Liv...well, Liv had seemingly hit it off with Ian's friend and teammate. There was no way she wasn't aware of what he did for a living. Not with the way Brandon had talked about the Rampage.

Liv nods. "Of course we do. But what does that have to do

with anything?"

"Someone found out."

I see the confusion flash across both their faces, and I know I'm going to have to elaborate more. I was hoping that would be enough. That they'd understand. But then again, this is a small town. There might be a lot of gossip among the locals, but they don't exactly pay attention to the tabloids. They wouldn't understand what something like this could mean for Ian's career.

"Someone found out we were together and went digging into my past. It's all over the news. All over the internet. Pictures of me from back then, quotes from friends who said I didn't even care that I hurt people. They've painted me to be this awful, self-centered party girl. And they're dragging Ian down with me."

A light clicks behind Liv's eyes, though Charlie still seems confused as to why it matters.

"So, his career is in jeopardy because of what some dumbass wrote?" she asks.

I nod. It's all I can do.

"And, now, you're leaving," she says, not even a hint of questioning in her tone.

I nod again.

"What did Ian have to say about all this?"

I shrug. "He's not seeing things clearly. He's confused and hurt but not thinking straight. This is what's best for him. If I disappear, he can pretend this never happened. They can tell people he had no idea, that I'd fooled him into believing I was something I wasn't. His life can go back to normal if I go away."

Liv shakes her head. "Do you realize how stupid that sounds? You're the one not thinking clearly."

"Lexi," Charlie says softly, breaking through the icy glare Liv is currently shooting at me. "You can't do this to him. You're crazy if you think his life will just go on because you disappear. He can't pretend it never happened because he can't pretend *you* never happened."

"You need to talk to him, Lex. You can't run away. It's not fair to either of you," Liv adds.

I shake my head. "No, you don't understand. This will ruin him. It's not just a possibility. It's a fact. He's too noble to tell me to leave. But, deep down, he knows it's what's best. Or, at least, he'll realize it soon. Once he starts to see reason."

"So, you're just gonna go? You're leaving Maple Lake, leaving behind the house you've worked so hard on? Leaving the bookstore? Leaving us?"

The tears start falling harder. "Don't do that, Liv. It won't be forever. Only until he goes back. I'll stay with Ella until then. Once he's back in Seattle, I'll come back."

I don't add that I'll only be coming back to sell the house. There's no way I'll be able to stay here, not when every inch of this small town is riddled with memories of Ian. There isn't a place in my home I can go that won't remind me of him.

Liv shoots me a questioning look. "How are you getting to Ella's? Wait, how did you get here? You didn't walk all that way in this cold, did you?"

I flush, my cheeks heating under the embarrassment of what I have to confess next. "Actually, I was hoping you could help me."

chapter twenty-five
tag

A pounding on my door pulls me from my wallowing on the couch. I lift my arm from my face, uncovering my eyes from where they were hiding from the light of day. I raise my head, turning toward the door. It's probably Margie, wondering what the hell my little stunt was about a few hours ago. I'm not really in the mood to talk to her, but on the off chance she's heard from Lexi, I go to the door.

As soon as I open the door, I'm surprised to find Liv standing on my front porch. She lifts a set of keys, the ring dangling from her index finger.

My keys.

My eyes shoot to the road behind her, seeing my truck is parked safely on the shoulder. My heart lifts a little as I scan the cab, searching for any sign of Lexi, only to be obliterated when I find she's not there.

"I don't understand. Why do you have my truck?"

Liv blows out a breath. "Because, *obviously*, Lexi gave me the keys."

"You saw her? How was she? Where was she? Where *is* she?"

Liv raises a brow at me. "Whoa, boy, calm down. She's fine. Well, physically at least. She stopped by the bookstore and begged me to drive her to Ella's."

I figured she'd go to her sister's. The only problem was, I had no idea where that was. I also had no fucking clue what Ella's last name was, so it wasn't like I could pull up Google and find her address. The only way I could think to find her was to find a phone book and start calling every single Ella and Drew listed in Grover until I got the right one. That was exactly what I planned to do, provided they still made phone books. And after I finished reeling in self pity.

But, now, with Liv standing here in front of me, telling me she knows where Lexi is...

"Let's go," I say, grabbing the keys and Liv's wrist, pulling her toward the car.

She digs her heels into the ground, using her other hand to pry my fingers from their hold.

"Excuse me, you can't order me around. Besides, she made me promise not to tell you where she was."

"Well, it's a little late for that, isn't it? You've already told me."

She nods. "I know. And I have every intention of telling you how to find her. But, first, we need to talk. You need to think things through before you go running off half-cocked and fully stupid."

"I don't need to think about anything. What I need is to get to Lexi."

She shakes her head. "No, you need to listen to me. She said some things I think you need to hear. And you need to think about what you're going to say to convince her she's wrong. Otherwise, you'll be fighting a losing battle, dude. She's absolutely positive that she's doing the right thing."

I hate the idea of waiting a single second before going to Lexi, but Liv is right. If I show up, wild with desperation and spouting off nonsense, Lexi will only dig her heels in deeper. I've seen how stubborn she can be. It's a miracle I've been able to get through to her at all. After this morning, her walls have probably been reinforced tenfold. I can't go running off—*how did Liv say it?*—half-cocked and fully stupid.

I turn and head back into the house, indicating Liv should follow behind me. I pull out a kitchen chair, nodding toward the one across from me.

She sits, her eyes taking in my disheveled appearance. "No offense, but you look like shit, dude."

A small laugh escapes my lips. That's probably the understatement of the century. "Yeah, been a bit of a rough morning. Now, what did Lexi say?"

Liv spends the next few minutes telling me about Lexi showing up at the bookstore, telling her and Charlie that the only way for things to go back to normal was for her to leave.

"You should've seen her face, Ian. She was scared, yes. And hurt as all hell. But she was so…I don't know quite how to describe it. Closed off maybe? Shut down? There was no getting through to her. And then, on the way to Ella's, no matter what I said to her, her only response was, 'It's what's best.' It was freaking spooky. Almost like she was running on autopilot. By then, she was almost completely devoid of any emotion."

A sharp pain shoots through my chest at hearing how much she's hurting. I've seen Lexi when she shuts down like that. Spooky is one way of putting it. She goes blank and doesn't say anything, though it sounds like she at least was able to form a canned response for Liv.

"I don't get it," I say, leaning forward and propping my elbows up on the table as I rub the heels of my hands into my eyes. "Does she really think I'll go home and pretend like none of this ever happened?"

Liv nods. "That's exactly what she thinks. She said those same words to me and Charlie when she was at the bookstore. She thinks that, if she just disappears, your life can go back to normal."

"Bullshit. There is no normal without Lexi."

Liv holds her hands up. "Don't look at me. I tried to tell her that, and so did Charlie. He told her you wouldn't be able to pretend like it never happened because there was no pretending *she* never happened. But, like I said, Lexi wasn't hearing any of it."

"I need to go over there. I need to talk some sense into her."

"I agree," Liv says. "But how?"

I shake my head, at a complete loss of what I can possibly say to Lexi to make her realize that none of it matters. None of what people are saying about me matters. Baseball doesn't matter. The only thing that matters is *her*. Without her, there is nothing. Without her, *I* am nothing.

"I don't know. But I'll have to figure it out. The longer we give her to stew and think, the more stubborn and hardheaded she'll become." I stand up, grabbing the keys from the table and tossing them to Liv. "You drive. I'll think."

The relief in Ella's eyes as she opens the door is palpable.

"Took you long enough," she says as she leans against the door.

"Sorry. Liv had to drive me over," I say, shooting a glance back over my shoulder to where Liv is sitting in my idling truck. "She doesn't believe in speeding."

Ella opens the door wider, letting me inside. "She's upstairs. Third door on the right."

I give her a hesitant look. "She might be angry I'm here…"

Ella smiles. "Oh, I guarantee she will be. Don't worry. I made Drew take the girls out for the afternoon as soon as she showed up. She and I needed to have a…talk."

I chuckle, thankful that Ella is in my corner. "Were you able to talk some sense into her?"

"Pfft, no," Ella says with a roll of her eyes.

It reminds me so much of Lexi, I can't help but smile.

I never thought the two of them looked much alike, but in that single eye roll, the resemblance is strong. They're definitely sisters. In attitude if nothing else.

"She refuses to listen to a damn word I say. I sent her to her room and have been watching the window, waiting for you to get here. I was about to come get you my-damn-self."

I take a reluctant step toward the stairs.

Ella gives me an encouraging nod. "Go on. I'll give you two

some space."

The stairs creak as I climb them. I take my time, each step slower than the last, my mind spinning. Now that I'm here, I realize I still don't have a clue as to what I'm going to say to her. How I'm going to get her to recognize the colossal mistake she's making. I imagine this must be what people felt like back in the day and age of pirates. It's like I'm walking the plank, and I have no idea if I'll sink or swim.

I tap lightly on the door when I reach it. She doesn't respond, but Ella said she was in here, so I gently place my hand on the knob, giving it half a turn.

Unlocked.

I turn it the rest of the way, gradually pushing the door open. Lexi is sitting on the bed, her face a mask of steely disdain. She looks as if she's been expecting me.

I take a step into the room, closing the door behind me.

"I saw the truck pull up outside. I should've known Liv was full of shit." Her tone is acidic, her words harsh.

All traces of the Lexi I've come to know over the last few weeks are gone. In their place is a stranger.

"Don't blame her. I made her tell me."

She gives a half-snort, her eyes darting away from me.

"You left." The words sound stupid, coming out of my lips, and I'm not surprised when she chokes out a laugh.

"You're observant."

"Why?"

Her eyes come back to mine, and I hate the look I see inside them. She's done more than rebuild her walls. She's reinforced them with ten feet of steel and concrete.

"Because this isn't going to work. You know it. I know it. So, why keep pretending?"

I take a step closer, wanting nothing more than to take her in my arms and shake her out of this emotionless trance she seems to have fallen into.

"Sure seemed like it was working to me. We had a little hiccup; that's all."

Again, I cringe at the absurdity of my own words. But, since I couldn't think of anything else, I figured I'd try downplaying the whole thing.

"A *hiccup*? You call having my entire life splashed on the front pages of every website and newspaper ever known to man a *hiccup*?"

I shrug. "Fine, maybe it was a…what's worse than a hiccup? A sneeze?" I give her my trademark smile, knowing that she's never been able to resist my dimples before.

But she doesn't crack. She shakes her head, her eyes rolling back in her head as she looks away from me again.

"Didn't anybody ever tell you that your eyes would get stuck like that?"

I'm trying to be funny and charming, hoping to get her to smile, desperate for a small glimpse of the Lexi I know.

I fail.

"Why are you here, Ian?" she asks, not a hint of amusement in her hard voice.

I stare at her, in complete shock that she can even ask me that question. "Because *you're* here, Lexi. Because you're here when you belong with me."

"I'm exactly where I'm supposed to be. You're the one who doesn't belong here. So, just go."

My heart fractures a little more with every word she speaks.

Deciding I can't handle even one more sharp word from her

lips, I open my mouth and spill my heart. "I'm not going anywhere, Lexi. Not unless you look me in the eye and tell me you don't want me. That nothing about these past few weeks meant anything to you. That you don't love me every bit as much as I love you. Because, Lexi, there isn't a single part of me that doesn't love you. You've invaded my life, stormed in like a fucking hurricane, and turned my entire world upside down. And I wouldn't have it any other way. So, fuck baseball. Fuck what any reporter has to say about you or me. None of it matters. Not without you by my side."

I watch her face as I trail off, and for a split second, I think I see her falter. She swallows hard, her eyes blinking rapidly, as if to ward off tears.

I strike again before she can recover. "You are the best thing that's ever walked into my life, Lex, even after everything that happened this morning. Even if I never set foot on a baseball diamond again, I will never, ever regret you. So, please, come home with me, Lexi. Come home, where you belong."

She's silent for a moment, and my heartbeat quickens as I realize I've won. She's going to give in because, as stubborn as she is, even she can't deny that what we have is special. That it's worth fighting for.

But, when her eyes lift to mine, I'm met with only blankness.

"The last few weeks have been a wonderful distraction, Ian. But that's exactly what they were—a distraction. I'm not cut out for this type of lifestyle. This morning has only further solidified that. It's not...worth it."

The final nail drives straight through my heart.

"You're saying I'm not worth it?"

Her eyes never leave mine as she shakes her head. "No. I'm so sorry, Ian. But it won't work."

I can't form a single word as I stare at her. I plead with her in my head, begging her to take back what she said. I blink hard, willing myself to wake up from this awful nightmare. But, no matter what I do, no matter how hard I try or how much I wish it otherwise, the fact remains that she just told me I'm not worth it. I'm not worth her having to deal with whispered rumors and scathing headlines. I'm not worth her putting herself out there. Me and my love are not worth it.

It hurts like fucking hell.

My chest aches, my heart shriveling into nothing, and I know I need to leave. I need to get the hell out of here before I do something stupid. Or worse, before I completely destroy my soul.

But I have to hear her say it. If I'm going to walk away, I need to know with absolute certainty that there is no chance.

"Say it then, Lexi. Tell me you don't want me. Look me in the eye and tell me you don't love me."

She stands, walking across the room until she's less than a foot away. Her eyes lock with mine, and I regret this decision. I should've walked away while I had the chance.

Because this girl? This girl isn't going to destroy me.

She's going to fucking *obliterate* me.

She doesn't blink; she doesn't cry. Fuck, I'm not sure she's even breathing.

But she opens her mouth and says the four words I hoped I'd never hear, "I don't love you."

I move in a haze, backing out of the room and down the stairs, silently slipping out the front door before Ella can stop me. I climb into the passenger side of my truck, grateful Liv agreed to stick around. We just thought there'd be three of us driving back to the lake house.

the Off-Season

Liv doesn't say anything when she sees me. There's nothing to say. I'm certain she can tell by the look on my face that things didn't go according to plan. And I'm glad this is the time Liv decides that prying isn't necessary.

We drive back to my house in silence. I climb out of the cab, not caring if Liv takes the truck home or leaves it here or what-the-fuck-ever she decides to do with it.

I walk up the stairs to my bedroom and collapse on the bed.

I'm immediately enveloped with Lexi's scent.

And I fucking lose it.

chapter twenty-six

lexi

One Week Later

I open the front door to my house, surprised to see how familiar everything looks. I was only gone for a week, but it felt like a lifetime.

A lifetime of pain and regret.

A lifetime of misery.

A lifetime of sorrow.

I half-expected to find everything covered in a thick layer of dust, my house boarded up and left behind, but that was only my heart.

Since the moment Ian walked out of my sister's house, I've been going through the motions, trying to live my life one day at a time. If that's what you want to call it. Mostly, I sat around Ella's, trying to help with the girls when I could, but more often than not,

I would find myself locked in the guest room, the sounds of my cries muffled by the pillow I kept firmly pressed against my face.

Watching his face crumple as I'd told him I didn't love him was the hardest thing I'd ever had to do. I'd wanted to throw my arms around him, kiss away all his tears, tell him I loved him more than he could possibly ever love me because he had brought me back to life.

But I hadn't done any of it. Because, while ninety-nine percent of the words that had come out of my mouth were complete and utter bullshit, the truth still remained. I didn't belong with him. It would never work.

Because he deserves better.

He deserves the type of woman he can take out and be proud of. The kind of woman who will always make him smile and never make him sad. The kind of woman who is the exact opposite of me in every single way.

Once Ella had realized he was gone, she'd stormed up the stairs, berating me for my stupidity. I couldn't blame her. I had known I'd just let the best thing that had ever happened to me walk out of my life.

But Ella doesn't understand. I'm not doing this for me. I'm not doing it because I'm scared. For once in my life, I'm being selfless. I'm putting Ian first.

I'm doing it for him.

In time, Ian will realize that. He'll realize that, despite the chemistry that exists between us, we're just too different. I could never fit into his world. And he shouldn't have to change himself to fit into mine.

So, I stayed away. I hid at Ella's until I was certain I wouldn't have to return here and face him. I was actually surprised when Liv had called late last night to tell me he was gone. I'd thought he'd stick around a little longer. Thought maybe he'd put up more of a fight. Liv had only had to utter two simple words for my heart to drop down to my feet.

"He's gone."

I'd expected it to hurt. I'd expected to be sad when I heard he'd finally left for Seattle. But what I hadn't been able to predict was the…intensity of it.

I don't just hurt. And I'm not just sad.

When Ella pulled up in front of my house only moments ago, putting the car in park before helping me get my bag out of the back, I wasn't able to stop myself from chancing a glance at his house.

The dark windows and drawn shades was a deathblow.

Now, standing in my kitchen and looking out over the frozen lake, I let the tears fall once more. I look over at Ian's house, all the outside furniture covered and the decorative lights no longer lit, I realize for the first time that he is well and truly gone.

Forever.

It's what I wanted. I lied to his face, told him I wanted him to go, that I didn't love him. But seeing it now, looking out over the aftermath of what I've done…

It's a pain unlike anything I've ever felt before.

Even after the accident.

Even after waking up and realizing what I did.

Even after all the hours of community service and my time in rehab.

And, yes, even after seeing all the photos of Lily during her recovery.

Nothing has ever felt like this.

And I'm not certain I can survive it.

the Off-Season

Turning my back to the outside world, I grab a glass from the cupboard and fill it with water from the tap. I suck it down in a few huge gulps, hoping it will do something to quell the lump currently blocking my throat. But, of course, it doesn't.

I would kill for a drink right now.

But, since there isn't an ounce of alcohol in this whole damn place, I opt for the only other thing that might help me forget.

After refilling my glass, I walk to my room, stopping in the bathroom along the way to grab the bottle. Once I'm settled on my bed, I twist off the top and shake out two of the sleeping pills I was prescribed after the accident—when my nightmares would keep me up, no matter how hard I tried to sleep. I didn't take many of them then, preferring the pain of my reality to living in a drugged stupor. Now though? Now, I want nothing more than to sleep.

I pop the pills in my mouth and chase them with the water.

When they don't kick in after five minutes, I follow them with two more.

Thankfully, that does the trick. Within minutes, my lids start to drift, the hammering in my heart quieting and the shaking in my fingers steadying.

I lie down on the pillow.

And I go to sleep.

chapter twenty-seven
tag

𝓘 roll the bite of my burger around in my mouth as Brandon babbles to me about God knows what. It's not that I don't care. It's just…

In the days since I left Maple Lake, my life has been on autopilot. Wake up, hit the gym, go to practice, meet with Ray, go to bed, and then get up and do it all over again. Every waking moment of my day is planned out for me, even down to each meal. Brandon and Ray have made it a point to make sure I'm never alone, except during those late hours when I'm supposed to be asleep.

But sleep is for those who aren't dying on the inside. It's for people who have their shit together and who haven't had their heart ripped out of their chest, stomped on, run over by a dump truck, and then set on fire. That is exactly how I feel right now.

the Off-Season

Remember when I said I didn't understand how people could forget about food? Yeah, I totally get that now. I eat when I have to, whenever the person who's currently assigned to be my babysitter says it's time for food. But, no matter what I put in my mouth, it all tastes the same.

Like loneliness and heartache.

Like resentment and bitterness.

Like nothing whatsoever.

I take another bite of the burger in front of me. It's a fantastic-looking thing. A week ago, I would have been salivating at the idea of being able to sink my teeth into the juicy meat, fresh bun, and crisp veggies.

But, now, it's just something I need to survive.

I wonder how much longer B is going to keep me out tonight. Even though I hate being alone with my thoughts—because, inevitably, they lead right back to *her*—it's still preferable to the alternative. Having to sit out in public, pretending like I'm not wishing I were back in Maple Lake every second of every day, is fucking awful. Having to smile for the cameras, telling people the whole thing was a big misunderstanding, explaining that Lexi and I aren't together anymore, is quite possibly the worst form of torture known to man.

Because just saying her name is enough to bring me to my knees.

Ray wasn't happy when I refused to tell people I didn't know about Lexi's past. He wanted me to tell the press she'd lied to me, that I'd been just as shocked as they all were. But I couldn't bring myself to do it. Because, despite everything that happened between us, I still love her. I will *always* love her. And, even though she shattered my heart into billions of tiny little pieces, I'm not willing to hurt her.

So, instead, we went with the alternative. I didn't tell them I didn't know, and I didn't call her a liar. But I did tell them things were over between us. I didn't tell them why or give any details on how it'd ended. I let them make their own assumptions. And, judging from the headlines, they fell right into the trap Ray had wanted them to. Everyone played me out to be the innocent victim, the man who had fallen for a snake.

And, when word got out about my anonymous donation to Lily's medical care, everyone started treating me like a goddamn saint.

I'll never forgive Ray for that one. He denies it wholly, but I know the truth. Releasing that information redeemed me in everybody's eyes. Fuck, even the asshole who'd written all those shitty things about me and the article about Lexi wasn't able to find anything negative about me donating money to a little girl.

I'm back on top, America's golden boy again.

But I feel like I'm six feet under.

I start picking at the bun on my burger when Brandon's voice finally gets through to me.

"So, that's when the alien said to me, 'Look, buddy, I don't care who you are. Lie down, and take it like a man.'"

My head snaps up, and my brows furrow as I look at my friend. "What the fuck did you just say?"

Brandon looks around himself, placing his hand over his chest as he feigns shock. "Oh, I'm sorry. Are you talking to me? You've been ignoring me for so long, I figured I'd start entertaining myself."

"Asshole," I mutter under my breath.

"How much longer are you going to sit around and sulk,

man?" he asks, his irritation evident. "I mean, I get that she gutted you like a fucking flounder. But, sooner or later, you've gotta move on."

I narrow my eyes as I look at him. "It's not that fucking easy, okay? It's not like I lost my favorite toy, and I'm pouting like a fucking five-year-old. She was *it* for me; don't you get that? And, now, she's gone. How the fuck am I supposed to move on?"

Brandon's eyes soften a little, and that almost pisses me off more. Because, if there's one thing I hate seeing on him more than anger, it's pity.

"Don't you fucking give me that look," I bite out. "Just eat your food, and let's get the hell out of here."

But B doesn't let it go. Of course he doesn't. Because he wouldn't be Brandon if he knew how to drop shit when he should.

"I know you loved her, man. You think I've known you all these years and don't understand you? You think I didn't see how different you were with her during the short time I was there? I know she was different. And I know you're not going to be able to forget about her. But you can't keep going like this. You've got to start living again. Because you're fucking bumming me out."

I chuckle, grateful that, even after his little heartfelt speech, he's still Brandon to the core. "I'm sorry I'm inconveniencing you."

He grins. "You should be. I'm a fucking joy to be around. But, lately, you make me feel like that might not be true. You're so mopey all the time. It's hazardous to my ego."

"And we wouldn't want that. Lord knows, your ego can't possibly survive another hit," I say with a sideways grin.

"True dat," he says with a nod. But then some of the joviality dims from his eyes, and his stare levels on me once more. "But, in all seriousness, dude, I think you might need to get some help. You're not yourself. I'm worried about you."

"I'm fine. It's just going to take a while, you know? It all ended so suddenly. One minute, we were lying in bed together, tangled up in sleep. And the next, all hell broke loose, and she was telling me she didn't love me. It happened so fast. With no warning."

"And you need closure," B observes.

The thought hadn't occurred to me until the word left Brandon's mouth, but yeah, that's exactly what I need.

I went to Ella's with every intention of bringing Lexi back with me. The thought that she might not return had never even crossed my mind. And, when she said those words to me, the ones that ripped through my flesh and cut me right down to the bone, I wasn't able to respond. I wasn't able to form a single word, my brain instructing me to get the hell out of there as fast as I could. In the battle of fight versus flight, I chose flight. And that wasn't like me at all.

But, still, she'd made her decision. She'd told me how she felt. I can't change that. But I need to have the same opportunity. We might not be together, but I still deserve one last chance to lay it all out there. Tell her how I really feel, without holding anything back this time. Maybe then and only then will I finally be able to move on. Maybe, if I tell her exactly how much she's come to mean to me, how much she's changed me, even in our short time together, then I'll be able to accept the fact that, even though we'll never be a couple, I'll have still said my piece. What I need is to put our relationship to rest, once and for all.

the Off-Season

"Brandon, you're a genius," I say, pushing back from the table and turning to walk out of the restaurant.

He shouts after me, but I don't stop. Now that the idea is in my head, I can't rest until it's done.

I stopped at an office supply store on the way home, grabbing three different notebooks, a package of fancy stationery, and a pen that cost more than any pen should have the right to. Don't ask me why. I just feel like something like this deserves special attention. I know Lexi won't see me. And, to be honest, I like the idea of being able to write it all down, making sure every word is perfect. E-mail seems too impersonal, not for what I need to say to Lexi. So, fancy paper and pen, it is.

I sit down at the desk, grabbing one of the notebooks first. I figure I'll write it all out in this, so I can scribble and scratch out whatever I don't like. Once I decide it's ready, I'll rewrite it all on the stationery. And then I'll mail it out.

Might as well spritz some fancy perfume on it while you're at it, too, you pussy.

I shove down the thought. It *is* a little...chick flicky. I mean, if this were a movie, I'd be rolling my eyes so hard right now. But, hey, maybe those movies aren't so bad. Because just sitting here with the pen in my hand has already caused a rush of peace to fall over me. Those romance dudes are smart.

I stare at the blank sheet of paper, not having the faintest idea of where to start. I toss around a few phrases.

Dearest Lexi…

My dear Lexi…

Dear woman who broke my heart…

I cross them all out and just write her name. Then, instead of debating every word and trying to sound like an eloquent fuck, I let it all out. I don't worry about what it sounds like. I decide that can all be fixed later. Right now, I need to purge.

Lexi,

It's been three weeks since you broke my heart.

I'm not going to sugarcoat it. Because that's exactly what it was. You took my heart, and you pulverized it with a few simple words.

Yet, I'm not sorry.

I can't even bring myself to hate you.

Believe me, I've tried. During those first few sleepless nights, I did everything I could to try to make myself curse your name. I tried to tell myself I wanted you to hurt as much as you'd hurt me. But, no matter how much I wished I could will the feelings into being, it didn't happen.

The truth is, I love you, Lexi. I've loved you since that first moment I saw you. And I'll continue to love you until the day I take my final breath.

I want you to know I meant every word that I said during our time together. I would've given it all up if you'd asked. I would've put it all behind me and moved on with you. Because nothing in this world means more to me than you.

That morning when it all came out, I was prepared to fight for you. I was prepared to fight the press, to go to battle to defend your honor. To prove to the world that you were not the monster they were trying to make you out to be. I wasn't willing to give you up. Not for anything.

Until you told me you didn't love me.

You had come into my life and spun my entire world on its axis. And then, with a few words, you knocked it completely off course. You took that decision away from me. You took away everything.

I'd like to ask if you ever really loved me or if you were full of it the whole time.

But I've decided it doesn't really matter.

Because, even if you played me for a fool, what I felt for you was real. You changed me, Lex. All my life, I wanted nothing more than to play baseball. I fucked around, had a good time, and didn't give a second thought to the repercussions as long as I could continue to play. And then, in a few short weeks, you showed me how much more there could be in life. You showed me that there was more to life than my career and fame. More to life than fortune and fancy cars.

So, for that, I'll forever be grateful.

But, Lexi, it's time for me to let you go. Since I've been back, I've been hanging on, holding out hope that something will bring you back to me. But I realize now that won't happen. It's only been three weeks, but I can't keep living this way. It's not fair to my team. It's not fair to my friends.

And it's not fair to me.

I will always love you, Lexi. But love can't be one-sided. No matter how much I wish I could, I can't love enough for the both of us. I would have given you all of me. Hell, I did give it to you. But it takes two to tango, as they say.

So, this is me, taking the first step toward letting you go. I needed to get it all out, tell you how I felt, and also to tell you good-bye. I don't know that I'll ever love another woman the way I love you. But I have to try. Because, now that I've had a taste of what life can be, how amazing things can be when you've found the right person, I can't live without it.

I've found the person I want to spend my life with.

She just doesn't feel the same.

I hope you find someone who makes you happy one day. I hope you find the person who makes you feel the same things you make me feel. I hope he makes you smile that gorgeous smile, and I hope he makes you laugh until your side aches. I hope he understands how amazing you are and appreciates the beautiful woman you are, both inside and out.

I love you, Lexi.

I hope you can be happy.

And I hope I can learn to be happy without you.

Ian

When I'm done, I read it over. It's messy, there are scribbles everywhere, and my handwriting is next to impossible to read. But, instead of rewriting it, using that fancy-ass paper and that expensive-ass pen, I tear out the sheet of notebook paper, carefully fold it, stuff it into an envelope, and print out her address.

The next morning, I drop it in the mailbox.

chapter twenty-eight
lexi

I read the letter three times, beginning to end, when it first arrived. And, in the four days since, I've lost track of the number of times I've studied Ian's words, examining each and every curved letter, every scribble, every imperfection. I have every single word memorized, down to the stroke of his pen.

Each time, different things stick out to me. The first time, it was his sadness. The fact that I'd hurt him so deeply. The second time, it was his accusations and how willing he was to accept what I'd said as truth. And the third…the third was the hardest time of all. When I realized he'd meant it when he said he was writing to let me go.

Ian is moving on with his life.

Without me.

I've kept all the curtains closed since I returned home from

Ella's, not able to even look at his house sitting there, empty. I've locked myself in my house, not answering the door when Margie comes knocking or when Charlie and Liv show up with dinner. I've completely closed myself off to the outside world.

And, in the days since receiving that letter, I've fallen off the deep end.

I know it. Ella knows it. Hell, I'm sure everyone in town knows it by now.

And, even though I hate knowing that I'm right back where I started after I woke in that hospital bed, I can't do anything to stop it.

I'm spiraling down that bottomless, dark hole—the one I clawed my way out of only weeks before. Only this time, I'm not sure I'll ever resurface.

I flip through the channels on the TV Ian helped me set up a few days before the end, not really paying attention to what I'm seeing. I don't even know why it's on, the sound muted because even that is too much for my pounding headache.

Speaking of which…

A literal pounding rings through my head, causing me to cringe. I press my fingertips to my temples, rubbing in small circles to try to ease some of the pain when it comes again.

Realizing the sound isn't in my head but at my door, I groan and roll over on the couch, pulling my blanket up higher on my shoulders and smashing a throw pillow onto my head to muffle the noise.

When will these people realize I don't want to talk?

Before I can begin to curse my neighbors' existence, my sister's voice comes through the door. "Open the damn door, Lexi. I know you're in there. Don't make me trudge through the snow to that damn garage and get a chain saw. You know I will."

And she's right. I know, if I don't get my ass off the couch and let her in, she *will* get in through other means. Even if it means hacking away my door.

I grab my cell phone, seeing that I have six missed calls from Ella and five voice mails. I switched it to silent and turned the vibrate off as well when I woke with this raging headache. I can only imagine what those voice mails say.

I moan as I climb from the couch and shuffle across the room. Ella's fist is raised, getting ready to pound on my door again, when it swings open.

She drops her hand, her mouth following suit, and stares at me. "You look like hell."

I give her a halfhearted laugh. I can only imagine what she sees. I haven't showered in…fuck, I can't even remember. Let's just say, it's been a while. And I'm certain my hair is a disaster. If the look in her eyes is any indication as she sneers at my head, I'd say it looks like a family of squirrels has taken up residence in my tresses.

"Thanks, sis. You sure know how to make a girl feel better," I say, dropping my hand from the door and turning to return to my post on the couch.

She steps in behind me, closing the door I left open, and takes in the catastrophe that is my living room. "My God, Lexi. What happened?"

I look at the smashed lamp, the empty paint cans I kicked across the room, and the rest of the debris I threw around the other night. The night I got Ian's letter.

"Um, I was robbed?" I try, knowing full well she won't believe me.

"What did you do, Lexi? All your hard work." She trails her

hand down a hole in the wall.

It got in the way of the wrench I threw. The wrench won.

"Are you drinking again?" Ella asks, her eyes shooting up to mine as panic fills them.

I shake my head. "No, Ella. I promise you, I haven't started drinking again. It's been hard as hell, but I've managed to stay on the wagon."

And it's the truth. Despite how much I've wanted a drink, I haven't touched a single drop of alcohol. Whether it's sheer willpower or only because I don't have any in the house and can't bring myself to leave, I'm not sure. I'd like to think the former, but it's most likely the latter. Still, I'm grateful. This sucks enough without having to deal with the disappointment of my sister.

She shoves my legs off the couch and sits down next to me. I sit up, propping my feet up on the coffee table and dropping my head back against the sofa.

"So, what's the plan, Lex? You gonna waste away in here? Hole up like Miss Havisham and pine away your days?"

"No," I say, not lifting my head to look at her. "Miss Havisham was the jiltee. I'm the jilter. There's a difference."

Ella sighs. "Must you always be so damn stubborn?"

"Must you always be so damn nosy? Nobody asked you to come over here and lecture me."

"No, but somebody has to. Because you're too damn hardheaded to figure it out on your own. And, because I love you and you're my sister, the duty falls on me."

"Figure what out? I'm fine, Ella. I just have a headache."

"You're not fine. You haven't left this house in weeks. And let's not even talk about the last time you showered. You smell, Lexi. Like, *really* smell."

I point toward the front door. "There's the exit. Feel free to use it."

She grabs my cheeks, surprising me and causing my eyes to pop open. She swings my face toward hers, her eyes hard as she glares at me.

"Stop being a bitch, Lexi. This isn't a game. It's not a joke. It's your fucking life."

I shove her hand away, rubbing my fingers along my aching chin where she gripped me. "I know that, *Ella*. You think I don't understand that? I'm the one living it. Does it look like I'm having fun?"

I gesture to the disaster around me. Ella doesn't soften though.

"So, *do* something about it. Stop lying around and feeling sorry for yourself. Get your ass to Seattle, and fix this mess you've made."

I slump back against the couch. "It's not that easy, Ella…"

"No," she cuts me off. "It *is* that easy. I know you've got this twisted delusion in your head where you think this is what's best for him, but believe me when I tell you, it isn't. I can absolutely guaran-damn-tee you that Ian is just as miserable as you are right now. You guys being apart doesn't make sense. So, get your ass up, and fix it."

"Even if I wanted to, you're wrong. He isn't sitting around, wishing we could be together. He wrote me a letter. He's moving on."

I get up from the couch, moving to the small side table in the hallway where I stored Ian's letter.

I pull it out and hand it to Ella.

She slowly unfolds it, giving me a worried look. "Why didn't you tell me you'd heard from him?"

I shrug. I don't tell her it was because it hurt too much to say it out loud.

Her eyes scan the page, and she's silent as she reads. Her hand comes up to cover her mouth the closer she gets to the end. And, when she finishes, she lifts her eyes to mine. They're wet with tears and a sadness I don't want to see. Because, now, she knows it's truly over, too.

"I love you, Lexi," she starts, her voice cracking on my name. "But, sometimes, you sure are stupid."

My mouth falls open, shock flooding through me at her words. "What the hell, Ella?"

First, she reads what is quite possibly the end of my life, and then she calls me stupid?

She lifts the letter. "This? This isn't him telling you he's moving on."

"Um, how do you explain the part where he says *exactly that* then?"

She shakes her head. "He said he's going to try to let you go. But, Lexi, did you read the rest of it at all?"

"Yeah, I've read it a few times." *Understatement of the century.*

"I know you've read it. But did you *read* it?"

I shoot her a scathing look. "Can you stop talking in riddles and get to the damn point already? I told you, I have a headache."

"He loves you, Lexi. And he's practically begging you to come to him. He doesn't give a shit about your past. And I believe him when he says he'd give it all up for you. That you're the most important thing in his life."

"He shouldn't have to give it up for me though."

"So, don't ask him to. He says you're worth it. You're worth giving up his dreams, his career, his life, so he can be with you. But you're telling me he's not worth the same? You wouldn't even have to give anything up. You only have to deal with being in the public eye a little more than you'd like. He's willing to drop everything for you. But you can't even handle a little public scrutiny?"

I shrink into myself, my eyes falling to the floor. When she says it like that, it makes it sound so awful. Like I gave up at the first sign of trouble.

I guess that is exactly what I did.

"It's too late, Ells. I've hurt him too much."

She reaches out and places her hand on my shoulder, holding up the letter again with her other. "This tells me it isn't. He still wants you, Lexi. He said it himself. You're his person. The one he wants to spend his life with. That doesn't change in a few weeks. He put the ball back in your court. Now, it's up to you to decide whether it's time to take the shot."

I quirk an eyebrow at her. "Was that a basketball reference? You realize he plays baseball, right?"

She waves a hand. "Tomato, *tomahto*. The point still remains. Are you going to swing for the fences? Or sit safely in the dugout, watching the game play out in front of you?"

I smile at her new attempt. "Much better."

And I know she's right. Ian poured his heart out to me. Now, it's up to me to do the same. I made the mistake of letting him go once. I won't do it again. If he's willing to fight for me, then I have to be willing to do the same. Like he said, love can't be one-sided. I've been holding back for far too long. It's time for me to get up to bat.

"So, what are you going to do, Lexi?" Ella asks.

A smile spreads across my face. "Hand me my laptop. I've got an idea."

chapter twenty-nine
tag

I stand, smiling for the camera, doing my best to look like the pretty puppet they want me to be. All the while, I'm thinking about how much truth there is to the saying, *Life goes on.*

It's been more than a week since I sent that letter to Lexi. There's no hiding from the fact that, at this point, she's received it. And either she read it and didn't give a shit or she threw it straight into the trash. I guess I'll never know for sure because I still haven't heard a damn peep out of her.

Yet here I am, shirtless and wearing nothing but a pair of trackpants, acting like my life didn't come to a screeching halt less than a month ago. Because, regardless of how much you might not want it to, regardless of how much it hurts…life truly does go on. It moves forward, hurtling through time whether you like it or not.

the Off-Season

"Now, turn to the left. Bend your arm up over your head, and look down to the right. Yes, yes, like that," the photographer shouts over the sounds of the room around us.

Everywhere I look, there are people in motion—a constant flow of raised voices, frenzied steps, and stress. It's fucking exhausting. Especially when all I want to do is curl up in my bed and sleep.

But Ray worked way too long and hard to book this gig for me to blow it now. When he called and told me the deal with Nike was back on, he wasn't even able to contain his excitement, giggling like a schoolgirl and telling me this was it. This was what was going to get me back on top for good.

Looking around at the people surrounding me, I'm not so sure. I mean, how is taking pictures of me in front of a green screen going to sell anybody anything?

A woman steps in front of me, spritzing my face and chest with water to give the appearance of sweat. I move to wipe the dripping mess from my chin, but Robert—the photographer—screams at me to stop.

"No! Don't touch it. That's going to drive people crazy. Millions of women across the world will soak their panties at the fantasy of being able to lick that off."

I shoot him an incredulous look. "That's disgusting."

Robert shrugs. "Maybe to you. But, believe me, nobody else will think so. Now, tilt your head back, and let me see that throat."

I drop my head with a groan, letting him take pictures of my Adam's apple for God knows what reason. I'm about to ask when lunch is because holy fuck do I need a break when my phone rings.

I straighten, pulling the phone from my pocket amid the protests of Robert and all of his assistants.

When I see Ray's name on the screen, I hold up a finger and turn toward the door. "Give me a minute. I've gotta take this."

As soon as I'm out of earshot, I press the phone to my ear. "You owe me big time for this, buddy. Where the fuck are you anyway? These people are driving me fucking batty. If Robert says one more goddamn thing about my junk, I'm going to punch him right in his."

Ray is silent through my tirade, not even laughing once at my unease, so I continue, "Do you know he won't let anyone call him Bob? Or even Rob? It's *Robert*. Who the fuck goes by Robert anymore?"

Still, nothing.

"Ray? You there?" I ask even though I know he is. He might not be speaking, but I can hear the bastard breathing. "You call to torment me? This'd better not be you calling to tell me you're not coming. I'll kick your ass."

"You need to pull up The Score," he finally says, referencing the news site that douche bag Paul Sharp writes for.

"Why the fuck do I need to do that? I don't give a shit what that asshole has to say about me now."

He's been surprisingly quiet about me ever since Ray leaked the info about my donation. Guess he hasn't found any more dirt worth digging into lately.

"Just do it, Ian," Ray intones and disconnects the call.

What the fuck?

I look at the phone as I pull it away from my face. *He didn't exactly sound pissed, so whatever Sharp wrote can't be that bad, right? But why the secrecy? Why the fuck couldn't he tell me what it was about and save me some time? Isn't that what I pay him for—to handle this shit for me?*

But, when I hear the sound of Robert's voice on the other side of the door, I duck into the bathroom and lock the door behind me. At least reading this bullshit article will buy me a little more time before I have to go back in there.

I open the browser on my phone and quickly type in the website. Sharp's article is the first thing I see when the screen loads.

WHAT HAPPENS IN THE OFF-SEASON

BY PAUL SHARP

I raise an eyebrow, wondering what in the hell has gotten into Ray. This doesn't even sound like it has anything to do with me. *What has his panties in a twist?*

By the time I finish the first sentence, I know that I'm wrong.

> *I've certainly made no secret of my dislike for Tag Taggart. Over the past several months, I've made it my goal to bring you the truth about his character, providing as many inside stories and updates as I could find following the charges brought against him. When those charges were dropped, I was convinced he'd gotten away with his crimes, and it only further fueled my fire.*
>
> *A few weeks ago, I brought you the story of Alexis Barnes, the woman Taggart had started seeing. I'd gotten the first look at the new couple, and when I'd dug a little deeper, I'd hit pay dirt. I'd literally struck career gold, and I hadn't stopped to consider the consequences before I broke that story.*
>
> *Today, I regret that decision.*
>
> *I can't tell you why I have such strong feelings against Taggart. I'm not quite sure myself. And, while he's still not my favorite person on the planet, I have to take this opportunity to apologize.*
>
> *So, I'm sorry.*

A few days ago, I received an e-mail from the same Alexis Barnes I wrote about in my article. It didn't take long for me to realize she wasn't the person I had made her out to be. And it didn't take long for her to convince me that Taggart wasn't half the villain I had always considered him.

I retract my previous statements regarding Barnes and Taggart. The damage is done, and there's nothing I can do to reverse that. Except maybe let her tell you the same story she told me.

Without further ado… Alexis Barnes.

My mouth drops open when I get to the break in the page. I'm not sure how to process all this information. *Lexi contacted him? After everything he'd done to hurt her?* And, while I always knew Sharp seemed to have some vendetta against me, seeing him admit to it, seeing the words in print, has validated my beliefs. *Would the bastard be fired now?*

But the thing that baffles me most is the fact that the following words aren't Sharp's at all.

They are from Lexi.

Are they for me? Or is she simply trying to defend herself, to pick up the pieces after I shattered her entire world?

There is only one way to find out.

My name is Lexi, and I want to start off by saying I'm not a writer. I'm not good with words. I prefer to keep things to myself, something I've come to perfect over the last few years. But it turns out, silence is no longer an option. So, here it is—the story of how I fell in love this off-season.

By now, you've heard the story of my past. You know about the night I drove drunk and forever changed the future of a sweet young girl and her family. I spent time in rehab after that accident, followed by six months probation, and community service. And I agree with you. I got off easy.

the Off-Season

But I can assure you, the rest of what you read was not true. Since the night of the accident, I have not touched a drop of alcohol. I live with the guilt of what I did every single second of every single day. Not a moment goes by that I don't think of her. I'm not the crazy party girl I was made out to be. I no longer drink at all. I don't go to bars. I don't go to parties. I don't do anything, except hang out with my sister and attempt to fix up my old, run-down lake house. And think of those I've hurt.

That is, until he walked into my life.

You all know who I'm talking about.

A few months ago, a man jumped out of the freezing lake behind my house and forever changed my life. With a single smirk and a smile, I was a goner.

I tried to keep him out. I told myself I didn't deserve happiness, not after what I did. I pushed him away every chance I got, yet, still, he persisted.

Ian Taggart changed my life.

He took my broken, shattered soul and started the process of putting it back together. And, while I'll never be completely whole again, I can say with absolute certainty that I have been mended. Ian took the pieces of my heart and sewed them back together. It's messy, the stitches loose in places and fraying in others, and while there are still a few small holes, it's there. The empty place inside my chest has once again been filled. And I owe it all to him.

I fell for Ian Taggart during the weeks we spent working on my house. His quiet acceptance of my quirks. His never-ending need to try to make me smile. The way he didn't ask questions he could tell I didn't want to answer. He was just...there. And, one day, I realized I didn't want him to be anywhere else. I didn't want to be anywhere else.

Ian brought me back to life. He showed me that it was okay to move on, to enjoy my life, despite my past mistakes. He taught me how to love again and how to accept love in return.

Until I forced him away.

The night I chose to drive drunk will forever be the biggest mistake of my life. But the day I told Ian to go, told him that I didn't love or want him anymore, will always be right up there with it. I was scared. Not just for myself. But also for Ian. I was afraid of what being with me would do to his career. I was afraid I was going to ruin him. So, I told him the things I knew he needed to hear in order to save him. I lied through my teeth, gutting not only Ian, but also myself in the process.

And it worked. Ian went back to Seattle, and I've tried to move on with my life.

Only there is no life without Ian.

Since the day he left, I've fallen right back into that dark hole where I started. I haven't started drinking again, but that doesn't change the fact that I'm still hiding from my life. Old habits die hard.

But I want to bury them once and for all.

So here it goes…

Ian, I understand if you never forgive me. I hurt you, and for that, I can never apologize enough.

But I just had to tell you one last time.

I love you.

The day you walked into my life was the first day of my new life.

I'm not the same person I was the day I met you.

the Off-Season

I'm better.

I'll never be perfect. And I'll always feel remorse for the hurt I've caused another family.

But I deserve to live.

And, if you'll still have me, I'd like to do it with you.

You know where to find me.

Lexi

My fingers are numb by the time I finish reading the story, my grip on the phone so tight, I'm surprised it hasn't exploded into a million pieces. My chest aches as I gasp for breath, and I realize that I'm crying. I don't know when it started, but the wetness soaking my cheeks is undeniable.

Throughout the past few weeks, since the day I left Lexi, I haven't let myself shed a single tear.

I let them fall, wiping them as they reach my chin before they can slide down on my bare chest. I think of the disappointment that would be on Robert's face if he could see me wiping them away. But I quickly shake it off.

I grab a few paper towels from the dispenser, wetting them in the sink and using them to clean the disaster that is my face. Once I'm satisfied that I look semi-human, I open the door.

And stroll right out of the building.

chapter thirty

lexi

I look around the room, taking in my nearly finished living room. Since the day Ella came over and I made my decision to contact that reporter, I've thrown myself into fixing up my house with renewed vigor. It takes some of the sting away over not hearing from Ian.

Sometimes.

It's been almost a week since the article ran, and there hasn't been a word. Not a single phone call, text, or e-mail. Not a letter. Nothing.

I can't say I blame him. I saw the look on his face as he backed out of Ella's guest room. It took everything in me not to run after him and tell him how full of shit I was. I'd lied to him so convincingly. Why should he believe anything I said to him now?

But I'll be honest. I thought the news story would sway him. I

the Off-Season

half-expected to see him show up on my doorstep the same day it ran. And, with each day that passes, I find myself growing more and more worried that I've truly lost him for good.

Getting Paul Sharp to run the article was easier than I'd thought. When I e-mailed him, I promised him a story his readers would eat up. I mean, who doesn't love reading a good love story? Especially when it involves one person practically begging for a second chance. Plus, as I told him, he sort of owed me one. He had taken my name and splashed it all over the internet, the vast majority of what he'd said untrue. I told him, if he helped me out, I wouldn't sue his ass for defamation.

But, honestly, he seemed to have lost some of his resentment for Ian, even before I contacted him. Considering all the ugliness Sharp had written about Ian in the last few months, I'd expected him to hold true to his accusations and tell me to give a lawsuit my best shot. But, instead, he e-mailed back almost instantly, asking if he could fly out to talk with me.

The reality of the man is much less intimidating than his online presence. He was a small, skinny man with thinning hair and clothes that didn't seem to fit quite right. I have a feeling he was the sort of kid who was bullied growing up. Most likely, by athletic men like Ian. It's easy to imagine how Paul could develop a certain animosity against people he thought were like those who'd tormented him in the past. And, for some reason, he'd chosen Ian as his target. Even though Ian couldn't be further from the type of person Paul thought he was.

But, even if I haven't heard from Ian since the story ran, at least one good thing has come out of it. Paul wasn't my only unexpected visitor last week. Two days ago, a knock sounded at my door as I patched the hole I'd made in the wall the night I lost my shit.

I dropped the tub of spackle and the tool I'd been using to smooth it on and rushed to the door. I flung it open, hoping to find Ian staring back at me. Instead, I got the shock of a lifetime.

Lily James and her mother were smiling at me from their spot on the porch.

It took a few seconds for me to wrap my brain around what was happening. And, when I did, I nearly fell over myself while trying to invite them inside.

We exchanged pleasantries for a few minutes before Lily got right down to it.

"I don't want you to be sad."

I almost slid off my chair when she spoke the words. "Wh-what do you mean?"

She looked at her mother for assistance, and the older version of her smiled over at me. "Lily doesn't want you to be sad over what happened."

My mouth dropped open, my thoughts running wild in my head. "I don't understand."

"Don't feel bad anymore." Lily's voice cut through my inner torment. "I'm not sad. And I don't want you to be either."

I looked at her mother, who was smiling proudly at her daughter. When her eyes turned to me, they shone with tears.

"Lily and I read your story. And we realized something. We never told you that we forgive you."

"H-h-how is that possible?" I stammered, tears springing to my eyes.

"We've had some hard times, Lexi. Lily has been through more surgeries than any young girl should ever have to endure. But look at her. She's the happiest little girl I know. That didn't change after that night. She has bad days, like anybody. But she doesn't let it stop her. Deep down, we know you made a mistake. Do I wish you hadn't? Every single day of my life. It nearly killed me,

watching my little girl struggle to get to where she is now. But, if your words showed me one thing, it's that you're a good person. You're a good person who made a terrible decision. So, we forgive you. And we think it's time for you to do the same."

Lily sat next to me as I cried, running her delicate fingers through my hair. And, when I embraced her, I felt those last remaining pieces of my heart regenerate. They left shortly after.

I'll never be able to forget what I did. But knowing that sweet girl doesn't resent me for permanently altering her life is the final piece I needed to heal. My heart is whole. For the first time in a long, long time.

She made me promise I'd come to one of her recitals next time I was in Chicago. And, even though I don't have a reason to go back there ever again, especially not after my so-called friends had betrayed me without a second thought, I promised I'd be there for her Christmas performance next month. I don't care if I have to make a special trip just for that. She's worth it.

My life is finally coming together, like my house, and for the first time in as long as I can remember, I'm actually excited to see where it takes me.

I only wish Ian were along for the ride.

I grab the vase I purchased online and head toward the entryway. I fill it with the decorative grass I also purchased, fluffing and fussing until it's exactly how I want it. I take a step back, surveying my handiwork. I still have a long way to go until the whole house is finished. But this room…this room is done.

It feels damn good.

Now, to decide what to do next—the kitchen or the bedroom. I'm weighing the pros and cons of each when there's a knock at the door.

This time, whoever is on the other side doesn't wait for an answer. The knob jiggles, and when it isn't met with the resistance of the lock, it turns all the way, the door swinging wide.

I look over my shoulder, and a smile spreads across my face.

Ian is standing in my doorway, a tool belt slung low on his hips, a ratty long-sleeved shirt and jeans the only things shielding him from the elements.

Realizing he must be freezing, I rush forward, pulling him inside and closing the door behind him.

He stands with his hands on his hips, taking in the room around us. "I like what you've done with the place. Here I thought, you might need my help. I guess, if my services are no longer needed, I'll be on my way," he says with a mischievous tone.

I grab on to his arm, pulling him back toward me. "If you take one more step toward that door, I'll handcuff you to the bed."

"In that case…" He trails off, pulling out of my grip and lunging for the door. After he places his hand on the cool wood, he turns around, holding his wrists together. "Ready for those cuffs, Officer."

I roll my eyes, giving him a lighthearted smack as I laugh. He pulls me against him, wrapping his arms around my waist and holding me in place.

My face falls as I pull back to look him in the eye. "I wasn't sure I'd ever see you again," I say, the playfulness of the moment gone.

"I wasn't sure you wanted to," he replies, his throat bobbing up and down as he swallows hard.

"When you didn't show up after the article, I thought I'd lost you."

the Off-Season

He gives me a slight smile. "Took me a few days to get things squared away. Add the freak snowstorm that hit Seattle, and I was grounded for longer than I wanted. Believe me, I would have been here sooner if I could have been. I finally rented a car and drove. Really could've used that damn truck I left next door."

My mouth falls. "That's a long drive."

He nods, his lips spreading into that charming grin I've come to love so much. "Worth it though. Because I get to do this."

His lips press against mine in the softest of kisses, as if he's testing the waters, gauging my reaction. When he pulls back, I stop him.

"I think we can do better than that," I say and pull him back to me.

This time...

This time, our kiss is everything.

He moves slowly at first, his fingers tangling in my hair as he tilts my head back to give himself better access. But it's been too long, far too many days since the last time I've felt this man's fingers on my skin. And I'm suddenly desperate for his touch.

"I need you, Ian," I whisper against his lips.

His eyes find mine, a fire igniting behind them.

His hands are gentle as they unbutton my shirt, his fingers tentative against the fabric. By the time he gets to the third button, I can't take it anymore. I grab hold of the thin material and yank it open. Grabbing his hands, I place them on my breasts.

"I need you, Ian," I say again. "Now."

He doesn't waste any more time, quickly shucking his jeans and driving inside me as soon as my ass hits the couch. He makes love to me fiercely, his every thrust as desperate and frantic as my own. I meet him every step of the way, my body rubbing against his, desperate for more friction. I can't get close enough, can't get enough of him. Can't believe he's actually here…

When he finds that perfect spot inside me, sending a wave of electricity through my body, I can't help the cry that springs free from my lips.

"Oh, God. Oh, Ian. Oh, God, I've missed you."

He stifles my words with his mouth, his tongue massaging mine as he swallows my cries. When I come apart beneath him, he moves faster, taking me to heights I didn't even know existed, extending my orgasm to an almost deliciously painful level.

He rocks against me a few more times before he stiffens, groaning out his release as he collapses into my body. I take his weight, relishing in the feel of him in my arms once more.

I am whole. I am complete. I am…loved.

Ian stretches out on the couch, pulling my back against his front so he's spooning me—his favorite position. He runs his nose up and down the back of my neck, nuzzling the tender flesh in the way he knows drives me wild.

"Thank you," he says when he reaches my earlobe, giving it a gentle nip.

"For what?" I ask as I shiver.

"For not giving up on yourself. And for not giving up on us."

I roll over, turning myself so that I'm facing him. "I'm sorry it took me so long."

He shakes his head before kissing the tip of my nose. "I would've waited forever."

"But what about your letter? About you letting me go?"

He pulls me against him, tucking my face into the crook of his shoulder and resting his chin on top of my head. "Never would've worked. You have my heart, Lexi. And there's no walking away from your heart. You need it to survive."

I smile against his warm skin, breathing in the rich scent of him.

A thought suddenly springs to my mind, and I push back, trying to wriggle out of his grasp. "Oh, I have something for you."

He wraps his arms around me tighter. "I have everything I need right here."

I giggle. "It'll just take a second. I promise I'll be right back," I tell him, breaking his hold on me and climbing from the couch.

He moans in protest.

I smile as I cross the room, grabbing the small box from the hallway table.

Ian sits up as I return, giving me a quizzical look when he sees the gift box. "You got me a present? Pretty presumptuous, aren't you, Miss Barnes?"

I shrug. "I like to be prepared."

I don't tell him how I was afraid I'd never get the chance to give it to him. That can wait until later. Later, the two of us need to have a very serious talk. Figure out how this entire thing is going to work, sort out all the heartache and misunderstandings of the past few weeks. I have a lot of groveling left to do. But, for now, I'm going to enjoy this.

I hand him the box and watch as he unties the ribbon.

When he opens the box, he turns to me, his brows furrowed. "A key?"

I nod. "To the house. The house next door is Brandon's. And, after all you've done to help me fix this place up, I want you to feel like it's yours, too. Like you always have a place to call home in Maple Lake."

He presses a kiss to my forehead. "You're my home. So, as long as you're in Maple Lake, it'll always be home."

I blush at his comment, heat and butterflies flooding throughout my entire body. I nod toward the box. "There's something else in there, too. Under the paper."

He pulls out the tissue paper, his confusion only deepening when he finds the hidden gift. "Uh, another key?"

"Take it out," I say, watching as he pulls the key from the box.

It's attached to a long chain, and engraved on one side is the word *love*. On the other is my name.

"I don't understand?" His words come out as a question.

I take the necklace from his hand and loop it over his head. "I know it's a little corny, but this is me giving you the key to my heart. I'm going to try, Ian. I'm going to try to knock down these walls I have for good. But, just in case, I want you to have this. I want you to always remember that, no matter what I say or do, I love you. And, if and when the day comes when I try to shut you out, I want you to use this. I want you to unlock those doors and remind me how lucky I am to have you. Because I am, Ian. I'm the luckiest woman in the world. Because you're mine."

He takes the key from my hand, looking at the words engraved in the metal. "I love it, Lexi. It's perfect."

"You're perfect," I say, my eyes dropping to my lap as I immediately cringe. "Oh, God, that was even cornier than the key."

He places his hand beneath my chin, lifting my face to meet his. "Lucky for you, I love corny. Almost as much as I love you."

His lips find mine, sealing his words with a soft kiss.

It might be the end of our conversation.

But this kiss…this kiss is only the beginning.

Of the rest of our lives.

epilogue

tag

Five Months Later

I grab my bat, hitting it against the heel of my cleat as I step out of the dugout. There's nothing like the thrill of the first game of the season. Especially when it's on your home field.

I raise my hand as I step out onto the field, grinning widely as the cheering grows louder. I take off my helmet, waving it over my head to let my fans know I am grateful for their support.

I never could have imagined this.

After Lexi and I returned to Seattle, I expected to have to run damage control with Ray. But we found quite the opposite. People loved Lexi's letter to me. By the time we got back to the city, everyone was already talking. She'd won them over with her honesty and her candor. And they graciously accepted her with open arms.

We've spent the last few months bouncing back and forth between Maple Lake and Seattle. Seattle is a necessity for my career, but it's no longer home. Home is a quiet lake town with a gorgeous girl and a run-down house. And I can't wait to get back there again.

I walk toward the plate, stopping short to take a few practice swings. When I'm confident I'm ready, I step into the batter's box. A loud cheer erupts as I look down to position my feet, and I look up to see Lexi's face on the Jumbotron. She smiles at me, giving me a tiny wave and blowing me a kiss, causing the crowd to go crazy.

I look at her, up there in the stands. And I can't believe how lucky I am. I came so close to losing her forever. And, now, here she is, watching me as I step up to the plate for the first time this year.

My two worlds have collided, and from the sounds of the crowd and the look on Lexi's face, they seem to have come together perfectly.

I catch the kiss with my hand before blowing one back. It's corny as hell, but a collective sigh goes up from all the women in the stands, and the men whistle. People seem to love Lexi and me. We've become baseball's golden couple.

It's a million times better than being the beloved playboy, I tell you.

Lexi beams down at me, her left hand reaching up to catch the kiss and pressing it to her cheek.

A soft flutter fills my chest at the sight of her empty hand.

If all goes according to plan, there will be a shiny new diamond adorning that fourth finger tomorrow morning.

Here's to hoping she says yes.

the end

also by megan green

The Wounded Love Series

Safe Distance
Soldier's Heart
Solid Ground

acknowledgements

As always, thanks goes first to my amazing husband, Adam. Without his never-ending love and support, I would never be able to do what I do. I love you more than words, babe.

To my family and friends, thank you for always believing in me. Thanks for always understanding when I have to hole up in my writing cave and finish a manuscript. Thank you for always being there, no matter what life throws our way.

To my lovely editor, Jovana, thank you for taking my disasters and helping polish them into something worth reading. You're absolutely amazing and I'm so glad I've found you.

To Julie Deaton: world's best proofreader. Thank you for taking such time and care with my work. You really help make it shine.

To the fantastically talented Megan Gunter at Mischievous Designs, thank you for making this cover what it is. You perfectly captured Ian and Lexi and I couldn't be happier with how it turned out.

To Alexandria with AB formatting, thank you for making the inside of this book as gorgeous as the outside. I love you.

Nichole – you've stood by my side throughout this whole journey, and I couldn't think of a better person to have in my corner. I know I give you shit, but you're truly one of the best people I've ever met. Thank you for just being you.

To my minxes – thank you, thank you, thank you. I can't thank all of you enough for the hours you've spent mentoring and supporting me. You are my safe place, the place I go when I'm struggling and know nobody will understand me better than you.

Thank you for being the best ladies in the business!

And finally, thank you to my readers. Thank you for sticking by me while I've been figuring out this crazy world. I hope you enjoyed reading Ian and Lexi's story as much as I enjoyed writing it.

To anyone I've missed, know that I love and appreciate you. My brain is in a deadline induced fog and not firing on all cylinders. I have the most amazing people in my life and wish I could personally thank each and every one of you here. But that would take way too much paper.

I know reading time is limited, so it means the world to me that you chose to spend a few hours with my characters. And if you enjoyed The Off-Season, you'll love The Cleanup – releasing July 2018. Brandon Jeffers is coming for you. I hope you're prepared.

about the author

Megan lives in Northern Utah with her amazing husband, Adam, and her spoiled rotten puppy, Scout. When not writing, chances are you'll find her curled up with a book or binge watching Supernatural. Besides reading and writing, she loves movies, music, animals, chocolate, and coffee—lots and lots of coffee. She loves hearing from her readers, so please drop her a line! You can find her here:

Facebook: https://www.facebook.com/authormegangreen
Twitter: https://www.twitter.com/MeganGreen616
Instagram: https://www.instagram.com/authormegangreen
Email: megangreenwrites@gmail.com

To stay up to date on her current projects and daily life, join her reader group here:
https://www.facebook.com/groups/920523784721273

Made in the USA
San Bernardino, CA
19 March 2018